2007

50¢

D1013237

WITHDRAWN

Broken Heartland

Books by J.M. Hayes

The Grey Pilgrim
Mad Dog & Englishman
Prairie Gothic
Plains Crazy

Broken Heartland

A Mad Dog & Englishman Mystery

J.M. Hayes

Poisoned Pen Press

Copyright © 2007 by J.M. Hayes

First Edition 2007

10 9 8 7 6 5 4 3 2 1

Library of Congress Catalog Card Number: 2007926447

ISBN: 978-1-59058-452-1 Hardcover

Poisoned Pen Press
6962 E. First Ave., Ste. 103
Scottsdale, AZ 85251
www.poisonedpenpress.com
info@poisonedpenpress.com

Printed in the United States of America

For Barbara,
who deserved Europe and the Riviera
and got Kansas and the Upper Sonoran Desert…
and bookshelves, lots and lots of bookshelves.

Sunday morning TV
Is filled with flags and God,
The symbols of the heartland,
The lightning and the rod.
   —John Stewart
      "The Wheel Within the Clay"

It was a beautiful morning, if your definition of morning included the predawn hours. Deputy Wynn's did. Especially when worries about keeping his job interrupted his sleep. On such mornings, he liked to sneak out of the bedroom without disturbing his wife, put on his uniform, crawl behind the wheel of the Benteen County Sheriff's Department black and white, and go cruising for speeders.

Two main blacktops ran all the way through the county, one east/west, one north/south. This being central Kansas, both went straight as arrows, or nearly. Neither one went anyplace particularly important, but Wynn preferred the east/west road. It was one of the first significant paved routes south of Interstate 70. Truckers occasionally liked to slip down here and make up time where they were less likely to encounter the highway patrol. And drug runners, he thought, not that he'd ever discovered any. Still, a deputy could dream.

Sheriff English didn't like him doing this. No one seemed to trust him to do anything on his own. That's why he only gave warnings to the vehicles he stopped. That way, there wasn't any paperwork to show he was out here. And no one could tell by checking the mileage on the black and white's odometer because it had stopped working just short of 300,000 miles.

Wynn had a favorite place to set up his speed trap. It was an old rest stop, complete with picnic tables and a single-stall toilet, just three miles east of the county line. He favored it because kids liked to park there and make out. Warning them against immoral behavior was lots of fun. More than once he'd copped a peek at fine young ladies in the altogether.

Much to his disappointment, the spot was vacant this morning. He pulled in behind the evergreens that masked the place from the road and killed the lights, but not the engine. The V-8 grumbled patiently as he rolled down his window so he'd hear a big rig coming.

A full moon peered though the windshield, and a light breeze—hardly cool even at this hour—touched his arm. It must be nearly sixty. Dawn would surely bring one of those perfect days of Indian summer. That or something dramatic, like a sudden blizzard. It was November, after all, and Kansas.

The road lay before him, straight and flat and full of promise, like a wish waiting to be filled. Wynn's wish was for some of those drug runners. He'd like nothing better than to bust someone hauling a load with a street value in the millions. That would get him a little respect and some job security, maybe even if today's election didn't work out. And people might stop calling him Wynn-Some. Wynn-Some, Lose-Some, folks said behind his back. They seemed to think, given the opportunity, Deputy Wynn would most likely lose.

Something flashed past his windshield. Wynn thought it was a black station wagon, one of those evil-looking new Dodge Magnums that bore more resemblance to a customized hearse than to the latest in alternative SUVs, but it was gone so fast that he couldn't be sure.

"Whoee!" Wynn let out a whoop. This could be it. He punched the accelerator, turned on his headlights, and activated his light bar. His lights illuminated first one ditch and then the other before he managed to correct his steering and the four-hundred-and-fifty-four cubic inch essence of Detroit heavy metal stopped fishtailing its back wheels.

The station wagon's taillights were already barely visible in the distance. The black and white might be old and inefficient by modern standards, but it had been built when gas consumption was an afterthought and muscle cars were the rage. Law enforcement needed to compete, and the Chevy still could. The Magnum, if that's what it was, could probably outmaneuver Wynn's patrol car, but there weren't many things on the road that could outrun it.

Wynn's chase went on for nearly ten minutes, covering a lot of the county since the deputy was doing well over 100 mph. But so was the station wagon. Wynn was gaining, but never enough to get a good look at the vehicle he pursued, especially when it turned its lights off. The chase went through three hamlets, each with a stop sign that both cars ignored. Fortunately, the sidewalks had been rolled up in all of them. The only traffic Wynn encountered was a pair of semis, one going in each direction. They wisely pulled over to make way.

Wynn was beginning to doubt he'd catch up before they got to Buffalo Springs. The last thing he wanted to do was go blasting through Benteen's county seat in high-speed pursuit. Even at this time of the morning, there might be a car on Main Street. If he was responsible for an accident there, Sheriff English might have his badge.

Maybe I can trick them, he thought. He turned off all his lights. They might think he'd given up, slow down some so he could get right behind them.

English would have more than his badge if he found out about this part, but if Wynn brought in a drug mule and hundreds of kilos of heroin or cocaine or even marijuana, he'd be the kind of law enforcement hero no one ever replaced. And there had to be something important in that vehicle for it to be running from him with its lights out like this.

He could still see all right. Or almost all right. Well enough for him to know they were coming up on the four-way stop at Jacobs' Corner—an experiment in middle-of-nowhere truck stops that had been out of business for more years than Wynn had been a deputy. In fact, the moon was so bright he could practically see colors.

It took Wynn a couple of seconds to understand he *was* seeing colors—flashing red lights. Two seconds, in which he covered nearly two hundred feet. He didn't realize what he was seeing at first. The lights were coming up the intersecting road from the south. He only caught a glimpse through the row of trees lining that road before he realized he was practically on top of the station wagon, too. He slammed brakes, grabbed for his headlights.

The red lights weren't flashing anymore, but something big and yellow was lumbering out onto the highway ahead of him. Ahead of the black station wagon, as well, which *was* a Magnum. With no time to stop, the Magnum accelerated instead, tried to get by, lost control, and started cart-wheeling through the ditch across the road from the old truck stop.

Wynn howled in victory as he realized he would catch his suspects. But his howl turned into a scream when a body flew from the tumbling Dodge. And the big yellow vehicle began flashing red lights again as it pulled to a stop, dead-square in the middle of the intersection. Wynn couldn't halt the patrol car before he got there. For some reason, he slapped on the light bar, as if the driver would see it and get out of his way when he realized it was a law enforcement vehicle that was about to t-bone him.

In the last seconds, Wynn saw red-and-blue-and-white horror-stricken faces flash into view along the line of windows in the Buffalo Springs school bus. They were turning toward him, mouths open to echo his primal cry.

The church went quiet when Sheriff English entered. It was the Buffalo Springs Church of Christ Risen these days, though it seemed to change names about as often as central Kansas changed weather. Well, no, you couldn't paint a new name on the sign that fast.

The interior was just a big open space, more like the floor of a gym than a site for hallelujahs. Pews were too comfortable, according to Pastor Goodfellow. Folding chairs were good enough. Then the church could rent out that space for meetings, such as the Tuesday morning pancake breakfast of the Buffalo Springs Chamber of Commerce the sheriff had walked into.

The sheriff was used to rooms going quiet when he came in these days. People never seemed to know what to say to him. Especially not with the election today.

"Sheriff. We weren't expecting you after this morning's disaster."

The voice was amplified and the sheriff looked up and found his opponent for office standing behind a microphone and a podium very much like the one he'd been about to pass. Damn! He'd forgotten all about the election morning debate he'd promised to participate in.

"Lieutenant Greer." The sheriff acknowledged his challenger. Lieutenant Greer was quite likely going to be the next sheriff of Benteen County. He was tall, handsome, rugged, and looked every bit the part. And he was a war hero. He'd brought home a bronze star after his last stint in Iraq. Sheriff English wouldn't mind losing so much, but he didn't trust Greer to enforce the law.

Greer continued. "I had intended my first question for you to be why you haven't hung a copy of the Ten Commandments in your office at the courthouse, but since your deputy just committed vehicular homicide, perhaps killing some of this community's precious youth, I think it's more appropriate to enquire why Deputy Wynn was conducting a high-speed pre-dawn pursuit with his lights off."

It was a good question. One the sheriff was still trying to understand. Wynn hadn't been able to tell him and, from what the emergency techs said, might not live long enough to get the chance.

Wynn-Some, Lose-Some had lost it big time this morning, but did Greer have to affix blame before anyone really knew what had happened out there? Wynn might have had some legitimate excuse. It was remotely possible.

The sheriff sighed. He'd come to speak to Pastor Goodfellow. The only survivor from the Magnum had mentioned the pastor's name. The sheriff was already near the empty podium. He didn't have time for a debate with Greer, but a couple of minutes wouldn't make much difference. He stepped behind his own microphone.

"Good morning," he told the crowd. "I'm afraid I owe the lieutenant and all of you an apology. As I'm sure you know, Deputy Wynn was involved in an accident at Jacobs' Corner today. There is, indeed, one dead. No one from the school bus, though some of those kids were seriously injured. I can't tell you any more just now, or take time to debate the many important issues you're being asked to decide today. Let me just remind you to vote, if you haven't already, and to please keep your minds open until we know what actually happened."

"Wynn-Some slaughtered an innocent motorist," Greer said. "He rammed a school bus filled with this community's children. We already know what happened. An incompetent deputy, who only had a badge because he was the son of the previous chairman of the board of supervisors, has disgraced this county. And that badge, Sheriff English, was issued by you."

The sheriff didn't like Lieutenant Greer. Greer was a born-again, holier-than-thou fundamentalist, quick to blame and point out shortcomings.

There were lots of born-again Christians in Benteen County. The sheriff got along fine with most of them. Every last one might be certain the sheriff could set his life right and save his soul if only he'd accept their beliefs, but when they suggested it, they did so more gently. Greer showed no patience for those who didn't see the world exactly as he did. And no patience with laws that didn't correspond to his belief system. That was the part that troubled English the most, that and the fact he couldn't just walk over and punch the blow-hard square on the nose.

"It was Deputy Wynn who organized that welcome-home parade for you, Lieutenant. Maybe that was when you should have pointed out your objections to his service to this county."

Greer's face turned beet red. He looked like he'd be willing to meet the sheriff half-way for the nose thing.

"Gentlemen, please!" Pastor Goodfellow stood behind his stack of pancakes and spread his hands. "Surely I don't have to remind you how to behave in the Lord's house."

Greer stepped back behind his microphone. "If your deputy's behavior isn't fair game for questions, Sheriff, then maybe we should consider yours. Isn't it true that both your daughters have had abortions?"

That was when the sheriff decided one to the nose wouldn't be enough.

◇◇◇

"This is a joke, right?"

"I'm sorry?" Mad Dog had just handed the highway patrolman his driver's license and was trying to convince Hailey, the wolf-hybrid on the seat beside him, that this wasn't the best time to growl. He had no idea what the officer might be talking about. He was still a little spacey after his three-day fast, and his stomach wasn't happy with the super-size burger with which he'd broken it.

"You're Mr. Dog?"

"Oh, that." He'd been born Harvey Edward Maddox, but his father ran off, leaving him no particular reason to feel attachment to the name. In high school, he'd been quite an athlete. The fans had started calling him Mad Dog and the nickname stuck. "No. No joke. I had it legally changed a few years ago."

Hailey was baring her teeth. She didn't like the trooper's attitude.

"You're sure it's not your companion's name?" Apparently the patrolman didn't like hers, either. And that wasn't going to improve Mad Dog's odds of getting out of this with a warning instead of a ticket.

"She's not dangerous," Mad Dog said. "I don't know why, but she's been grumpy ever since we got back into Kansas."

"Both of you remain in the vehicle," the trooper said. He turned and went back to his cruiser. Mad Dog watched him enter information on his computer while Hailey continued complaining in Mad Dog's ear.

Mad Dog had been speeding a little. Eighty, maybe ninety. The Mini Cooper cruised so effortlessly on the wide-open stretches of asphalt that crisscrossed central Kansas. His foot hadn't been as heavy as he wanted, though.

He'd come down off that mountain in the middle of the night with a feeling he desperately needed to get home. He'd spent days purifying himself. He'd fasted. He'd done everything the old Cheyenne medicine man had told him he should to prepare himself for a vision. Instead, he'd gotten a premonition. He was still trying to figure out that dire portent, and not paying much attention to his speedometer until he saw the sudden blaze of flashing lights in his mirror.

Not for the first time, Mad Dog regretted leaving home without his cell phone. He really wanted to check in with his brother, or someone in Buffalo Springs. Find out whether there was any legitimate cause for the sense of dread he felt. He'd left the cell behind on purpose, though. If you were on a spiritual quest, staying connected to the outside world seemed inappropriate. But then an awful sense of impending doom overwhelmed him as he sat on the Cheyenne sacred mountain and watched the remnants of a Black Hills' sunset fade and a sky full of stars come out of hiding.

Mad Dog hadn't been able to load himself and Hailey in the Cooper and blast straight home. Not after three days without food. Having the vision you've been seeking while you were behind the wheel of a speeding Mini could be disastrous. So he'd stopped at the first food outlet he came to. He'd called the Benteen County Sheriff's office from there. All he got was the recorded message. He still wasn't used to that. Before the county's financial crisis, his brother had tried to keep someone there to answer the phone at all times. Now, there was only a message giving the sheriff's personal cell number with instructions to call only in case of a legitimate emergency. Mad Dog knew his brother would answer if he called, but the sheriff hadn't been sleeping well as it was. The last thing he needed was to be awakened by a call from a brother whose concern was based on nothing more than a gut feeling fueled by three days without food.

"You're Englishman's Mad Dog." The patrolman was back at Mad Dog's window and this time Hailey hadn't announced his return.

"Uh, yeah. Englishman, he's my brother." Their mother had married again. Or maybe just found someone to father her second child—that's what most of the community thought. The rumor was that Sheriff English got his name because of the nationality of his daddy, since their mother hadn't taken time to ask his name. Mad Dog couldn't argue with that. Their mother had been something of a flower child, well before people like her began congregating in Haight-Ashbury. Then, when everyone began calling Harvey Edward Mad Dog instead of Maddox, it hadn't taken long for his little brother to get stuck being Englishman. The difference was Englishman hadn't liked the handle people hung on him.

"Sheriff English is something of a legend in central Kansas. And so is his brother." Mad Dog wasn't sure he liked the way the officer phrased that last part. The man handed Mad Dog back his license and registration. "Keep your speed down, Mr. Dog. And tell your brother good luck with today's election. From what I hear he's going to need it."

Doc Jones, the Benteen County coroner, wasn't in his office at the back of Klausen's Funeral Parlor. The sheriff could hear the whine of an electric motor from farther down the immaculate white corridor. He didn't like thinking about what that meant the coroner was doing, and he didn't like going where the sound required, but he needed to see Doc.

It was as bad as he'd expected. Doc was bent over a cadaver with a gaping hole in its chest. The body had no face because its scalp had been peeled forward while Doc used a small circular saw to cut through the top of the skull. The smell of burning bone might have been enough to make the sheriff gag, but he wasn't capable of smelling much at the moment.

English stood in the door until Doc's shaggy eyebrows rose as his hang-dog face straightened into Doc's version of a welcoming smile.

"What happened to you?"

"I think the medical term is, 'bloody nose,' but you're the doctor. I figured I should let you make the diagnosis."

Doc put the saw down and came around the stainless steel table. "Lot of blood on that handkerchief," he said, "which seems to be covering a nose. Offhand, I'd say you got it right." He stopped to remove the surgical gloves he was wearing and replace them with a fresh pair. "Let me see."

The sheriff uncovered and Doc reached up and wiggled the sheriff's nose from side to side.

"Ouch! That hurt like hell."

"It's not broken," Doc said. "But you best cover back up until I get something to pack it with and find you some ice. Otherwise, you're gonna drip all over your shirt. What happened?"

The sheriff reapplied his handkerchief. "You've been coroner too long, Doc, if that's the best bedside manner you can manage."

"I *have* been coroner too long," Doc said. "I've been telling myself that all morning, ever since I started doing an autopsy on this dead teen." He nodded toward a chair near the door. "Sit over there and tilt your head back, then tell me who popped you in the nose."

The sheriff took the chair. "I'm not really here about my nose," he said. "I hadn't heard from you and I thought I'd better see what you can tell me about this kid."

"All right. But first, the nose. The dead will wait, and you're not gonna be the most efficient law enforcement officer if you're running around holding a bloody rag to your face. Who punched you?"

"Our next sheriff, but it's more like I tried to hit him and he blocked me and I kind of ran into his elbow."

That interrupted Doc's normal cool efficiency. "You what? You tried to slug your worthy opponent? That's not like you, Englishman. What happened?"

"He got a little insulting."

"Our local war hero is often insulting. But I haven't heard of you making a habit of trying to punch him out. You been taking those antidepressants I prescribed for you?"

The sheriff hadn't even filled the prescription. "This time, it wasn't me he insulted," the sheriff said. "It was my daughters."

"Oh," Doc said, getting that sad look again. "You mean…?"

"He accused them of having abortions," the sheriff said, "and I kind of lost it." The tough part was that one of the girls had gotten an abortion. And most folks in Benteen County, except a silent majority of women, had turned solidly pro-life. Not that the sheriff wasn't. He just thought the question was more complicated than the pro-life, pro-choice arguments made it. And, frankly, he hadn't thought the decision was up to him. Doc obviously didn't buy the pro-life arguments. He'd performed that abortion, and many others.

"Too bad it's not Lieutenant Greer's nose I'm treating," Doc said. "If it wasn't already broken, I might have corrected that myself."

Hailey started growling again when Mad Dog was still a quarter mile from his driveway.

"Hey, what's this about?" he asked. "We're just coming home." Though the truth of it was he felt like a marching band was parading across his grave. If he had a ruff on the back of his neck, his would be standing up as rigid as hers. Something was wrong but he didn't know what. The place looked fine.

Or it did until he got past where the evergreens blocked the view of his front yard. That's when he saw it.

Somebody had erected a sign in his yard, right out by the fence near the road. He knew what it was before he got close enough to read it. He'd been seeing them along the highway, off and on, all the way home.

The thing was about six feet high. It was mostly white—white posts, white background. All white but for the black and red of the lettering and the figure. The figure was a child, just its outline except for ears, all in black with no detail. No indication whether it was a girl or a boy, either, though it was supposed to be naked. From the proportions, the kid would be about six, but that wasn't what it represented. And that wasn't what you concentrated on, since the child on the sign had been dissected—head, arms, legs, all amputated and bleeding. Just spurts of blood around the pieces and the sexless trunk, and quite a puddle underneath. "My Mom Chose Abortion," that's what these signs usually said.

Mad Dog felt a fire in his gut. He was Cheyenne. He was absolutely opposed to abortion. Life began at the moment of conception. That was a canon of Cheyenne world view. But that didn't mean he wanted someone putting one of these grotesque pieces of trash in his yard. If he found out who….

And then he was close enough to read this sign and realize it was a little different than most. He stopped his Mini Cooper in the drive and got out, though not before Hailey used his lap as a springboard to exit first. She trotted to the sign, hackles raised, sniffing it and the grass nearby.

Whoever had put it up was long gone. If anyone were still here, Hailey wouldn't be running around memorizing scents. She'd be sinking her teeth in someone's ass. And Mad Dog wouldn't be calling her off.

He went to the thing and applied a boot. When that didn't work, he tried a shoulder. He had to back off and get a run at it before wood cracked and a four-by-four splintered. The sign twisted and broke free of the other post as he continued applying pressure. Even after it was lying on the ground, invisible to anyone but him, he didn't feel satisfied.

"Hailey," he said. "Let's go get an ax and some gasoline and matches." He wouldn't feel clean until this thing was converted to ash. Not even then. The idea that someone would put one of these disgusting things in his yard, that was bad enough. But this one had been personalized. Turned, it seemed, into the lowest sort of mudslinging he'd ever seen in a Benteen County campaign. This sign said, "Sheriff English's Daughters Chose Abortion."

Mrs. Kraus still hadn't managed to check all the messages on the sheriff's office answering machine. The phones had been that busy since she came in, precisely at eight because the county budget could only afford to pay her an eight-hour day, five days a week—absolutely no overtime. Even so, her paychecks were two months behind.

All the messages she'd gotten to had been questions about Wynn's accident with the school bus and the Dodge that had gone off the road. There could still be something important on there, but every time she tried to check, the phone rang again.

"Sheriff's office," Mrs. Kraus rasped in a voice as smooth as barbed wire.

"I just wanted to call and extend my sympathy to all of you over there about poor Wynn-Some."

It took Mrs. Kraus a minute to place the voice. "Is that you, Agnes Wagner?"

Agnes hadn't spoken to Mrs. Kraus for three years. Not since the county-backed scheme to build a wind farm went down in flames. The plan had turned out to be a scam and it cost Agnes Wagner all of her small investment. Nearly every resident lost money on the deal. Mrs. Kraus, too. Even some misappropriated county funds had disappeared. That boondoggle had been the responsibility of the former Benteen County Board of Supervisors, all of them recalled and replaced now, not the sheriff's office. In fact, Sheriff English had uncovered the plot and saved most of the county's money. That hadn't kept Agnes Wagner from blaming everyone who worked at the courthouse, probably even the janitor.

"Why, yes dear, it's me," Mrs. Wagner said. "I just wanted to tell you all I'm praying for you and…."

Here it came.

"Well, dear. I was wondering if any of those poor children on the bus died, and if you could tell me who they were?"

"So you can call their parents and offer your sympathy to them as well?" Mrs. Kraus was pretty sure it was more so Agnes could call her friends and scoop them with the latest gossip. There was a reason Mrs. Kraus hadn't felt hurt at being cut off by Agnes these last three years.

"Of course, dear."

And Mrs. Kraus hated being called dear, at least by someone who didn't mean it.

"Well, *dear*," Mrs. Kraus began, on the verge of telling Agnes to stuff her sympathy where the sun didn't shine. The other line rang, interrupting her. And, offering what she thought was an even better exit. "The list of dead and dying, it's so long, and there goes the other phone. I know you wouldn't want to keep me from departmental business."

"I could hold," Agnes said.

"No, I couldn't ask you to do that," Mrs. Kraus said. "But thanks for your kind thoughts."

Mrs. Kraus punched a button, hanging up on Agnes Wagner and connecting herself to the line that was ringing. "Sheriff's office," she said.

"Vote for Greer," someone said, then laughed before the line went dead or she could tell him off.

Politics always seemed to bring out the worst in folks, but this election was beyond anything she'd seen before. How had the opposition found someone as self-righteous and vicious as Lieutenant Greer, then persuaded so many folks to buy into his Old-Testament, unforgiving brand of Christianity? It was exactly contrary to the version she'd been brought up on, where turning the other cheek was the preferred option. What was wrong with Kansas? And, more particularly, Benteen County? The evangelical crusade against infidels and Democrats seemed to have found its ultimate level of insanity here.

She took advantage of the momentary silence to play another message from the department's answering machine.

"This is Mr. Juhnke over at Buffalo Springs High," a nasal voice said. "Sheriff, I thought you should know. That school bus your deputy ran into, it wasn't checked out to anybody. Whoever was using it didn't have authorization."

"Young Caucasian male," Doc said. "Maybe fourteen or fifteen. He wasn't carrying any documents, but most of his clothes were made in Latin America."

The sheriff tried to concentrate on what Doc was saying instead of the person he was saying it about—a wrecked, partially autopsied body lying on a stainless steel slab a few feet away. At least the sheriff's nose wasn't leaking anymore. Doc had stuffed it with cotton and given him one of those artificial ice packs.

No matter how many years English had spent on this job, he'd never learned to handle the way sudden violence turned living, breathing humans into empty containers like this one.

"Anything in his pockets?" The sheriff's voice sounded like a cartoon character's with all that cotton jammed in his nostrils. It might have been funny in other circumstances.

Doc shook his head. "I went through everything and did an external examination before I started cutting. Truth is, I'm not likely to be able to help you much. I can tell you what he ate last and how long ago, but you already know when and how he died. Acute blunt-force trauma. Kid must have been trussed up and thrown in the back of that vehicle. He wasn't belted in, so when the car rolled he was thrown out a window. Then the car crushed him, but he was probably dead already."

"Trussed?" That took the sheriff by surprise. He hadn't noticed any bindings at the scene. Of course he hadn't spent much time on the kid once he knew the boy was beyond help. There'd been so many other victims.

"You probably wouldn't have noticed that, would you? I found a little piece of sliced plastic embedded in one of his wrists. Part of one of those disposable plastic pull-tight strips they use for handcuffs these days. Marks on his ankles make it look like he was bound hand and foot. The plastic probably got cut off him when he went through the window, or just tore free as he tumbled across that field."

"You're saying this kid was being abducted? Held against his will?"

"Looks that way," Doc said. "Guess I should have let you know that sooner, huh?"

The sheriff started to tell him so, then stopped himself. If he'd known at the scene, maybe he could have concentrated more on questioning the driver of the Dodge. But Doc hadn't known at the scene, either, and both of them had been too busy trying to keep Wynn and the kids from the bus alive until the emergency vehicles arrived. He hadn't had time for an interrogation. Now, with the driver transported to a hospital in Hutchinson, and with the sheriff working this investigation single-handed, knowing before this moment wouldn't have helped him one bit.

"The driver was belted in up front where he had air bags. Still, he did things to his knee that'll remind him of last night for the rest of his life. When I found the plastic, I called the hospital in Hutchinson. The driver's still in surgery. They said he wasn't likely to wake up for HPD to question him before mid-afternoon. I did ask them to call back and let me know when he starts recovery. That was the guy who asked for Pastor Goodfellow, wasn't it? You find Goodfellow? He know anything about this?"

The sheriff was glad he hadn't chewed Doc out. The emergency medical techs who transported the driver had known he was under arrest and in need of questioning. By the time Doc found the plastic, there was nothing more to do from Benteen County. Just call the cops in Hutch and make sure they questioned the man as soon as he came out from under anesthetic.

"Greer and I had our little misunderstanding before I got to Goodfellow, so we didn't talk much. The pastor claimed he knew nothing about the guy or the Dodge or the kid."

Doc leaned against the counter where his autopsy tools were laid out. The bone shears gleamed. "Goodfellow speaks Spanish. He evangelizes among the new Latin majority down in Garden City and some of the other meat-packing communities where English has become a second language. You'll probably find most Hispanics in this part of the state know our pastor."

The sheriff pulled his notebook out and checked. He'd forgotten the driver had appeared to be Hispanic, though it was in his notes that way. The man hadn't been carrying any identification and there'd been no tags on the Dodge.

"Remember?" Doc said. "Goodfellow tried services in Spanish here. Didn't work because our Latinos don't speak Spanish anymore."

That was because Buffalo Spring's last economic boom had been more than fifty years ago. People had been leaving the county ever since, not migrating to it.

The sheriff's cell rang. It was Mrs. Kraus. She told him about the school bus, as well as her opinion of the low-lifes who'd been tying up her phone since she got in.

"Just what I need," the sheriff said, "another mystery to solve."

He was feeling overwhelmed. Aside from Wynn, who was in an ICU in Wichita, the county's financial crisis had left him with only two other deputies. One of those was on indefinite leave in Winfield, trying to persuade his aging parents to trade the house they kept accidentally setting fire to for a place in a retirement community. The other, a wanna-be chef, was home heaving his guts out after one of his recipes failed. Mrs. Kraus had said that deputy wouldn't be in until his fever broke and he could get more than ten feet from the nearest toilet.

"Things are getting complicated, Doc. That school bus had no business being out there. Now I've got that to look into, as well as this kid." He glanced at the crushed and carved body on the stainless steel table. "Can you tell me anything else about him that might help? I don't have much to go on."

"Well, there is one thing," Doc said. He bit a lip for a moment as if searching for a way to put it. "Took me awhile to realize it," he said, "'cause he's so banged up and all, but this boy's real unusual."

"How's that?"

"He was perfect. Other than what the accident did to him, and being tied up, this kid didn't have any blemishes. No cavities, no fillings, no missing teeth. You'd expect some old wounds, but I haven't even found a scar on him, to say nothing of birth marks or other defects. I mean, it's weird. He doesn't even have a pimple."

When Mad Dog looked around, Hailey wasn't there. She'd been sniffing the grass moments ago, just a few feet away. Had she caught a scent and decided to follow it?

He called her name, not that she usually came when wanted. She was mostly wolf, not dog. She didn't do obedience. When he needed her, that was something else. When he needed her, she was always there.

He left the Mini in the drive and headed for the house. Maybe she was thirsty. Maybe she'd gone to the galvanized steel tub he kept filled for her by the back door.

As Mad Dog passed the lilac bushes in front of the house, a splash of color caught his eye. Red, on his front door. There wasn't supposed to be any red on his front door. Paint, he thought at first. Then he got closer and realized it wasn't exactly red and it sure wasn't paint. It was more the rust shade that blood turns when it dries. And it had been applied to his door to spell one word—"Pagan."

Mad Dog was starting to get seriously angry. The sign in his front yard, that was bad enough. But somebody had painted their intolerance on his door in blood, and left behind the paint brush. One of the squirrels that lived in the big trees that dotted his yard had been gut shot, its tail dipped into the death wound to paint the message.

This was almost like killing a pet. The squirrels in his yard were half-tame. Hailey delighted in chasing them, and they delighted in teasing her from just out of reach. It seemed to be a game both sides had agreed to play without the normal consequences. Hailey might cut them off from a tree they were headed for, but she always let them get away. And when they stayed too close to the ground to stop and brag about their escape she showed them how high a wolf could jump, but she always managed to avoid snapping her powerful jaws on one. Even when they threw sticks or hedge apples at her.

The little corpse had been dead a while. This must have been done shortly after he left. He was surprised the kid he'd hired to keep an eye on the place hadn't cleaned it off.

Mad Dog tested the front door to be sure it was still locked. It was. And the windows all proved to be closed, unbroken, and secure, as he made his way around to the back door.

That's where he found Hailey. By the water tub, along with more dead squirrels and a few dead birds. Hailey's hackles were up. She was staring at the tub and growling deep in her chest. Mad Dog wanted to join her. The water was green from the discarded bottle of antifreeze that had been dumped into it.

Jesus, she hadn't drunk any, had she? No, she couldn't have. From her stance and attitude, she'd recognized the threat and the evil behind it. He didn't take any chances, though. He turned the poisoned water over and got a hose and diluted the stuff until he'd turned his back yard into a muddy mess. He still wasn't satisfied, but he didn't know what else to do. He'd have to ask someone, the local vet, maybe. But first, he needed to make sure Hailey came inside and got fresh water, safe water, straight from the tap. And he needed to call Englishman. Tell his brother about the greetings he'd found in his yard. And warn him, because Mad Dog was pretty sure that however viciously he'd been attacked, Englishman was the real target.

Heather English parked her Honda Civic in the lot behind the Benteen County Courthouse. It was a dazzling fall morning. She stepped out and stretched, a bit stiff after the three-hour drive home from Lawrence. She was a first-year law student at KU. Bright sun, gentle breezes, lots of color in the leaves welcomed her. It was always good to come home, but it was odd to drive past so many election posters urging voters to pick someone other than her father for Benteen County Sheriff. He'd been getting reelected by narrow margins for as long as she could recall, but this year's signs had a nastier quality than she remembered. Politics in general had been moving that direction for years, but when it was your dad, that made the insults personal.

Englishman's Chevy pickup wasn't in the lot, but Mrs. Kraus would know where he was. Heather went in through the back door, anxious to find him. She was sure he was all right, but she'd woken with the oddest feeling this morning. Her dad had talked her out of skipping school to come home for Election Day. He'd suggested she wait and maybe stretch out the Thanksgiving break. But the moment she opened her eyes this morning, she'd had no choice except to come back. She'd never felt anything like it before. It was woo-woo stuff, like Uncle Mad Dog was always talking about. She believed in the spiritual stuff her Uncle Mad Dog described, but nothing like it had ever happened to her no matter how hard she tried. Not until this morning.

"Heather!" Mrs. Kraus stood behind the counter in the dusty old sheriff's office and greeted her with a smile as big as the Kansas sky. "What are you doing here? Does Englishman know you're coming? Did you hear about Wynn?"

She felt a little reassured. If something had happened to her dad, Mrs. Kraus didn't know about it. And that wasn't likely. Heather decided to answer the last question first.

"I heard on the radio as I was driving back. Is there any word? Do you know how Wynn's doing? Or the kids who were on that bus?"

Mrs. Kraus' smile disappeared. "Wynn's critical, but stable. I was on the phone with his wife not long ago. They flew Wynn to a hospital in Wichita. The doctors think he's got a good chance to make it, but he won't be telling his side of the story anytime soon. Would sure help your dad if he could."

"Is Dad okay?" Heather had wanted to lead with that question, but she'd been trying to persuade herself that the feeling she'd woken with could be explained by the anchovy pizza her study group had split last night, along with some pithy thoughts on the limitations of tort liability.

"Oh, sure, honey. I mean, you know he's not been sleeping well and he's shook up by all this, and overwhelmed as usual, but he's fine. He'd be better if I could find him a deputy to help sort through this mess."

Englishman hadn't been sleeping or eating well since her mother died. Before, really, while he was sheriff and caregiver and searcher after miracles. Heather knew about her dad's deputy problems, too. Englishman had only had one qualified deputy in all his years in office. The woman had saved Heather and her sister from a bomb. After that, she got lots of better offers from other law enforcement agencies. Then Benteen County's finances turned so desperate they stopped issuing regular paychecks. Heather didn't blame the woman for moving on.

"Dad's working this case by himself?" She hadn't thought it would be that bad. The county budget included three deputies—not trained police professionals, but nice guys who did their best. Wynn was in a hospital, but that still left two. "Where are Gaddert and Frazier?"

"Gaddert's on leave to deal with his folks. Frazier's latest experiment in gourmet cooking missed the mark. He's out with food poisoning."

"How can Daddy investigate the car Wynn was chasing and the bus accident, all by himself?"

"Well, he's got me." Mrs. Kraus squared her shoulders and pulled herself up to her full four-foot-ten. Heather knew the old woman was a huge asset, no matter how tall she stood.

The phone rang. "Dang!" Mrs. Kraus said. "I had the state troopers on one line and the hospital in Hays, where they took the people from the school bus, on the other. Somebody's gone and got impatient on me."

"I'm sorry. Deal with business. You get that line and I'll see if I can keep the people on the other one happy." Mrs. Kraus grabbed a phone and Heather started around the counter.

"Heather?" someone said. Heather turned and discovered a neighbor, who lived a block down from the English house, standing in the doorway behind her.

"I was just about to vote," the woman said, "only someone told me the most disturbing rumor. Maybe you can help."

That phone needed attention, but Heather had been taught to be polite. "Yes?"

"That person told me Englishman is an atheist. Is that true?"

Heather tried to decide how to answer that. Englishman wasn't exactly on speaking terms with God. She'd once heard him say he and God shared mutual doubts. And that was before Mom died. The God Englishman believed in wasn't much interested in tracking the flight of every sparrow, or even humanity in general. In this woman's world, that was atheism.

"Uh, no," Heather said. She thought that was technically accurate. "Daddy's no atheist. My sister and I were raised as Episcopalians, if that helps."

The woman's face turned prune-like. "Oh my," she said. "Isn't that pretty much the same thing?"

The sheriff pulled his Chevy out of Klausen's parking lot and turned right on Main Street. It was too warm for fall. Indian summer, he supposed. Mother Nature teasing you with what she was about to take away.

There wasn't much traffic on Main. Good thing, since he was working his cell phone as he drove. He hated people who did that, but he needed to do several hundred things at the moment, among them making sure the authorities in Hutch realized the driver of the Dodge was probably a kidnapper.

There never was much traffic on Main these days. The street was empty of cars, but littered with the first dead leaves of fall. That and the black walnuts kids liked to roll out in front of motorists. When you ran over them, they exploded with a sound like the crack of a rifle. The sheriff recalled strewing a few walnuts in his own youth. He and his friends had thought it was great fun to watch people duck and start searching for snipers. Since 9/11, the prank had a new edge to it. Not that that had stopped anyone.

There hadn't been a hard enough frost to bring down all the leaves yet. Bright yellow and red, they clung to the tops of the mature trees that lined the street. Lower down and nearer the trunks, they were still a tired green. The condemned, awaiting execution.

The sheriff ran over a couple of walnuts and finished his call before he turned in at the high school. The first of its buildings had been erected on the east edge of town back before the Great Depression. The school was still on the east edge, since the city had pretty much stopped growing soon after. The sheriff found a spot in the parking lot, not far from the signs that indicated the gym was a polling place today.

A single crow sat on a ledge above the entrance to the high school. It watched him silently as he passed through those familiar doors. The bird looked like it wanted to tell him something. Since this was Election Day and the evangelical right had targeted him, "nevermore" would be appropriate.

The sheriff turned down the hall toward the principal's office before he remembered the cotton Doc had packed in his nose. He wasn't about to walk in there sounding like Elmer Fudd. Instead, he stepped into the boys' room and carefully removed the packing from each nostril. The right one started bleeding again. The dispenser was out of paper towels, so he stepped into a booth to look for toilet paper.

The restroom door opened and someone entered.

"Are you crazy?" a cracking adolescent voice asked. "What if someone finds us in here?"

The sheriff could remember sneaking into this very room several times when he should have been in class. Secretly making plans to raid a girls' slumber party, for instance. In his day, those raids had been pretty innocent. Boyfriends stole a kiss from their girls, would-be boyfriends tried to get attention by setting off firecrackers or sneaking up to windows and holding a flashlight under their chins to look spooky. No one ever got hurt. Except when one of his buddies had run from an angry chaperoning father, an impressive burst of speed that was spoiled by the clothesline in his path. And then, it was mostly hurt pride, though his friend had spoken with a peculiar squeaky voice for a few weeks afterward.

"Don't worry about it," another voice said. "Worry about what happens if you talk about last night."

That got the sheriff's attention. Wynn had run into a school bus during that night. But that wasn't necessarily what the boys were talking about. The sheriff decided his nose could use a bit more quiet pressure here in the stall.

"I won't say anything," the younger one whined.

"Swear to God," the other demanded.

Whatever it was, it was serious to these two.

"I swear."

"And I condemn my soul to eternal damnation if I break my word," the older prompted. "Say that, too."

Everyone in the sheriff's class had been Christians. Everyone in the county was, with the exception of Mad Dog, a couple of Jews, a converted Buddhist, the Muslims who ran the hardware store over in Cottonwood Corners, and a few closet agnostics and atheists. But English and his classmates hadn't worried much about eternal damnation. That was something new. The sheriff didn't like it much. English didn't like anything that required everyone to believe the same as everyone else. When you had a brother like his, you tended to be aware of stuff like that.

"I...." The first voice didn't care for that version of the oath.

"Swear it," the second boy said. "Swear you'll never tell any-body where you were last night, Chucky, or I'm gonna personally shove you through the gates of hell myself."

Chucky. That must be Chucky Williams—his old man had only been a couple of classes behind the sheriff. English was pretty sure there wasn't another Chucky in the county, though there were several Chucks.

How many times had he heard lives threatened in these hallowed halls while he was growing up? None of those had been serious threats. This probably wasn't either, but it did seem to be getting out of hand. He dropped the bloody toilet paper in the bowl and took hold of the handle of the stall. The door stuck and he had to yank a couple of times to get it open.

"Holy shit," Chucky said.

"Somebody's in here," the other finished.

Both of them were out the door before the sheriff could get a look at them. And no one was in the hall when he exited the restroom. He knew how many potential escape routes they had. He'd never catch them, but Chucky should be easy to find. And he'd recognize the other voice if he heard it again.

Could something else have happened last night that required such a solemn oath of secrecy? It could when you were in your teens, he decided. But when he looked across the hall at the windows facing Main Street, the crow was sitting on the sill. It was staring in, watching the sheriff and turning its head from side to side as if it couldn't believe he'd let a clue like that get away.

Heather answered the line Mrs. Kraus wasn't on. "Benteen County Sheriff's Office."

"Who's this?" The brusque voice was an older man's.

"My name's English," she said. "Who are you?"

"Oh, sorry, Sheriff," the man at the other end of the line said. "I wasn't expecting a woman."

He thought she was Sheriff English. What a kick. She should tell him, but he still hadn't identified himself.

"And you are?"

"Sorry. Hell of a morning here in Hays. Can't remember the last time we had to expend so much energy doing some other jurisdiction's work for them."

This guy had an attitude. She hadn't told him she was the sheriff. His mistake. Let him live with it. She didn't say anything and he correctly interpreted her silence.

"Okay. I know. Little county like yours hasn't got much manpower, but we don't exactly have a generous budget either. I'm Under-Sheriff Pugh. Sheriff passed your request on to me, not that I ain't got more open cases than Carter's got liver pills."

Carter? Liver pills? And *man*power? This Pugh must be a serious coot with a tint of misogyny.

"And?" Heather said.

"Yeah, I'm getting to it." He paused and she heard him thumb through a notepad. "I questioned everyone who was on that bus your deputy rammed. A couple are gonna be kept for more treatment. Rest should be released by this evening." He recited a brief litany of their injuries.

"They all say they were coming from choir practice at Bible camp," he continued. "Kinda early for choir practice, if you ask me, which you didn't. Your bus driver didn't end up here. You'll have to check, see where another ambulance might of took him."

"Names?" Heather kept it short and sweet. She didn't trust him not to recognize how young she was. Twenty-two, now, but she didn't feel like a full-scale grownup. Not most of the time, anyway.

"You mean the kids? I didn't ask who was driving the bus. Figured you would of established that at the scene."

"Yeah, kids," she agreed. He read off the list and she wrote them down on a sheet of scratch paper. She didn't have to ask him how to spell them. She knew them all. She and her sister had been babysitters for every single one.

"Anything else?"

He sighed, like she'd demanded he give up the rest of his precious day. "Well, they all agreed your deputy was running without lights until just before he rammed them. Why'd he do that, Englishman? Why'd…?" He paused a moment. "Say," he said, "if you're a woman, why do they call you Englishman?"

"Inside joke," she said. "You got anything else for me?"

"Ain't that enough?"

"Thanks for your generous cooperation." Heather hit the disconnect button. Beyond his rudeness and attitude, there was something about their conversation that bothered her.

"Mrs. Kraus." The woman had just hung up her own line. "Didn't you tell me everyone from the accident but the driver of the Dodge and Wynn-Some were transported to Hays?"

"That's right." Mrs. Kraus was making notes of her own and the phone had just started ringing again. "Why?"

"Then where's the bus driver?"

Mrs. Kraus raised an eyebrow and shook her head. Then she raised her phone and answered it.

So who was the bus driver? And what was this crap about choir practice at Bible camp? The county's only Bible camp was never open except in summer, and a church choir shouldn't have anything to do with Buffalo Springs High. You couldn't use a school bus to transport a church choir, could you? Wasn't that mixing church and state?

Then, what Mrs. Kraus said destroyed her train of thought.

"Mad Dog. Calm down. What d'ya mean, attempted murder?"

The sense of impending doom that had brought Mad Dog speeding down from the Black Hills was nearly forgotten by the time he got off the phone with Mrs. Kraus. His brother, Englishman, she'd assured him, was alive and well and out there trying to solve the mystery behind this morning's accident. When Mad Dog told her he might check in with Englishman on the sheriff's cell, Mrs. Kraus advised against it. Englishman needed a free line so he could get updates from the office and the localities to which the injured had been transported. And he needed to be left alone to do his job since he was a one-man department this morning.

Mad Dog decided he'd found what he dreaded. What pulled him off that mountain must be that obscene political muck in his front yard and on his door, and the attempt on the life of his beloved Hailey. If Englishman was too busy to help him solve those crimes, Mad Dog would do it himself.

Armed with his own cell phone, so he wouldn't have to drive back to the house to contact Englishman or Mrs. Kraus, he and Hailey started back to the Mini Cooper. Halfway across the front yard, Mad Dog changed his mind. He sprinted back past the house toward the barn and a view of the pasture beyond. Antifreeze in Hailey's water could as easily be duplicated in the cattle tank where his small buffalo herd drank.

The water in the trough also looked green, but just from the moss that lined it. The liquid itself was as clear and pure as always. There weren't any dead bison lying around, either. The ones he could see all looked reassuringly fat and sassy. He couldn't see all of them, of course. They had a full section to graze on.

Mark Brown was the kid he'd hired to keep an eye on the place and do chores while he was gone. Mad Dog wanted a word with him. The assault on his home hadn't taken place this morning. The dead squirrel and poisoned animals were too desiccated for that. Mark should have dumped the poison, disposed of the dead animals, hosed off his front door, and taken down the offensive sign. Mad Dog wanted an explanation and an apology.

"Kid" wasn't quite the right word for Mark. He was in his mid-twenties. Mark had gone off to major in agronomy after Buffalo Springs High. Apparently he'd been better at parties than studies. He hadn't brought home a degree. He'd been helping his folks farm these last few years—a bit on the lazy side but with a good heart. Or so Mad Dog thought when he left his farm and buffalo herd in the young man's care.

Mark would probably be at his folk's place. Farmers didn't get out much, except to pick up supplies or deliver crops. And there wasn't much entertainment to be found in Buffalo Springs. The Browns' farm was on the next section north, surrounded by acres of winter wheat that stretched from the road like an immense treeless lawn. A cluster of evergreens and a couple of rusty maples marked the Browns' homestead, a sprawling ranch-style house surrounded by modern metal outbuildings. But the house was empty and the buildings were closed up and silent. Mad Dog wandered about and shouted a few hellos, without effect.

He got back in the Mini Cooper and went north another section. The Browns farmed that one, too. And, sure enough, there was a tractor tilling some low ground near the creek. Mad Dog pulled up beside the fence, got out, waded through a weed-filled ditch, and waved.

Mark's dad finished the row he was working, then parked his rig and walked over to join Mad Dog at the edge of the field.

Hailey ignored Brown, checking the ditch for quail, pheasant, bunnies, or grizzly bears for all Mad Dog knew.

"Didn't expect you home so soon," Brown said, keeping a wary eye on Hailey's bushy tail. Brown knew Hailey well enough and he liked dogs and all, but he'd never quite warmed to the idea of a wolf-hybrid. Hailey knew him, too, which was probably why she was staying busy elsewhere. She didn't dislike him so she didn't go out of her way to make him nervous the way she did with some folks.

"Just got back," Mad Dog said. "I was looking for Mark."

"Figured," Brown said. "Thought he'd be at your place. Me and his ma haven't seen him since you asked him to sleep over at your house while you were gone."

Mad Dog hadn't asked Mark to do that. In fact, he hadn't even left Mark a key. All he'd asked was that Mark check on the place and the buffalo every day, feed them some alfalfa and grain, and call Englishman if there were any problems. Still, maybe the lie Mark told his parents was a white one. Maybe he had something going with a young lady or…. Mad Dog couldn't imagine an "or," not in Benteen County.

"No, I missed him. He might be running an errand in town. Mark doesn't have a cell phone, does he?"

"Nope," the farmer said. "Not unless he's found himself a job that pays a lot better than I do."

Mad Dog nodded. Cell phones were common enough in central Kansas now, but spoiling your kids wasn't. If Mark were a better laborer, maybe, but the Browns probably felt they were being kind just giving a grown-up boy room and board. From what Mark had said, Mad Dog didn't think the old man even paid his son regular wages.

"If you see him, tell him I'm back," Mad Dog said. "Ask him to get in touch and we'll settle up."

"I'll do 'er," Brown said. He turned back toward his tractor as Mad Dog climbed the barbed wire.

"Church," Brown said.

Mad Dog looked back and nearly lost his hold on the upper strand while its barbs were uncomfortably close to his crotch.

"Mark's been hanging around that church near the courthouse a lot lately. That'd be the first place I'd look if he's not where he's supposed to be."

Mad Dog must have looked surprised. Not because he hadn't thought Mark was religious. Most folks in Kansas were inclined to seek heavenly intervention from droughts, floods, tornados, hail, late and early frosts, and the other extremes of nature. Mark just hadn't seemed the sort to attend weekday services.

"The oldest Epperson girl practices piano over there most every day," the senior Brown said. "I reckon it's got more to do with her than any spiritual calling."

◇◇◇

Heather took several more phone calls. Every one was from an angry or nosey citizen, wanting to know what the hell Deputy Wynn had thought he was doing and why he'd hit that bus and whether any of the local children were dead. And who were the people in that other car, anyway? It was Election Day and her dad had said this one was going to be extra tough. She made herself be polite, even when the callers weren't. But she was starting to get frustrated, and a little anxious. She still hadn't proved to herself that Englishman was all right. She hadn't seen or talked to him. It was going to take seeing him in the flesh, she decided, before the last of the bad feelings she'd woken with would go away.

Mrs. Kraus was taking the same kind of calls. Only her patience had long ago worn thin. "That's not public information," she said. Or, "I'm not at liberty to say." As well as the occasional, "Don't you have anything better to do than keep me from my job?"

Mrs. Alexander was Heather's current caller. The woman lived across Main Street from the school and she was convinced the sheriff had just pulled in there to inform the administration that every child on that bus had died.

"No, ma'am," Heather said. "In fact, I just heard from the authorities in Hays that, other than a few broken bones, none are seriously hurt."

"Well then, young lady," Mrs. Alexander said, "what's your father doing wasting time at the school? Is he campaigning for a few last-minute votes right at the polling booths?"

Heather had had it. "No, I think he's trying to find out why those kids were out there so early this morning. If not, he's probably getting ready to serve those eviction notices the commission authorized for past-due property taxes." That shut the woman up. Mrs. Alexander had refused to pay her property taxes since she lost money in the county's wind farm debacle. The line went dead and Heather wondered whether she'd just lost her dad a vote. Probably not, considering the tone the call had begun on. She left the line off the hook and went over to her father's desk. She knew where he was now. And she would go see him, reassure herself that he was fine so she could stop that nagging fear at the back of her brain. And after she saw him, she knew what she would do then, too.

When she turned, she discovered her dad's opponent, Lieutenant Greer, accompanied by Newt Neuhauser—Greer's sidekick and likely the next under-sheriff—with Pastor Goodfellow, coming through the door.

Greer had been so far ahead of her in school he'd never noticed her. And he'd been the kind of guy who didn't notice anyone who didn't worship him, or get in his way. From the way he smiled at her, Heather was sure he didn't know who she was. The smile went away when Goodfellow nodded to her and said, "Good morning, Miss English. I thought you were off at school."

"I was," she said, and left it at that. She had no desire to explain herself to these three.

Mrs. Kraus cleared her latest phone call and offered the trio a greeting. "What can I do for you *gentlemen?*" The way she emphasized the last word made it clear she thought they were anything but.

Heather put her own phone back on the hook. "I've got to go," she told Mrs. Kraus, and went around the counter toward the men bunched by the door.

"No need to get testy, Mrs. Kraus," Greer said. "I don't plan to fire you when I'm elected. You can stay on till your Medicare kicks in…or has it already done that?"

"Excuse me," Heather said. "You're in my way." Goodfellow and Neuhauser had stepped aside to let her pass, but Greer was blocking the door.

"We just came to get an idea of the layout," Pastor Goodfellow apologized. "If the lieutenant wins, we plan to set up a desk for me over here. I'll be available for Christian counseling whenever I can spare the time. As a volunteer, of course."

Greer didn't comment. He was staring at Heather. She'd watched men undress her with their eyes before. No big deal. She knew she was attractive and had a good figure. But this felt different, more like a strip search.

"Wow," Greer said. "Looks like Englishman's daughter is all grown up."

"Some of us do that," she said. She had her mother's short temper and wise mouth. It was going to get her in trouble one day. "Now, if you'll let me by…?"

He stood his ground. "You see your daddy," Greer said, "tell him I'm sorry if I busted his nose. But old men ought to know their limits."

The morning's anxiety snapped back. Had this bully really hurt her dad? She tried to brush past but he put a hand on her arm to stop her.

And then he was kneeling on the floor as she decided whether to break his finger. Englishman had insisted she take those self-defense courses. This war hero should have been smart enough to avoid the hold she'd put on him, but he'd underestimated her and placed his hand where she could control it.

"You best let go of me, little girl. Else, broken finger or not, I'm gonna have to hurt you when I get up."

And that was a problem. He was probably a lot better trained at this stuff than she was, to say nothing of the eighty pounds he had on her. She could make that finger very painful, and she knew a few other tricks that were likely to hurt just as bad, but there wasn't much chance she could stop him cold and, if she didn't, his size and strength were going to make the difference. Then he could hurt her.

"Let me go now or you're gonna end up bleeding all over this room," Greer hissed.

"No she's not," Mrs. Kraus said. Heather looked over her shoulder. Mrs. Kraus had her Glock in a two-handed shooter's grip centered on Greer's belly. "Why don't you go on and leave, Heather. This man's gonna stick around and explain to me why he's assaulting a young woman right here in the sheriff's office and why I shouldn't arrest him and maybe lock him back in one of our cells for the rest of Election Day."

"Now, now," Goodfellow said. "The lieutenant was only teasing."

"Yes, teasing," Neuhauser said, his voice hard. "Weren't you, Lieutenant."

Greer glanced from Heather to Mrs. Kraus and her Glock. Heather thought he might be angry enough to kill all of them, but he agreed with Neuhauser and Goodfellow. "Yeah," he said. "Just joking around."

"It's been fun," Heather said. "But I really do have to go." She released her grip and went out the door. Behind her, she heard Goodfellow suggest that Mrs. Kraus put the gun away.

"I'm gonna need a few minutes to think on that," Mrs. Kraus said as Heather went down the hall toward the back door.

Heather wondered if she would be able to come home again if Greer won this election. All of a sudden, that seemed like a legitimate question. Probably, she thought, but not if she'd followed her instincts and snapped the bastard's finger.

The principal's office was located in the ugly blond-brick addition that made an odd link between Buffalo Springs' red-brick two-story elementary and high schools. It had been added in the fifties when the community's student population was still rising.

The bell rang and Englishman found himself threading his way through a mob of hobbit-sized kids. This part of the school had become the junior high—now, middle school—shortly after it was built. The principals' offices—three, one for each level—occupied subdivided classrooms about midway along the addition's main hall beside an absurdly short water fountain.

The sheriff acknowledged waves and greetings from most of the kids before ducking into the security of the secretary's office.

"Oh, Sheriff English," she said, rising and offering her hand. "I'm so sorry." Her sympathy for his wife was two years late and it embarrassed both of them.

"Is Mr. Juhnke in?" he asked. Juhnke was the high school principal and the man who'd called about the buses.

"Yes, but he's with someone. He'll be free in a few minutes if you could just have a seat."

"It's kind of important," the sheriff said. "Maybe you could let him know I'm here."

Her blush freshened and she ducked into one of the offices. When she returned, she was followed by a sour-faced teen, who took the seat the sheriff might have otherwise occupied. Juhnke came out and offered his hand, then guided the sheriff inside. Diplomas lined a wall above a collection of file cabinets. Textbooks, interspersed with dusty trophies, decorated shelves on either side of a window with a marvelous view of the faculty/staff parking lot.

"Any word on my students, Sheriff?"

"Not that I've heard, but you and I both would know it if there were bad news."

Juhnke didn't seem reassured. "Then I assume you're here about the bus?"

The sheriff nodded.

"I don't know what it was doing out there. Or why those kids were on it. We aren't missing any bus drivers or teachers. Everyone showed up as usual this morning. Fortunately, we've got a spare bus for emergencies."

"Whose bus was missing?"

"Swenson's. He called me when he came in. By then, I already knew what had happened to it."

"Who has keys?"

"Each driver has his own set. Spares are in a lock box in the bus barn. The drivers all know the combination. So do most of our teachers and some students, I'm afraid. We haven't been security conscious about that. Now we will be." He shrugged. "Locking our barn door after the horse was stolen. Isn't that how it goes?"

The sheriff was beginning to think he should have called instead of taking the time to drive over. "So you have no clue who might have stolen it?"

"Well, one of the drivers came in early. Had a fouled spark plug yesterday and he brought a replacement to install this morning. He said a car and a truck were in the lot near the barn. Weren't there when he came back."

"Did he recognize them?"

Juhnke looked pained. "Just the car. It was Mr. Gamble's."

The sheriff felt his eyebrows go up. "You mean…?"

"Yes," Juhnke said with more than a hint of irritation. "Our music teacher."

The sheriff knew Gamble. Gamble had been working hard for his opponent. One of Greer's campaign promises was to force the high school to let Gamble teach an Intelligent Design course.

"Mr. Gamble won't want to talk to me," the sheriff said, "but it seems we need to have a conversation."

Heather felt odd, stepping back inside Buffalo Springs High. Like she'd overslept and was late for a test. All that was needed to complete the script of her occasional nightmares was for her to be dressed in her nightshirt, or not dressed at all. She couldn't quite catch herself before one hand checked her blouse and the other her jeans. No, she was really here, back where she'd always had to be on her best behavior. It was bad enough that Dad was sheriff, but Mom had taught and served as vice principal inside these very walls.

She turned and aimed herself toward the principals' offices. That was where Englishman would have gone. She knew he was still here. She'd parked beside his tired old pickup in the parking lot.

There was a new row of pictures above the lockers that lined the hallway. She hadn't seen them before. Valedictorians along one wall, salutatorians on the other. Her picture appeared to be in both locations for the class of 2002. That wasn't true, of course. She had been the runner-up. Her sister, the second Heather in the family, had gotten downright manic about pleasing her foster parents with good grades. Heather Lane, or Two of Two as they'd decided to call each other when a pair of Heathers in the family turned confusing, had shown One of Two who really was first in the English household, academically at least. And Heather English hadn't minded. It had been a friendly competition. There were no hard edges to either of them, even though they'd decided to number themselves like *Star Trek Voyager*'s sexy and dangerous Borg crew member, Seven of Nine.

Heather was near a branch in the hall, studying her sister's picture and marveling, yet again, at the remarkable resemblance between them. They looked like twins, though they weren't even real sisters, just distant cousins. That, and the shared name, had caused them all sorts of troubles, and afforded all sorts of opportunities. Heather remembered the time she'd scheduled two dates on one evening and how Two had filled in. The guys found out, of course, but neither figured out which of them got the girl he'd asked and which got the substitute.

Mark Goodfellow, Butch Bunker, and Chucky Williams came bowling around the corner and literally ran into her.

"Whoa, guys, slow down," she said. They looked surprised to see her, and not very happy about it. At least Mark and Butch looked that way. Chucky just looked desperate.

What was going on here? Mark and Butch were seniors. Jocks for Jesus and starters on the football team. Chucky was just a sophomore, and kind of a dweeb at that. Not someone a pair of lettermen like Mark and Butch would hang with. She noticed their hands were locked on Chucky's elbows. If not hang with, maybe torment.

"'Scuse us," Mark said, trying to edge around her. He was Pastor Goodfellow's son and he'd learned to put on a respectful front.

She looked in Chucky's panic-stricken eyes and side-stepped, blocking their way. "What's the hurry, guys? I used to babysit for you, remember? Haven't seen you in ages."

Like she'd care. Mark and Butch had been bullies as long as she'd known them. But no way was she leaving Chucky to their tender mercies. She reached out, found where the guys held Chucky and began gently prying their fingers loose, taking their hands in her own. The boys looked surprised. She gave them a dazzling smile and tried to look fondly into their eyes. Neither of them returned her gaze. They were focused, laser-like, on her boobs. Maybe she should have buttoned at least one more button on her blouse.

She clasped their hands tight and bounced up and down a little, giving their twin stares a bit of payoff. She bounced a couple of steps backwards, too, pulling them behind her and leaving Chucky free and unnoticed. Chucky might not be in competition to join her and Heather in the picture gallery, but he recognized opportunity when it slammed him upside the head. He ducked back around the corner and she heard the echo of his footsteps as he ran for it.

"Hey," Butch said, dragging his gaze away to look for their designated prey.

"You did that on purpose," Mark said, turning and heading for the corner.

"So," Heather asked, "you guys still bed wetters?"

Butch turned back and pushed her. Hard. It took her by surprise and left her off balance, so she only kicked him in the shin instead of where she'd intended. It must have hurt like hell, though.

"Leave her be," Mark said. "Help me find Chucky."

Butch had quite a limp when he turned to obey. He took the time to glance over his shoulder and favor her with a glare. "I'll see you again," he said.

No doubt about it. Heather had to admit that coming back home to live some day was turning into an increasingly risky proposition.

M ad Dog parked the Mini in front of the Church of Christ Risen. Beneath the name, the sign bore another message, "All Are Welcome Here." That was an exaggeration. It didn't apply if you were a homosexual, pro-choice, believed Darwin's theory wasn't a hoax, or were attempting to practice Cheyenne shamanism. He decided to test the message anyway and held the door open for Hailey. She bared impressive teeth, growled low in her chest, and trotted back across the street toward Veteran's Memorial Park. He didn't blame her. He'd left the windows down in the Mini. She could jump back in and curl up on a seat if she got bored.

Mad Dog hadn't been in the building in years. But he'd spent a lot of time searching for a spiritual element to fill his life. He finally found it in his mother's genealogy. She'd been an intelligent, well-read woman who marched to the beat of a different drum. She would have fit right into Bohemian or Beatnik society. Neither existed in Benteen County, so she hadn't fit in at all. She explained herself by telling folks she was a half-breed Cheyenne. It hadn't been completely true, but it gave the locals something to blame her eccentricities on. In reality, her Cheyenne half turned out to be equal parts Cheyenne, Sans Arc, Mexican cowboy, and Buffalo Soldier, but Mad Dog was convinced she'd latched onto the right ancestor to claim. She'd been Cheyenne at heart, and when he started studying Cheyenne culture and religion, he'd discovered he was Cheyenne, too. Christians weren't the only ones who could be born again.

The church bore a distinct resemblance to a warehouse. The foyer was utilitarian, a place to stomp the snow off, trap heat or cold, and block the wind. Inside, there was just a big open space. Today it was filled with rows of empty tables and scattered chairs. This was Tuesday. Didn't they hold Chamber of Commerce breakfasts here? That would explain the lingering odor of grilled sausage that hung on the air. And the platter of cinnamon rolls on the end of one of the tables against the west wall—the only tables currently being used. Half a dozen people were working phones there. They were using phrases like "Vote your faith," which made him sure he'd stumbled into the evangelical right's get-out-the-vote headquarters. He felt like going over and asking if any of them knew about the sign in his front yard, but he wasn't looking to cause trouble for its own sake. Besides, these people were openly proclaiming their politics. The ones who had assaulted his property weren't likely to work that way.

The volunteers were busy with their phone scripts. If any of them noticed him, none of them said anything. He cruised through the auditorium and took the hall on his left. He could hear the faint strains of a piano playing an unlikely honky-tonk tune back there.

The piano player had nice hair and good posture. She was so caught up in her music that she didn't notice when he entered the choir room. She was alone. Mad Dog had hoped to find Mark Brown in her audience, but there were just the two pictures on the wall in front of the piano. Jesus on the left, Reverend Aldus P. Goodfellow on the right. Aldus P. was the father of the Buffalo Springs pastor. The old man was a famed televangelist, known to millions. Mad Dog found a seat. The eyes on both portraits seemed to follow him across the room. Jesus' eyes hinted at forgiveness. Aldus P.'s glared, clearly having pegged Mad Dog as someone destined to suffer hell's eternal flames.

Mad Dog had never understood the appeal of the elder Goodfellow. Maybe he tapped some universal guilt, some need folks had to be punished for the things they'd gotten away with—the lies that worked, requited covets, or failure to deserve the devotion of a first puppy. Aldus P. had raged from his pulpit directly into people's living rooms, promising damnation for the mildest of sins, but selling redemption. In Mad Dog's youth, while he searched for spiritual answers, Aldus P. Goodfellow's verities never appealed to him. But they'd appealed to plenty of others. Even when the old man began suggesting nuking Godless Communists and, more recently, purging the earth of every Muslim. The specifics of his plans put even Hitler to shame. But he'd maintained a substantial following until age slowed him down.

The girl at the piano finished her tune and did a neat segue into something innocuously classical. Mad Dog decided it was time to proceed with his investigation. He cleared his throat and the girl cleared the bench. She stifled a screech and grabbed her attractive chest in surprise.

"Oh," she understated, "you scared me. I'm glad it's only you."

Mad Dog didn't think the "only" was a put down, considering what she'd just finished playing.

"Wasn't that Kinky Friedman? When did the Church of Christ Risen add 'They Ain't Makin' Jews Like Jesus Anymore' to their hymnal?"

"Dad!" Heather couldn't contain the relief she felt at seeing Englishman obviously safe. Not that he looked good. The weight he'd lost and the dark circles under his eyes emphasized his high cheekbones. His puffy nose was new to her. But his startling blue eyes were filled with life, and the pleasure of seeing her.

Mrs. Kraus had reassured Heather, but there'd been that premonition. Her father and Mr. Juhnke were exiting the principal's office when she spotted them and flew into her father's arms.

"Hello, Heather." Mr. Juhnke took the safe route. He'd never been sure which of the sisters was which.

Englishman returned her hug, then held her at arm's length and tried to look disapproving. "What are you doing here? Is everything all right?"

That was what she'd wanted to ask him, but now the horrible sense of concern she'd felt about the possibility of losing a second parent was finally beginning to fade.

"Sure, Dad. I just wanted to come spend Election Day with you. Help you celebrate."

"What, my retirement?" But he smiled at her and she could tell he was glad she'd come, even if she was cutting classes.

"It's great to see you," he continued, "but I'm in the middle of a busy morning."

"Yeah," she said. "I heard about Wynn. I helped Mrs. Kraus answer some calls over at the office when I got in. One was from a deputy in Hays." She told them what the man had had to say, though not who he'd thought he was saying it to. She could see tension bleed out of both men as she explained that none of the kids on the bus were seriously hurt.

"And I heard how shorthanded you are," she said. "Actually, that's why I'm here."

She reached in her fanny pack and pulled out the stuff she'd brought from his office. "You need a deputy, so I got you one."

"Really!" She could see the excitement in his eyes. "Who's that, honey?"

What she'd brought from the office was a shiny old badge bearing the logo, BENTEEN COUNTY DEPUTY SHERIFF. He had lots of spares since no one was using them at the moment. And she'd stuffed in his old set of handcuffs. The ones you could open with anything you could insert in the keyhole. She already had a can of pepper spray, so she'd left his spare pistol. She wasn't keen on guns.

"Me, Dad." She pinned the badge on the inside of her jacket. "Swear me in. Okay?"

◇◇◇

Hailey was visiting the courthouse. Since it was warmer outside than in, someone had propped the front doors open, making it simple for the wolf to enter.

There was an unusual crowd inside the foyer, waiting to vote at the booths lined up across from the door to the sheriff's office. Hailey watched for a minute, even let an elderly woman she knew stop to pet her. She didn't wag her tail, but she didn't bare her teeth either.

Agnes Wagner presented herself at the table, had her registration verified, signed in, and was presented with a ballot. She took it to the farthest booth. Hailey observed it all with the intensity her ancestors reserved for lonely caribou calves.

Agnes took her time. Several booths near her were occupied more than once while she laboriously studied the names and propositions and carefully checked each against a list she'd brought to spur her memory. She finally finished and walked to the man by the ballot box.

"Morning, ma'am," he greeted her. He reached out and took her ballot. "Here," he said. "Let me put that in the box for you."

Agnes smiled and fluttered ancient eyelashes at him. He let the ballot drop to his side as he reached out to guide her toward the door with his other hand. Hailey's lips curled as he turned back to the ballot box. When he reached to insert Agnes Wagner's ballot Hailey put herself between him and the box. Her teeth flashed and she took the punch card out of his hand.

"Hey!" the man said. Several people turned to see what had caused the exclamation. "Nice doggy," he said. "Give that back now."

Hailey made a rumbling sound in her chest and drew back her lips to let him see how long her canines were. She turned and trotted across the lobby into the sheriff's office. Mrs. Kraus was on the phone. The wolf padded around the corner of the counter as the man from the ballot box trailed her through the door.

"Can you make that dog put that down?" he said.

Mrs. Kraus shook her head. No one ever made Hailey do anything. "Actually," Mrs. Kraus told the phone, "I don't care to take a voter survey just now because this is the Benteen County Sheriff's Office, you ninny." She slammed the phone back in its cradle and glanced at Hailey.

"Where's Mad Dog?" she asked. "And what kind of trouble have you gotten into?"

"Just make the dog put that down," the man said, advancing into the room. "Then I'll take care of it and there won't be any problem."

One of the precinct observers was close on his heels. "Actually," he said, "you're supposed to let the voters put their ballots in the box themselves. You shouldn't touch them at all."

"Innocent mistake," the man said.

Hailey dropped the punch card at Mrs. Kraus' feet. "What the...," she said. "There isn't just one punch card here. There's a bunch, and all of them are punched identically." Mrs. Kraus looked up accusingly. The man from the ballot box wasn't there anymore.

"My God," the precinct observer said. "Are you saying he was stuffing the box?"

Hailey opened her mouth and did that happy panting Mad Dog thought was canine laughter, then turned and trotted out of the office and headed for the front door.

"Get me one of the written ballots," the observer was saying. "I want to know who's trying to rig this election."

There was a commotion in the foyer. Hailey wove through people's legs. As she went outside, Mrs. Kraus was saying, "I remember noticing Englishman is number eighteen on the punch card. Lieutenant Greer's just after him. All these cards are punched nineteen."

Englishman wasn't as thrilled about having a daughter for a deputy as his daughter was about becoming one. Heather should have expected that. But he was short on options, and smart enough to realize she'd do a better job than most people he could get. This was her community and, because she'd grown up a sheriff's daughter, she had a slightly different view of it than most. Trouble was, he also had a different idea of how to use her.

"Start with the Dodge," he'd told her, dismissing her idea of checking out the Bible camp. "There are plenty of other things I need your help on before that." She thought maybe he didn't want her going out there alone.

"I checked the Magnum's visor for registration," he said. "Looked in the glove box, which was empty, but I got too busy to search the whole vehicle. Start there, then the phone needs to be worked. Someone's got to talk to each of the kids on that bus, and their families. Choir practice at three in the morning? Sure. So where were they actually coming from, or going? And Wynn's family. Call them, too. See if he told his wife or father what he thought he was doing out there."

Englishman tore a couple of pages from his notebook and gave them to her, along with a spare pen so she could make notes. She felt stupid for not thinking to bring a notebook of her own.

"Mr. Juhnke and I are going to have a chat with Mr. Gamble, who happens to lead the school chorus. His car was parked near the bus barn when the first driver arrived this morning. And there's a student I want to talk to. But you start with the Dodge and then make those phone calls. And report back to me. In an hour, say, or the minute you learn anything I need to know." She might have forgotten a notebook, but she did have her cell phone.

She found her Civic in the parking lot. Checking the Dodge wouldn't be as glamorous as peeking in windows and testing doors at the Bible camp, or flashing her badge at anyone who thought she had no business nosing around. But it would help her dad in an important way. And she did have the badge she'd wanted. She was official. She'd find someone to flash it to before the day was out.

But those calls…. That wasn't going to be fun, or easy. The people she talked to wouldn't be able to see her badge over a phone. Even when she explained her new official capacity, she wasn't likely to inspire confessions. She would still be Heather English in their minds—the sheriff's kid, not the latest member of Benteen County's law enforcement team.

Chucky Williams was getting a trombone out of the trunk of the family Ford as she headed toward Main Street. She waved, but he ducked down and pretended not to see her. He was probably embarrassed that she'd had to save him from a bad case of bullying. Gratitude apparently didn't last very long in teenage boys. Nor had Chucky's commitment to the clarinet. Hadn't he tortured her with that instrument when she last babysat for him?

Heather turned right on Main and glanced back at Chucky, now nearly to the entrance to the high school. It startled her when she hit a black walnut. But not half as bad as it startled Chucky. He hit the ground like he was in downtown Baghdad.

It had been the clarinet. She remembered now, because he'd complained he couldn't play brass instruments because they made his lips numb. So why had he changed to trombone?

She smiled at herself as she avoided more walnuts with a bit of slalom-like steering. Was this what being a deputy did to you? Turned you distrustful of clarinetists who traded for trombones? If there'd been time, she would have gone back and made him explain. Lord, Heather thought, she hadn't been in law enforcement ten minutes and already she was developing a cop's inclination for suspicion.

The Epperson girl was tall, almost as tall as Mad Dog, and pretty, with a figure guaranteed to draw passes. Mad Dog understood Mark's interest in her, even if she proved unable to speak in complete sentences.

"Nobody else has called me on this," she said—a complete sentence. Mark was onto something here. "I'm not sure whether they don't pay attention or they just don't recognize what I'm playing."

"If I had to guess, I'd say Kinky Friedman isn't widely known by Pastor Goodfellow's flock. But that was pretty obviously not 'Amazing Grace.' I'm surprised you haven't had complaints."

She shrugged. "None yet. I give them 'Amazing Grace' on Sundays, and I play for choir practices. Maybe they put up with my practice sessions rather than risk losing me."

"You're good," Mad Dog said, "but they could find another decent piano player. And I'm thinking they will, if they catch on. The people who run this church don't have much of a sense of humor."

"Or forgiveness. Yeah, I know. But I don't really care anymore. I turn twenty-one next week, and then I'm outta here. My uncle runs a bar in Vegas. He can use a piano player. He says if I dress right, play a few bawdy songs, and flirt a little, I can make fifty bucks an hour in tips. No way to match that in Kansas."

No legal way, Mad Dog had to admit. Not that it was his business. "Actually," he said, "I didn't drop by to act as a music critic. I'm looking for Mark Brown. His dad said I might find him hanging around you."

She smiled. "Yeah. Mark's nice. I've spent some time with him lately. But I haven't seen him since Friday."

"His dad hasn't seen him either. Mark was supposed to be looking after my place while I was out of town. He doesn't seem to have done that either. You have any idea where he might be?"

She put a long, supple index finger to her chin and bit her lower lip. "No," she said. "Friday, that's when I told him about Vegas. He took it kind of hard. I thought that was why I hadn't seen him. That he was off pouting somewhere."

Mad Dog remembered how much it hurt when the girl you loved told you she was through with you. Still hurt, in his case, since the same girl had gone and disappeared on him twice now. The second time was just a couple of years ago, when the wind energy company she'd tried to bring back to Benteen County went bankrupt, sending her and her money to a nation where the U.S. had no extradition treaty.

"When you say he took it hard…?"

"No way." She understood what he was alluding to immediately and waved a hand in dismissal. "Mark's not the suicidal type. Besides, I told him from the start we were only temporary."

It seemed Mad Dog might not be the only guy who refused to hear what he didn't want to. "But you haven't heard from him and neither have his folks. And my place got trashed. Does that sound like Mark to you?"

"You're starting to scare me."

Mad Dog had been looking for a thoughtless boy who hadn't fulfilled an obligation. But this was turning into something else. He didn't think it was possible, but he had to ask. "Mark wouldn't take his anger at you out on me and my place, would he?"

"No. Mark really likes you. He thinks you're way cool. He's been telling me how he wants to have a wolf and raise buffalo of his own some day."

"Then where would he go? Who would he talk to when he realized you weren't going to turn into forever?"

She stopped biting her lip and started on her finger. "I don't know." She shook her head. "Most of his old buddies have moved away. He and Galen Siegrist graduated together. They're fairly close."

Mad Dog said he'd ask Siegrist.

"Or Mr. Gamble."

"Gamble, the music teacher at the high school?"

"Yeah. Mark's got a nice voice. He talked about improving it so we could pursue a music career together. But that was weeks ago. And Gamble would probably make him sing hymns, not honky-tonk or heavy metal."

"I should hope so." A mellow baritone interrupted them and Mad Dog turned to discover Pastor Goodfellow in the door to the choir room. That was a relief. For just a second, he'd thought he'd seen old Aldus P. Goodfellow's lips move in that brooding portrait on the wall.

◇◇◇

Mr. Juhnke led the sheriff to the soundproofed room behind the high school's assembly hall stage. Juhnke knocked, politely, but he didn't give anyone time to answer before opening the door.

Chorus was not in session. Three young girls were sitting on the risers where singers usually stood.

"And so I said, like in your dreams...." The blonde one trailed off as she realized she'd lost the attention of her audience.

"Where is everyone?" Juhnke said.

The blonde got to her feet. She was wearing a modest navy blue skirt, a white blouse, and penny loafers. Were penny loafers back?

The sheriff wasn't good at keeping track of the names of kids in the community. They grew up too fast. But this one was pretty obviously a Showalter. He'd had a classmate, a Showalter, who'd looked almost identical to this one, right down to the penny loafers.

"Uh," she said. It was obvious she didn't want to field this question. "Some of them were hurt in that bus crash this morning."

"So that leaves, what, six missing?" Juhnke said. "And Gamble. He's supposed to be teaching this class. Where is Mr. Gamble?"

The girl fluttered her hands, another Showalter trait. Lord, the sheriff thought, this would be his Showalter's granddaughter—proof he didn't need about how time flew.

"I haven't seen him all day."

Juhnke was incredulous. Also embarrassed, if the sheriff was reading him right. This was Juhnke's school and he was supposed to know what was going on. He was the man in charge, but things were happening on his watch that he wasn't aware of. That was bad enough, but having the sheriff right here to witness his failure, that made it intolerable.

"Let me get this straight," Juhnke said. "You girls are enrolled in chorus this hour, right?"

There were bright red splotches on the Showalter girl's cheeks. Her companions kind of sidled off, out of Juhnke's direct gaze, as if he might somehow, later, fail to recall their involvement.

"Yes." The girl's voice cracked a little.

"But your teacher and some of your classmates aren't here and so you're just sitting around chatting and not reporting their absence to the office?"

"Well, they usually aren't here."

"Excuse me?" Juhnke seemed on the verge of a Krakatoa impersonation.

The sheriff decided to get involved. "You know where they are?"

"Well, sure," the girl said. "Mr. Gamble left me in charge, so I didn't think there was anything to report."

"Where are they?" the sheriff prompted.

"Our voices, they aren't full enough," she tried to explain.

Juhnke was red as a Kansas sunset and sputtering. Maybe Krakatoa wasn't big enough. Maybe he would mimic a super-nova.

"Tell us where they are, please," the sheriff said.

"Choir practice. It's a cappella."

"Choir?" Juhnke's voice was all funny and high pitched, like steam coming from a safety valve. The girls jumped, but he hadn't really gone off. Not yet. "Choir, not chorus?"

"Where's this choir practice held?" the sheriff asked again.

"In the basement, Sheriff English, sir. In that old classroom next to the boiler."

"We don't have a choir," Juhnke stammered. "And we haven't had classes in the basement for years." The sheriff didn't think Juhnke was going to explode, after all. Not until he found Gamble, anyway.

"You don't have one of the school buses you had yesterday, either," the sheriff said. "Come on. Let's take a look."

Heather found the Dodge wagon out behind the Texaco. Except it wasn't the Texaco anymore. Now it was just GAS –FOOD, thanks to Texaco's merger with Chevron. Gas–Food didn't work for Heather. She wanted the Texaco back. She wanted Buffalo Springs to be just the way it always had been. She knew, when she let herself think about it, that what she really wanted was a Buffalo Springs with her mother in it. She sighed and parked around by the entrance to the restrooms. When she got out and advanced on the Dodge, she kept a hand on the edge of her unbuttoned jacket, ready to flip the badge and justify her presence. No one paid her any attention.

The school bus wasn't there. It must have been towed back to the bus barn.

The Dodge was almost unrecognizable. Heather wasn't a car expert, but it was the only vehicle back there that was new, black, and covered with chunks of fresh earth and vegetation.

She tried the driver's door. It wouldn't open. Neither would the back door. They weren't locked, they were buckled.

There wasn't any glass in the windows, but she didn't want to crawl in if it wasn't necessary. Too many shards, even if it was safety glass. She tried the rear lift gate, but it wouldn't budge either. The back door on the passenger's side was open a crack. She got both hands on it and pried and it reluctantly gave way. She looked for blood, oil, or other unpleasant substances that might spoil her clothes, didn't see any, and crawled inside.

Englishman had checked the glove box and the sun visor for registration papers. That didn't mean she shouldn't look there again. She wormed her way between the front seats, brushing aside the spray of safety glass with her jacket sleeve. Nothing in either location, nor in the doors' cubby holes either. She did find a crumpled Jack-in-the-Box sack under the driver's seat, empty but for dirty napkins. She crawled out of the car and set it out on the grass to take back as evidence.

The back seats were folded down to increase storage space. Presumably, the boy who died had been tied up and tossed back there. She opened both back seats, though, just in case. And found nothing. She folded them down again and ducked back inside to examine the rear. There was a storage compartment under the carpets there. Only, of course, it was meant to be opened from the other direction. The floor accordioned up toward her. She was still young and limber, though, and she managed to open it without cutting herself on the jagged strip of roof that appeared to have been opened by a gigantic can opener. There was something in there, netted to the passenger's side—a compact ice chest, it looked like. Getting it out and into her half of the rear compartment was another struggle.

Someone had wrapped the ice chest with clear tape and then written, over and over again, "Sealed for delivery," along the edge in magic marker. She thought the handwriting was something the recipient would recognize, and was meant to ensure this package would arrive unopened.

Now, what to do with it? Benteen County didn't have a crime lab. The chest had to be opened, though her dad wasn't likely to think she was the one who should do it. But he was busy, and once she knew what was inside—drugs, money, a decapitated head—Heather would know what to do next. She should call Englishman, she supposed, not that he could do anything with it she couldn't do herself. She got her cell phone out and thought about it for a minute. Then, since her phone took pictures, she documented the container before her miniature Swiss Army knife slit neatly through the tape.

It was cold in the ice chest, but there was more water in there than ice. It should have gotten where it was going before now. A small box swam atop the ice water. And an envelope. She made digital images of both, then opened the box. It was filled with four tiny test tubes. Each held a nearly colorless fluid. None were labeled. She took another picture before closing the box and returning it to the chest.

That left the envelope. It was unmarked on the outside and sealed, but there was no point in stopping now. She used the knife again. A single sheet of plain white paper lay within. It wasn't addressed to anyone and it wasn't signed. But she knew who should get the test tubes now—Doc at the coroner's office, if he was there. She'd call first, right after she called Englishman to tell him what the note said.

This was getting seriously weird. She reread the paper as she photographed it with her cell phone. It didn't sound any less strange when she read it out loud.

"I will not guarantee the integrity of stem cells transported in this manner."

◇◇◇

"Someone changed the lock." Juhnke was still steaming. No doors in Buffalo Springs High should fail to open to his ring of keys.

The sheriff was getting tired of traipsing around the old building on Juhnke's heels. He didn't even know if this mystery choir had anything to do with his deputy's accident, though it was certainly suspicious. If it wasn't related, he needed to turn his attention lots of other places, and quick. "I could shoot it open," he offered, putting his hand on the butt of his .38.

"Oh no," Juhnke said, taking him seriously. "That's not necessary. There's another entrance."

"I know," the sheriff said. "The outdoor stair at the back of the building."

"Of course, they could have changed locks back there, too."

"Yeah," the sheriff said, "but there's a way into the cage that surrounds the stairs that doesn't require a key. Once inside the fence, we should be able to see what's going on through the windows. If we can't and your keys won't open the basement door, I know how to jimmy those windows."

Juhnke raised his eyebrows.

"Hey, I was a student here. Remember?"

"And a trouble maker, it sounds like."

The sheriff led the way down the front hall and out the exit. "Not really. But this is a small school and an old building. All of us knew its secrets."

"Everyone but the administrators, apparently," Juhnke said.

Someone ran over a handful of black walnuts on Main Street. The explosive cracks rang across the school yard and the sheriff grinned as Juhnke ducked. Grinned, until he noticed there weren't any cars on Main. No one was there to run over walnuts and cause gunshot-like explosions. Nothing explained the sounds, except maybe a real gun that might be somewhere inside the school.

◇◇◇

"Mad Dog," Pastor Goodfellow said. "You're the last person I expected to find visiting God's house."

Mad Dog could believe that.

"Morning, Pastor. Seems to me every house is God's house. Besides, you've got that big welcome sign by the front door. I didn't think anyone would mind."

"We welcome all who come here to accept Jesus. Is that what brings you?"

Mad Dog shook his head. "Not today, thanks. I'm not inclined to join a faith whose followers would put an obscene sign in my front yard, kill small animals, and poison the water bowl by my back door. I was looking for Mark Brown. He's supposed to be keeping an eye on my place. His dad thought he might be here listening to Ms. Epperson practice the piano."

Goodfellow favored him with a patient smile. "Each of us is granted free will. We may use it to accept Jesus, or not. But I assure you, no true Christian would do the things of which you accuse us. As for Mark, alas, he hasn't accepted salvation here either. Nor has he been present in this house of worship today, as you can see for yourself."

Another man stuck his head in the door, a little fellow with a bad comb-over. "Don't waste time with this guy. Just get him out of here."

Mad Dog didn't recognize the man. "So the welcome sign is only for show?"

The man who wanted Mad Dog gone didn't answer. He just looked at Goodfellow and said, "I mean now," before he disappeared back into the hall.

"My apologies," Goodfellow said. "Mr. Dunbar could have been more polite, but I suppose he's within his rights. He's a representative of the political action committee renting our facilities today. Since they've brought in local volunteers who are trying to put your brother out of a job, your presence could hamper the enthusiasm of their efforts."

Mad Dog nodded. "Not a problem, Pastor. I've been thrown out of better places. You prefer me to use a back door?"

Goodfellow's smile was weak. "If you don't mind," he said, "there's an exit at the end of the hall."

The Epperson girl grabbed her purse and put her arm through Mad Dog's. "I don't think I want to be here anymore, either," she said. "Let's go. I'll help you find Mark." She edged Mad Dog out of the practice room and into the corridor. Dunbar was tapping a foot, arms folded, a few steps back into the church.

"You know," she told Mad Dog, louder than was necessary for him to hear, "I wasn't planning to vote. But now I want to go right over and cast my ballot for Englishman."

They went out the rear exit into bright sun and a gentle fall breeze. Someone slammed the door behind them.

◇◇◇

Screams. More walnuts that weren't walnuts. Shouts. Pounding footsteps. A kid, a boy with red hair and pimples, came careening around the corner. When he saw the sheriff and the principal he stopped and pointed behind him. He made some vague whimpering noises and then started to cry.

"Gunshots," the sheriff said.

"Yes," Juhnke said. "I think so."

"You have a plan for a situation like this?"

"We evacuate everyone to the gym, or the lunchroom if the gym isn't safe. Then we lockdown. No one goes in or out until it's over."

The sheriff nodded. "Do that," he said, "and take this boy with you." The boy was still trying to tell them things that the sheriff needed to know, but the kid was unintelligible in his terror. The sheriff couldn't wait.

The shouts and cries seemed to be coming from behind the school. Maybe down in that basement where the nonexistent choir was supposedly practicing. The sheriff took no chances. He pulled his .38 and went around the corner, crouched in a shooter's stance. Two more boys were hiding against the wall near the back of the building. When they saw the sheriff, one threw himself on the ground and the other just froze. But only for a moment. Then he ran toward the sheriff.

"In the basement," the boy was saying. "Someone's killing people in the basement."

The sheriff made sure this kid, and the one on the ground, didn't have anything in their hands. When guns started going off in a school, they were probably being fired by kids who might look just like these two.

"Who's shooting?" the sheriff asked. "How many guns?"

The kid shook his head. "I don't know. But they got Freddie. We were in the shop, out back." Vocational Agriculture and shop classes were still taught in the metal building behind the school. The sheriff had built his mother a pair of awful end tables there that she had prized all her life.

"Freddie came stumbling up the steps and fell down." The kid gestured to where his friend still hugged the ground. "We saw him and heard the shots and we just ran for it."

There were still a lot of voices coming from back there. No more gunshots, though. The sheriff was thankful for that. "Get your friend," he told the boy. "Take him around front and go to the gym. I'll cover you."

The sheriff and the boy went to the corner, where they practically had to claw the second kid off the ground. "It's all right," the sheriff told them. "I'll take care of it. This is my job." He kept one eye on the boys and one on the corner, his .38 up and cocked. Once off the ground, the second boy was ready to run. The two of them disappeared around the front of the school.

It *was* his job, but how would he do it on a day when he didn't have any deputies? The sheriff took a deep breath and peered behind the building.

Another boy lay on the paved drive between the main building and the shop. His tan shirt was stained with blood and he was feebly trying to crawl away.

One thing at a time, the sheriff told himself. He grabbed his phone and hit the button that dialed his office.

"Mrs. Kraus," he said. She was trying to tell him something about a problem with the election but he didn't give her the chance. "There's been a shooting at the high school." She shut up in mid-sentence. "Get the highway patrol to send us any available officers immediately. And get an ambulance. Call Doc and tell him we've got at least one wounded. Then find me a deputy...but don't send Heather."

He slapped the phone shut, holstered his gun and went. There was a kid out there who had to be extricated from the killing zone.

◇◇◇

Heather called her dad first. He had either turned off his cell or was on the line, because it went straight to his voice mail. She knew how busy he must be, so she gave him a brief summary of what she'd found and what she planned to do with it. When she called Doc at the coroner's office, his line was busy. He must have a cell, but she didn't know the number. When she tried to get it from Mrs. Kraus, the lines to the sheriff's office were busy, too. She tried Doc again. No answer this time. Then the sheriff's office was still busy.

What should she do with the ice chest full of stem cells? Secure and cool them, she supposed. But where? Doc must have left his office. The courthouse didn't really have proper facilities. So….

Heather marched the cooler into the Gas – Food. She flashed her badge at the woman behind the counter. Heather had been wanting to do that.

"I need to commandeer some space in your cooler," Heather said.

The woman's jaw dropped. Heather faintly remembered her as the mother of a girl who'd been two or three classes ahead of her. "Lord, Heather, I thought you were off in school. You come home to work for your daddy now?"

"It's just temporary."

"Well, honey, you don't need to commandeer a thing. You want some space back in that cooler, you're welcome to it."

Commandeering would have been more fun, but Heather smiled and thanked the woman and put the ice chest on the counter. "I need to keep this cold until I can get it to Doc Jones." She looked around the interior of the Gas–Food. "It might be important to a case we're investigating, so I need to protect the chain of evidence."

The woman looked impressed. Thanks to whoever had sent the cooler, Heather knew exactly how she was going to do that. "I'll need a roll of packing tape and a magic marker." The clerk's face creased with doubt and Heather clarified her request. "I'll pay for those," she said.

The woman found her a two-inch-wide roll of clear tape and a black marker.

"Or would you prefer fuchsia?"

"Black, thanks." Fuchsia didn't seem serious enough.

Heather resealed the package and scrawled her signature and the date on the tape. The thing couldn't be opened again without her knowing about it. She used enough tape to be sure. The stuff was so hard to handle coming off the roll it ended up covered with her fingerprints. Her seal was at least as effective as the original.

"Now," Heather said, "show me where we can put this."

The woman took her down a narrow hall to a door that led into the back of the glassed-in cooler where beer and sodas and a selection of lunch meats and cheeses were displayed. They found a spot above a shelf filled with cases of Coors. Heather reeled off more tape and attached it to the shelf. Again, she signed and dated the tape in a couple of places, then covered her signature with yet another layer of tape.

"My, honey, you are being cautious with that. What's inside?"

"I'm not sure." That was true. Heather didn't know whether the test tubes really contained stem cells. "But it's nothing for you to worry about. It won't hurt anyone who doesn't open it." Heather was sure it would be left alone here, but a little insurance never hurt. She followed the woman back to the counter and paid for her purchases, including plastic evidence bags—food storage bags, really—for the Jack-in-the-Box sack and the original tape that sealed the cooler. She got herself a notebook, too.

After determining the clerk's shift wouldn't end before nightfall, Heather reassured her, "I'll be back for it before then. Or Dad or Doc Jones will come pick it up. Don't let anyone else touch it. In fact, it'd be better not to tell anyone it's back there."

"Not to worry, honey. I'll see it isn't disturbed." Heather would have preferred being called Deputy, but honey would have to do. "Where you off to in such a hurry, you've got to leave that?"

Up to that moment, Heather hadn't even admitted it to herself. Most of the reason she didn't want to take it over to the courthouse and stick it in the refrigerator beside Mrs. Kraus' brown bag lunch was because she wanted to continue investigating. Despite her father's instructions about the Bible camp, Heather yearned to look for herself. And then, a couple of the kids who'd been on that bus, the ones the deputy over in Hays had told her were being released and would soon be home, lived out that way.

Heather wanted to test her interrogation techniques, and flash her badge a few more times. She hoped to solve the mystery of what that busload of kids had been doing out there at three in the morning. It wasn't just about enjoying the power of her badge, it was about helping Englishman. Hey, that's what a daughter did when she loved her dad.

The sheriff was going to take a quick look at the kid's wound before moving him, but bullets began slamming into the metal wall of the shop even before he got there. He hunched down and tried to make himself a lot shorter than normal and grabbed the kid by the arms. A bullet whined off the concrete lip to the stairwell, too close, as the sheriff dragged the boy back toward the corner. He could feel the next one ripping his flesh, but it never came.

He heard laughter, high-pitched, hysterical maybe. And then a voice from the basement, cracking, one that hadn't finished changing yet.

"Ally ally out's in free, Sheriff. This time, anyway."

The sheriff was gasping for breath by the time he got the wounded boy around the corner. His heart felt like it would tear a hole in his chest and go pounding out toward the football field.

The boy had been grazed along one hip. The bullet had plowed a nasty furrow through jeans and flesh. That one was causing a lot of bleeding, but it wasn't as dangerous as the gaping exit wound on the boy's other side, just below the last rib.

Freddie King, Buffalo Spring's star tackle, was still conscious, though. He stared at the sheriff through disbelieving eyes. The sheriff peeled out of his jacket and used the garment to fashion a sort of compression bandage that concentrated on the hole in the boy's abdomen, but covered the entry wound in the small of his back, too. The sheriff used his belt to cinch it as tight as he dared.

"Who shot you, Freddie?"

Freddie was panting as hard as the sheriff. It made him hard to understand. "Am I gonna die?"

The sheriff didn't think so. There wasn't enough blood to make him think the bullet had hit a major artery. And the wound wasn't bubbling, nor was Freddie coughing up blood. It had missed heart and lungs. Which didn't mean it might not be life threatening. It depended on how soon he got medical care.

"You're going to be fine," the sheriff said, trying to make a wish sound like a certainty. "Who did it? Are there hostages?" The sheriff had a million questions, but Freddie had other concerns.

"It hurts, Sheriff," he said. "Oh God, it hurts."

A beige station wagon nearly lifted off the inside wheels as it took the turn into the parking lot in front of the school. The sheriff knew that Buick.

"Doc Jones is here, Freddie. He'll fix it. He'll stop the hurt."

Freddie didn't seem to hear him. "I thought I'd made it, but he just let me get to the top of the stairs before he shot me."

"Who, Freddie?" The sheriff stood and waved and Doc's Buick jumped the curb out front and came careening around the building before locking up brakes and showering them with gravel.

There was another shot from the rear of the building. And the sound of breaking glass—one of the windows in the shop.

"No fair peeking." It was the same man/child voice as before.

Doc was out of his car, black bag in hand. The sheriff returned to the corner of the building and looked for fresh bodies. There weren't any, but the bottom right pane on the door to the voc-ag classroom had a hole in it.

English didn't think it would work, but he had to try. "This is the sheriff," he yelled. "Throw your gun out and come through the door with your hands raised."

A volley of bullets tore out the nearest window and headed for the northeast corner of the county.

"You throw your gun in," the cracking voice said. "You surrender to me."

"Doesn't work that way," the sheriff said. "Freddie's gonna be all right. Why don't you come out now, before things get out of control?"

The boy laughed at him. "Just 'cause Freddie's okay doesn't mean everyone is."

"Don't make me come get you." Jeez, like he was talking to a child. Well, he was.

"You better not try, Sheriff. I got more in here. Some aren't hurt yet. You come in, that's gonna change."

Okay, this wasn't working. Time for a different strategy. "Who are you?" the sheriff yelled. "What's this all about?"

"You don't know, do you, Mr. Sheriff Englishman? Sometimes I don't think anybody knows who I am. After today they will. After today, all kinds of people are gonna know me."

That's when the sheriff realized he'd heard that voice before. Earlier today, in a restroom in this building while removing Doc's packing from his nose.

"Chucky Williams," the sheriff said. "Do you know what your folks are gonna do when they get hold of you?"

There was a moment of silence before Chucky answered. "Nothin', Sheriff. Not anymore. How do you think I got this gun out of the house?"

◇◇◇

The Epperson girl had actually voted first thing that morning—for Englishman, she told Mad Dog. Mad Dog had voted by mail. That meant they didn't have to go to the courthouse after all. Just as well, since the entry was jammed with people raising voices and shaking fists at one another. Politics as normal in twenty-first century America, Mad Dog thought.

"I guess I'll try Mark's friend, Galen Siegrist," Mad Dog said. "Did you really want to come along?"

"Yeah, really." She followed him to the Mini Cooper. "Hi, Hailey." The wolf was waiting in the front seat. "I'm Pam Epperson. Do you mind if I come for a ride with you?"

Pam—that helped. Sooner or later, Mad Dog had known he'd have to come up with something more than "the Epperson girl."

"She's not outgoing," Mad Dog explained, opening the door for Pam. Hailey made a liar out of him by delivering a slobbery kiss to Pam's outstretched hand. "Not usually, anyway." Hailey bounded into the backseat and the girl got in the car.

"She's beautiful," Pam said.

"So are you," Mad Dog would have said if he were a few decades younger. Instead, he got in, started the car, and aimed it toward Main.

"I may actually be able to help," Pam said. She and Hailey were exchanging nuzzles. Mad Dog had never seen Hailey take to a stranger so easily before. She usually didn't growl or bare her teeth, not unless people deserved it. But she tended to be standoffish, maybe allow a pat or two before retiring into regal privacy.

"Galen's kind of paranoid. If he thinks you're looking for Mark because Mark screwed up, Galen probably won't help. But since he likes me, and he's got the hots for my favorite cousin, he'll tell me where Mark is. If he knows."

As Mad Dog turned right on Main, he thought he heard someone run over a bunch of walnuts. A car pulled out of the old Texaco's lot and headed south as they approached the stop sign in front of the Gas – Food. It was a silver Civic, just like the one his niece, Heather English, drove. And the driver looked a lot like her, too.

"Look," Pam said. "I think that's Galen's truck."

"Where?" Mad Dog didn't know what Galen drove, but looking for the truck in question took his mind off both the Civic and the walnuts.

"There." It was a blob of color disappearing into the distance on the westbound blacktop. Mad Dog couldn't even tell if it was a pickup.

Pam looked at him and grinned. "I've heard your Mini is fast. Is it fast enough to catch that truck?"

It had been a very long time since a pretty girl sat beside Mad Dog and encouraged him to speed. But not long enough for him to have forgotten how.

"I need your help."

Doc's plea tore the sheriff's attention away from the grim possibilities of what he might find when he had the chance to check Chucky's house.

"This boy needs to get to a trauma center," Doc said as he opened the back gate on the Buick and wheeled out his stretcher. "But we can start replacing some of the blood he's losing and get some antibiotics and painkillers in him. I'll get a helicopter on the way as I take him to the clinic." Doc was trying to retire from practicing medicine, except for his duties at the coroner's office, but he still had an office at the clinic downtown. So did two other doctors, though both alternated weeks with similar clinics in adjacent counties.

Doc gestured toward the school. "Are there more in there need tending to?"

"I think so. Chucky Williams—he's the one with the gun—claims there are more wounded. From what he said, his parents might be hurt, too. If you can find somebody to check on them, they might need help."

"Jesus!" From Doc, it wasn't a prayer. The two men got their arms under the wounded boy and lifted him gently onto the stretcher. The sheriff helped Doc guide it back into the Buick, where they locked it in place and tied the boy down. "I'll see how the clinic's staffed. Maybe I can send someone to the Williams place from there. Whatever, I'll be right back. Don't do anything stupid. I don't want to be cutting bullets out of you."

"If you can find me any help, bring it. I need to get the exits to that basement covered before I decide how to get Chucky out of there."

"Right." Doc finished strapping Freddie in and hung the IV bags where they could continue flowing into the boy. Freddie wasn't talking anymore. He was just groaning.

Doc and the sheriff didn't exchange more words. There weren't any. Doc jumped behind the wheel, threw the Buick in reverse, turned in the parking lot, and headed for Main. The sheriff went back to the corner to check on Chucky.

"Who's down there with you, Chucky?" he called. "What's this all about?"

"Just me and the choir, Sheriff. And it's about time. I've put up with these bullies way too long."

Keep him talking. At least for now. While he was talking, he wasn't shooting and the sheriff knew where Chucky was.

"Who?" English called. "Who's in the choir? Who are the bullies?"

"Freddie. But then you already know that."

"Are there more? Can I talk to somebody? You're claiming you've got hostages down there, but for all I know you've already killed everybody. Maybe there's no reason for me and my deputies not to come down there and bring you out." There weren't any deputies, of course, but maybe Chucky didn't know that.

Chucky said something, soft and low and not to the sheriff.

Another voice, trembling. A girl's. "There are three of us he hasn't hurt yet. But he shot three down here. I think Mr. Gamble and Butch and Mark are all dead."

Butch—that would probably be the Bunker kid. The sheriff had had several run-ins with that young troublemaker. Who was Mark? Not Goodfellow, surely. Not the pastor's son.

"Butch Bunker? Mark Goodfellow?"

"She said all you need to hear, sheriff. Now you know my hostages are for real."

"I know that, Chucky. I know they're for real. I know you're for real. So, now, how do we go about solving this?"

There was a long silence.

"What do you want?" the sheriff called. "What do you hope to get out of this?"

The silence continued for what seemed like forever. When Chucky finally answered, his voice sounded young and frightened. "That's a good question. I just wanted to do what was right. Now, I don't know."

"You're a juvenile, Chucky. This doesn't have to be the end of the world for you," the sheriff lied. If someone was dead, Chucky was going to spend the rest of his life behind bars. And if several were dead, he was likely to be tried as an adult and get strapped to a gurney while the state dripped poison in his arm. "But you've got to give up now. You've got to let me get help for those who are hurt and bring the rest out of harm's way."

"Too late, Sheriff. But I got three girls in here. You don't want them hurt. So maybe I am gonna want something. A million dollars and a plane, maybe. Don't go anywhere. I'll think on it and let you know."

The sheriff, who hadn't planned on going anywhere, suddenly wanted to be any place on earth other than Benteen County.

"I'll be here, Chucky," he said out loud. Until I get enough backup so I can come in after you. He kept that last part to himself.

Heather should have expected it, of course, but she was surprised to find the gate on the driveway to the Bible camp locked. And it wasn't like her new badge came with a universal skeleton key or a lock picking set.

She'd attended the camp years ago, back when it was more ecumenical than evangelical. She knew the drive led along the trees that bordered Calf Creek until it turned in where a lazy oxbow left room for the boxcars that had been converted into dormitories. If she went around the section, there was a small cluster of houses a farmer had built for his grown-up kids in a back pasture he wasn't grazing anymore. He'd bladed a road into them and they were just across the creek. One of the annual projects when she attended camp was renewing the rope suspension bridge that linked the camp and the side of the creek with the houses. She could park in there, show her badge to anyone who wondered what she was doing, and walk to the bridge. It probably wasn't more than two hundred yards.

She got out of the car first, though, and examined the path that led through the gate. Tire tracks, sure enough. And some big ones, double-wides, like on the back of a school bus. Or a large farm truck, or even some pickups, these days.

Heather had expected her father to call back. She checked her cell to be sure she still had a good signal and hadn't missed any calls. She even thought about calling him again, or Mrs. Kraus. But she didn't want to tell either one where she was. Especially not Englishman, after he'd specifically told her to leave the Bible camp alone.

Not yet, she decided. Not until after.

The houses weren't as appealing as she recalled. They mostly looked unoccupied. No curtains parted, no doors opened, no curious eyes followed her Civic as she piloted it as close as she could get to the creek. The path was right where she'd remembered. But it hadn't been used much. Not for a long time. It was almost knee deep in grass, with bigger weeds on either side. Not the easy access she'd had in mind. She'd have to get a change of clothes and a shower soon after this hike. There'd be chiggers. Probably ticks as well. It was hard to believe that ticks hadn't been a big problem when Englishman and Uncle Mad Dog grew up. Hardly any deer then, they'd told her. There were deer everywhere, these days. Enough for road-killed venison to be a common dish all over the county.

Well, hell. It was a beautiful day and the leaves were changing. Some of the weeds had died back after recent frosts. Maybe the chiggers and ticks had, too.

It was dark and noisy once she penetrated the cottonwoods along the stream bank. Enough leaves up there, however golden, to cut the sun and rustle in the wind. Birds, too, complaining about her presence. She even scared up one of those deer that had come back to the Great Plains bringing the great ticks.

The stream bank was steep, the water coffee dark and flowing with the rush of freshly opened catsup. The buildings and boxcars were where she'd expected them, though there looked to be more now. The rope bridge, on the other hand, didn't look like it had received much attention recently. Not that any of the ropes were broken or badly frayed. The posts to which they were affixed were weathered, but solid. The structure just looked old and tired, and it drooped a lot closer to the muddy water than it had when she was ten. Or maybe the muddy water didn't look as appealing as it had then. Jeez, they'd gone swimming in that stuff. And probably swallowed a gallon or so as they giggled and wrestled and swung out and let go, Tarzan-like, to plop into that deep hole under the ancient catalpa just upstream.

She didn't get her feet wet. Not quite, though it was closer than she liked since Uncle Mad Dog had told her water moccasins were making a comeback, too. Wild and woolly Kansas seemed to be returning to its natural state. Or a new natural state, as the population continued to drop, generation after generation, out here in the rural counties. Progress meant fewer people raised more crops. And only the monster corporate farmers could survive. You couldn't support yourself on a quarter-section anymore. Nor a section, and so there were little wooded patches where homesteads used to be until the houses fell down or got moved. Or not even wooded patches where the ground could be forced to yield a few more bushels of grain. The deer didn't mind. They liked grain fields better than endless acres of grass. The deer were thriving. So were the ticks.

Things hardly seemed wild at all, on the far side of the creek. Someone had mowed around the buildings recently enough for a foursome to play through on their way to the nearest green. The boxcars were a series of freshly painted bright colors now, with names above the doors like SERAPHIM and CHERUBIM. But there was a silence to the place, in spite of the wind in the trees and the chatter of birdcalls. It felt empty of people. Doors were closed, drapes pulled. The camp looked just like it was supposed to—closed for the season.

And then something chirped that wasn't a bird. Heather went around a corner and found the cluster of parked cars. Someone was at the door to one of them—the one that had just chirped as the electronic key worked its locks.

"Hold it right there," Heather said, flipping open her jacket and showing her badge. Maybe it would get more respect this time.

The Mini Cooper was fast, but with a hundred pounds of wolf and an extra passenger on board, not as fast as it could be. And Mad Dog was no lightweight. He'd been a big guy back in high school when he led the Buffalo Springs football team to the best record in school history. He was bigger now.

Even so, the blob Pam Epperson had told him was Galen Siegrist's truck was clearly recognizable by the time it turned north. After that, the truck's dust was too thick for Mad Dog to close the gap. He hung back, in relatively clear air, and contented himself with knowing they only had to go five miles from the highway.

The Siegrist place looked more like a rural corporate headquarters than a traditional farm. The house was low and modern and sprawling. Lots of reflective glass in a brick façade next to a four-car garage. Hardly any vegetation, just a row of neatly trimmed dwarf evergreens along the front and a perfectly manicured postage-stamp lawn with a couple of saplings that were either dead or had already lost their leaves. There wasn't a mature tree within a quarter mile of the house. When young Galen took over, he'd bladed the old farmstead and started fresh. The result was cold and sterile, and Mad Dog didn't blame Galen's parents for moving to town.

The outbuildings didn't include the traditional barn or silo. Instead, there were pressed metal warehouses and immense circular-metal bins. Galen's Dodge was parked beside the entrance to the nearest warehouse, still enveloped in a cloud of its own making as Mad Dog pulled into the driveway. But for the dust and the Dodge, there was no sign of life.

Mad Dog parked upwind of Galen's truck and he, Pam, and Hailey all got out.

"Mark was always trying to get Galen to throw a party out here," Pam said. "The house is huge, mostly unfurnished. Plenty of room for a band and dancers in the front room. But Galen's pretty conservative about that stuff. Besides, he's always got about three days' work that needs doing in only one."

"Sounds like a fun guy to hang around with." Mad Dog said.

"That's why he'll talk to me. He's hungry for the stuff he's afraid to do. He's always had a thing for me, but I have a life. That makes me too wild for him, except in his imagination. My cousin's more his speed, but she mostly ignores him 'cause this isn't the lifestyle she dreams of, except for his money. About the only adventures Galen has anymore come second-hand from Mark."

"In there?" Mad Dog asked, starting toward the nearest warehouse.

"I think so, but hang on a minute." Pam fumbled in her purse and pulled something out, then she was hiking up her dress and Mad Dog, embarrassed, found himself turning to study the pattern in the stamped metal wall. Dress back where it was supposed to be, she appeared beside him.

What was that about?

She smiled and said, "Galen's been a little weird lately, so, just in case...."

Mad Dog didn't know what she was talking about and decided this was one of those times it might be better not to ask.

"Okay," she said, "let's see if anyone's home."

Mad Dog drew back a fist to rap on the door, but she just reached down and turned the knob. He raised an eyebrow.

"If Galen didn't want people to come in, he'd lock his door or put up a doorbell."

Mad Dog didn't think that was necessarily so. This was central Kansas and hardly anybody locked their doors, or failed to keep a shotgun handy in case some stranger took advantage and walked in uninvited.

"Anybody home?" Pam called. Her voice echoed back from the building's shadowy depths. The place was filled with farm machinery—several four-wheel-drive tractors to begin with. At least $300,000 each. It reminded Mad Dog how different farming had become in his lifetime.

A door opened and Mad Dog realized there was a small office back behind the nearest tractor. Galen stood in the entrance. "What are you doing here, Pam? And why's *he* here with you?"

That didn't sound like a welcome.

Mad Dog was ready to answer, but Pam had taken charge. She went toward the office and Mad Dog fell in behind her. "Hey, Galen. We're looking for Mark. You seen him?"

"Why? What do you want with him?" Galen didn't step out of the entry to his office or invite them in. Nor did he seem inclined to offer any help. Mad Dog wondered if Pam would be as successful as she'd thought.

"We can't find him. He was going to call me this weekend and he hasn't. That's not like Mark."

"Well, you dumped him pretty hard, Pam. What did you expect?"

"So you have seen him," she countered. "Otherwise you couldn't know that. Well, where is he?"

"Uh…." Galen was the master of conversational repartee. "I don't know."

"Then why's his pickup parked over behind that tractor?"

Mad Dog looked and, sure enough, there it was. When he looked back, Galen had a pistol in his hand and it was aimed at them. "Dang!" Galen said. "Now see what you've gone and made me do."

"You haven't got the balls to shoot us," Pam said. Mad Dog didn't think this was the moment to question someone's manhood. It was time for Mad Dog to step in and calm this down, only Pam and Galen were proceeding as if he weren't present.

"I will if I have to," Galen said. "But that's not my preference."

Pam tried to interrupt again but this time Galen managed to still her with what he had to say. "Mark's fine and you can see him in a few hours. With any luck. But right now, I'm gonna have to put the two of you on ice until this thing's over."

"Where is he?" Pam said, at the same moment Mad Dog was asking something else.

"What thing?"

"Can't tell you." There was no way to know which question Galen was answering, or whether he'd just answered both. Galen wagged the pistol to his left and pointed toward an opening in the wall of the warehouse. A corridor led, presumably, back toward the grain bins.

"Both of you, down that way, now." Galen pulled back the pistol's hammer to show he meant business. Mad Dog tried to think of what his choices were. If Pam had it right, they could just refuse. And Mad Dog could go over and take Galen's gun away. But if she were wrong....

A bullet threw up sparks at their feet before whining over and crashing through the wall behind them. That convinced Mad Dog not to argue.

"All right," Pam said, "but my cousin's never going to speak to you after I tell her about this."

"That's not my main worry right now," Galen said. "Down the hall."

They went. He told them to stop when he got to the third bin. It had a door that was open a few feet above the surface of the corridor, and metal steps so you could get to it easily enough.

"In there," Galen told them. "It's empty. Roof door's open so you've got ventilation."

Mad Dog stepped up and peered inside. It wasn't completely empty. There were still clumps of grain on the floor. Some stuck, here and there, to the ribbed metal sides further up. And there were inner and outer doors. He was pretty sure the inner one wouldn't have handles on the grain side, and he could see the heavy metal tabs the lever locks on the outside would grab. It was big for a prison cell, but it would make an effective one.

"Not yet," Galen said, stopping Mad Dog before he climbed through. "Empty your pockets."

Mad Dog did. Nothing much there—cell phone, billfold with a couple of hundred dollars in it, a little pocket change, and the keys to his Mini. Nothing more dangerous than his miniature Swiss Army knife. Galen made him set it all on the ground beside the steps.

"It'll be here when I let you out."

"When's that?" Mad Dog asked.

"Soon as I can." It was more of an answer than he'd expected.

"Now you, Pam."

She shrugged and twirled around to demonstrate. "No pockets, Galen, that's why women carry purses." She set hers on the ground beside Mad Dog's stuff and the two of them crawled through the door into the cavernous bin. Mad Dog didn't go far, hoping for a chance to grab Galen before the inner door closed. Galen was going to need both hands on those levers.

"Both of you, over against the opposite wall." It had to be thirty feet over there. So much for the grab. Considering how she'd behaved to begin with, Mad Dog was surprised at how compliant Pam had become. He followed her across the bin. They were almost there when the door started to close behind them. Of course, that was when the cell phone in Pam's crotch began ringing.

Chucky hadn't made any demands. And the sheriff still didn't have a plan. There were other ways into that basement, and not just through the locked door the principal's keys hadn't fit. But for now, until he had some help, he had to watch this exit, the most likely one. Chucky might not know about the others and might not have a key to that locked door. If the sheriff left, there was nothing to keep Chucky from coming out and going hunting.

"Talk to me, Chucky," the sheriff called.

"Nothing to say."

Good. He was still there. Doc should have made it to the clinic by now. Mrs. Kraus would have called for backup from out of county. Surely he'd be getting help soon.

"That's okay. Just talk to me now and then. Let me know nothing's changed down there."

"Maybe."

The sheriff would accept that for now. Chucky was there, not headed out another exit.

Tires squealed on Main and the sheriff turned in time to watch a Corvette take the turn into the Buffalo Springs High parking lot in a controlled power slide. For half a heartbeat he found himself hoping. And then he knew whose car it was. The Vette blasted across the parking lot and came to a halt at the edge of the front curb. The doors flew open and two men jumped out. Newt Neuhauser was on the sheriff's side. Soon-to-be Sheriff Greer was on the other. Both of them came out of the car with weapons—Neuhauser with some kind of Dirty-Harry-sized pistol in a shooter's stance, Greer with a short-barreled shotgun high and tight on his shoulder, the way they did it in Iraq. The two of them performed a synchronized sweep, fields of fire never overlapping.

"Clear," Greer said.

"Clear," Neuhauser repeated.

"What's going on?" Chucky called from the basement. "I heard a car come in real fast."

"Ambulance," the sheriff said, "for when you turn your hostages loose. You ready?"

"Not hardly."

The sheriff looked at Greer and Neuhauser and raised a finger to his lips. He might not want these two, but he had them. Greer was probably competent, combat experienced at least. And from the way Neuhauser came out of the car with the lieutenant, he looked competent, too. The sheriff didn't know much about Neuhauser's background. The man was an outsider, a buddy of Greer's who'd come to help him win the sheriff's office. Greer and Neuhauser—well, maybe he could use them.

The two joined the sheriff at the back corner of the building. Neither had uttered another word after the sheriff urged them to silence. Greer leaned down close. His voice was soft and eager.

"We hear the Williams kid is pulling a Columbine."

The sheriff nodded, though what Chucky had done didn't seem as carefully planned.

"He alone?"

"Except for hostages," the sheriff said.

"Where?"

"Basement."

Greer had gone to school here, too. "Ah." The lieutenant nodded. "So we've got to get through the fence and down the stairwell, then through the windows or doors to take him."

"That's the problem," the sheriff agreed.

Greer smiled. "No problem." Keeping one hand on the grip near the shotgun's trigger, Greer used the other to open his jacket. He had a bandolier under there. An assortment of little metal globes hung from it.

The sheriff's eyebrows shot up violently enough to lap his head. "Are those grenades?"

"You bet." Greer sounded proud of himself. "Grenades, flash bangs, tear gas, the works."

"Where…? How…?" There weren't enough questions. Greer wasn't on active duty. He shouldn't have access to armaments like these. In fact, it was a violation of the law.

"After hunting insurgents, I feel naked without them."

As if that explained it. The sheriff's mind was racing. He ought to arrest Greer right now, but those grenades opened all kinds of possibilities.

"Let's go get him," the lieutenant said.

"Whoa." They needed a plan. They needed to know where Chucky was in relation to his hostages. They needed….

"Whoa? No wonder it's going to be so easy to replace you as sheriff. I'm going in. Come if you want."

"Look." The sheriff tried to be reasonable. "What if he's using his hostages as shields? It's going to take a minute to get down there. What if he panics and starts shooting them?"

Greer didn't care, and his reply made a point. "What if he starts shooting them anyway?"

Okay, the sheriff thought. But they still needed a plan. One of them should get around the building. One should probably blow that locked door to the basement and go in that way with all of them entering together, making their assault as nearly as simultaneous as they could.

"Hell with it," Greer told Neuhauser. "Keep him out of my way."

The sheriff felt that massive pistol snuggle into the nape of his neck.

"Put your gun down, Mr. English," Neuhauser whispered as Greer slipped past, choosing a grenade and edging closer to the corner of the building.

The sheriff obeyed. He'd been pointing his .38 at the sky. Now he lowered it until it was centered on Greer's back.

"Touch that trigger, Mr. Neuhauser," English said, "and neither the lieutenant nor I will be available for the next term as sheriff of Benteen County."

Heather found herself staring at her mirror image as it straightened from behind the nearest car in the parking lot, the dustiest one of the half dozen there.

"Heather," she said. The other Heather, her adopted sister, wasn't supposed to be here. She was a fifth-year senior finishing her degree in anthropology at the University of New Mexico. That was in Albuquerque, a six-hundred-mile drive away.

One of Two looked at Two of Two and Two of Two looked back. "What are you doing here," they chorused. "You're supposed to be in school."

And then the absurdity of it hit them and they both grinned and went around the car and hugged each other. Heather number one said, "I've got the badge, so you have to answer me first."

Heather Lane said, "Okay, if you promise to explain about the badge." She got a nodded acquiescence and went on. "I woke up about two in the morning in a panic. I felt sure something awful was going to happen to Englishman if I didn't prevent it."

This sounded disturbingly familiar.

"It was silly," Two continued, "but I couldn't shake it off. And I couldn't go back to sleep. So I finally grabbed some clothes and got in the car and pointed it this way." She looked sheepish, and tired, like someone who'd just driven hundreds of miles in a hell of a hurry on too little sleep. "Have you seen Dad? Is he all right?"

"This is like so weird," One said. "I woke up with the same premonition you did. But I saw Englishman over at the high school just a little while ago and he's fine."

Some of the stress went out of the second Heather's face. "That's what Mrs. Kraus said. Englishman isn't answering his cell. I started calling just before I hit the county line. When I couldn't get him, I called the office. Mrs. Kraus said he was real busy, that Wynn ran into a school bus and Englishman was investigating that and it was Election Day and all and so I shouldn't worry. She told me to just put in my normal school day."

"I'll bet she was surprised to discover both of us had come home unexpectedly."

"Yeah," Two said, "only that was kind of weird. She never mentioned that you were home or that you'd been worried about Dad, too. When I told her I'd be at the office in a few minutes, she said Englishman wasn't there. And then she said something about the school bus Wynn hit having been stolen. It was supposed to be on its way to the Bible camp so Englishman was coming out to look into it. She said I'd probably find him here. And if I didn't, I should wait. He'd be along shortly."

"That's odd. What she told you about the bus is all true. But Dad told me there was no reason to check the Bible camp now. In fact, when I offered to look this place over, he gave me another errand." That required further explanation about Wynn and the bus and the reason Heather English was carrying a Benteen County deputy's badge, as well as what she'd found in the Dodge station wagon.

"By the way," One said, "how'd you drive in here?"

"What do you mean? The gate was open. I just turned in and followed the road."

The gate hadn't been open when Deputy Heather tried it a few minutes before. Someone had unlocked it. She felt a little of that creepy feeling slip back into her consciousness and raise hairs on the back of her neck. Had the gate been unlocked by someone going out, or coming in?

"What's the matter?" the second Heather asked.

Benteen's newest deputy eyed the parked cars, the cabins, and the dark shadows under the trees along the creek. "I've got a feeling," she said, "we're not alone here."

The sound of breaking glass from the cabins confirmed it.

"What the…?" Galen pushed the door back open and stuck his head in the bin. "Pam, have you got a cell phone in your underwear?"

She shrugged. "Latest technology."

"Gosh darn it to heck," Galen swore. "Let's have it."

Mad Dog started sidling, trying to put himself where Galen wouldn't notice as he crept close enough to the door to make a try for the gun. Pam was holding Galen's attention. She turned around and hiked up the front of her dress. Even from where Mad Dog stood, she revealed a lot of skin. Mad Dog tried to keep his mind on the gun. Side step, slide the other foot, repeat. It was a big bin.

The cell phone rang again as Pam took it from its hiding place. From where Mad Dog stood, his view was even better than Galen's. Gun, he told himself, but his eyes kept returning to a pair of legs even Charlize Theron would have envied.

"Don't answer it."

She glanced at the phone. "No one I care to talk to anyway."

"Throw it over here."

Step, slide, step, slide. Pam threw the phone so that it didn't quite get to the door. Perfect, Mad Dog thought, stepping and sliding. Galen was going to have to lean way over to reach it and Mad Dog was going to get close enough to….

"Get back against the far wall," Galen said. He'd swiveled in the doorway and was pointing the gun at Mad Dog's face. There went the step sliding. Mad Dog retreated.

When Mad Dog was too far away to do anything, Galen bent and picked up the phone. He tossed it over his shoulder and wiped his hand against his shirt as if he feared contamination.

"Don't be more stupid than you already are," Pam said. "I didn't get any cooties on it."

Galen flushed and the phone rang one more time before giving up. "Unclean," Galen hissed. He didn't seem to realize that when you had the gun, you didn't have to explain yourself. Kid's got issues, Mad Dog thought, but he didn't offer to help sort them out.

"Cleaner than your mind, Galen Siegrist." Again, Mad Dog thought she was picking a bad time to test the limits of Galen's temper.

"You are a slut, Pamela Epperson. I know. Mark told me."

"Told you what? Mark and I…hell, hardly anything happened between us."

"You and he…," Galen sputtered. "The two of you were lovers."

"Just missionary position," Pam said. "Well, all but that once."

Galen turned half a dozen shades brighter than red. "I've got no time for this," he said. "And I can't take any more chances. Out of those clothes."

Now it was Pam's turn to sputter.

"Hey, you can't…," Mad Dog protested. But of course, Galen could. He had the gun.

"Way you've looked at me, I always thought you wanted to get me naked," Pam said. "And behind a pointed gun is the only way it was ever going to happen." She reached for her throat and started undoing buttons.

"I don't want to see you naked, you Jezebel. You can keep your underwear on, long as I can tell you don't have anything hidden in it."

She stepped out of the dress. Her bra and panties were examples of minimalism. They weren't hiding anything but the good stuff, and that, just barely. She removed her shoes and tossed them to the door. "What," she said, "no body cavity search?"

Galen's color heightened still further. Mad Dog was pretty sure Galen would glow if only it were dark.

The gun swiveled to point at Mad Dog. "You, too, old man."

"Can't," Mad Dog said.

"Can't?" Galen's voice was getting high and a little hysterical. "Why's that?"

"I don't wear underwear," Mad Dog said. He blushed. Pam's eyebrows went up and a little smile appeared on her lips.

Mad Dog wasn't entirely surprised when Galen laughed and told him to strip anyway. What Mad Dog chose to wear, or not, under his jeans made no difference to Galen.

◇◇◇

Lieutenant Greer looked down the muzzle of the sheriff's .38 and shook his head.

"Jeez," Greer said to Neuhauser. "You don't know our sheriff very well. He doesn't shoot innocent people who aren't a threat to his life. He may hate my guts, but he's not going to pull that trigger, even when I reach out and take his gun away from him."

The sheriff wondered if Greer was trying to convince himself, but the man was right. For half a second, the sheriff considered just winging the bastard, but then the lieutenant gently pushed the sheriff's gun so that it was aiming at the school wall. He didn't take it, though.

"In fact," the lieutenant continued, "though he won't like it, our sheriff will probably provide me with good backup."

What do you do when the options run out? The sheriff wasn't willing to kill either of them, especially when Greer's wild plan just might work. But he had no intention of letting them take over.

"You're both under arrest for interfering with an officer in the performance of his duty."

"Whatever," Greer said. "As soon as this is finished, we'll all go over to the courthouse and you can charge us and we'll post bail."

"And, Mr. Neuhauser," the sheriff continued, "if you don't get that pistol out of the back of my neck, I'm going to charge you with pretty much everything in the book and see how you like our eight by eight iron cells."

"Sorry," the man said. He stepped back, putting enough distance between himself and the sheriff so he wouldn't be easy to disarm. The sheriff felt like continuing to read them the riot act, but Greer didn't give him time.

"Wait for me," the lieutenant said. "Don't follow until I give you the all clear."

"Right," Neuhauser said. The sheriff didn't say anything. He would go in right behind Greer, unless the lieutenant's corpse was in the way.

"Let's boogie," Greer said. He peeked around the building to remind himself where the stairwell and the fence were. He pulled the pin on a grenade, rolled it around the corner and ducked, clutching another grenade as he did so.

Neuhauser and the sheriff grabbed wall just as the earth moved. Greer threw himself around the corner, behind the second grenade. Flash-bang, the sheriff guessed, because Greer wasn't afraid to expose his body to it and because a deafening concussion further assaulted the sheriff's ears.

The sheriff left Neuhauser hugging the wall and followed Greer. He rounded the corner just in time to hear the lieutenant's shotgun and Chucky's automatic rifle open up simultaneously. There was so much dust in the air that the sheriff couldn't tell what was going on for a moment. The first grenade had left a hole in the chain link surrounding the stairwell, just as Greer intended. But it wasn't as big as it should be. And something was hanging in it, blocking the opening.

Christ! It was Greer, hanging there, the light jacket he was wearing caught on strands of twisted wire. He was dangling in the stairwell. Not that deep, at least. His waist was roughly at ground level. But his feet, God, they'd be hanging down near the windows, down in Chucky's field of fire.

That's when he realized Chucky wasn't shooting anymore. Greer wasn't doing any shooting, either. His shotgun was at the bottom of the steps, lying in a pile of shattered glass and pieces of window frame. Hell, even part of the door was down there with it.

"You alive?" the sheriff asked directly in Greer's ear. He didn't get a response, though he could tell the man was breathing. And bleeding from the head. The sheriff put his arms under Greer's and yanked. The lieutenant was heavy, but the sheriff was benefiting from as much adrenaline as his system could produce. Greer slowly emerged from the hole in the fence, and the sheriff dragged him back around the corner.

"Is the lieutenant dead?" Neuhauser asked.

"Not yet," the sheriff said. "But we could still get lucky."

It was cool in the grain bin. Not cold, because it must be getting close to noon and the sun was beating down on the bare metal and conducting a little heat. It would probably be pretty comfortable by mid-afternoon. But tonight….

"What are you doing?" Pam was standing against the wall on the sunny side, absorbing the warmth. Mad Dog was busy checking seams on the opposite wall, trying to do anything to keep his mind off the young woman in the minuscule underwear on the other side of the bin.

Not that he was a prude. Back when he was part of that commune down in Oklahoma, he'd spent most of a summer running around bare-assed in the company of seriously attractive and equally unclothed young women. But he was older now. Old enough to know better. Old enough to be this girl's father….

Still, it wouldn't have been a problem, but shortly after Galen took their clothes and left them alone together, Mad Dog noticed a certain part of his anatomy didn't care whether Pam was too young. He felt preliminary stirrings that had been a lot more common back in the decades before Pam was even born.

He told himself their situation was difficult enough without him parading around with an erection and started a detailed inspection of the bin's construction. It occupied his mind and turned the offending member from her view. And his search even stood a chance in a billion of getting them out of here.

"Looking for a weak point," he said, recalling how wispy her underwear was. The memory diverted blood flow in an unfortunate direction.

"Like this," he said, forcing himself to focus on a flawed rivet he'd just discovered. If he only had a really good pry bar, he might be able to pop it, then start working on the seam. Given a few uninterrupted months to work on the spot, he might get them out of there.

"Like what?" Her voice came from just over his shoulder and he was suddenly sure he could detect her body heat radiating along his right flank. Damned blood flow.

"Uh, here," he said, pointing out the rivet and trying to make sure she only noticed the cold metal instead of….

"You really think you can do something with that?"

She was right beside him, now. He couldn't turn away. That would be too obvious. He let his right arm fall to his side in a masking position.

She wasn't just too young. He was Cheyenne. Cheyenne were not promiscuous. They didn't have casual sexual relationships. Not that she would be interested in an old man like him, anyway. But if she noticed how interested part of him was… well, it would be humiliating. And that very thought should have been enough to reverse the blood flow process, but she was leaning in close to examine the rivet and something very soft and hardly contained by lace and gauze brushed his arm. More blood left his brain.

She turned and looked at him. At least she was looking at his face. "Mad Dog, do you think you could do something with that?"

He'd forgotten her question. He took a deep breath and tried to lock his eyes on hers, and not that cleavage only inches away.

"Yeah." His voice sounded husky even to him. He tried again. "If I had my knife or some piece of metal to work on it with."

"There's a metal hook in my bra," she said. She reached up and undid it and he lost control of his eyes. She handed the translucent garment to him and he took it. There wasn't much more to the hook and eye arrangement than there was to the bra itself. Just some thin wire that would bend before it even scratched the rivet.

"I don't think this is hard enough," he said, voice even huskier.

"But that sure is," she said. He managed to get his eyes back on her face and discovered her own had traveled elsewhere. When he'd taken her bra, he'd uncovered himself.

She smiled. "Thanks," she said. "I was beginning to think I wasn't your type."

He dropped his hands and tried to hide himself.

"Hey, don't be embarrassed. I'm flattered." She put her arms around his neck and slid up against him.

In spite of all his will power, his arms reached out to welcome her. Her mouth opened and found his and then she stepped back a little and dropped her hands to her waist.

"Let me get out of these," she said. A last filmy cloth slid from her hips to her ankles. And then she was back in his arms and nothing separated them. There was only one way they could get closer and she rose up on her tiptoes as she nibbled at his mouth, hips doing a subtle bump and grind to guide him and make it happen.

Mad Dog didn't want it to happen. But his hands found her hips and pulled her to him and he knew there was no way to stop it. What his intellect wanted didn't matter. Sometimes the body has a will of its own. Nothing on earth would keep them from....

The door to the bin swung open on creaking hinges.

"Heather," Heather English said. "Would you move your car back over and block the road into the camp where it goes between those two trees? And then stay with it?"

"What," Heather Lane said, "you're going in alone?"

"I may flush somebody. If I do, you'll have them trapped. I'll call if I need help. Is your cell on and charged?" Her sister showed her that it was. "If I need you, I'll call. If I'm not there when you answer, sneak in and maybe bring a tire iron, just in case."

"You're scaring me," Two said.

"Nah, I'm being dramatic. Something weird is going on, and somebody died in that accident this morning, but it's not like anything dangerous is happening. Not in Benteen County."

The other Heather smiled. "Well, be careful," she said. She got in her car and backed toward the gap in the trees.

Deputy Heather fumbled her cell phone and pepper spray out of her fanny pack, then slid between cars and melted into the grove that surrounded the camp. The deeper she went, the more the trees thinned and individual buildings became visible. She slipped from trunk to trunk, pausing at each to search for any sign of movement and to examine the cabins for broken windows.

She would have missed it but for the breeze. A curtain fluttered in the window of a candy-cane striped cabin near the center of the camp.

Heather hadn't done much hunting growing up. Hunting wasn't a girl thing in Benteen County, and after Vietnam her dad hadn't been interested in killing for sport. But she'd played her share of cops and robbers and hide and seek and seen thousands of movies. She had a pretty good idea of how a cop should approach a probable breaking and entering. She continued slipping from cover to cover, even more carefully now, as if someone might stick a gun out that window and begin sniping at her at any moment. And she checked around her as she advanced, in case there were other people in here or whoever broke that window had moved somewhere else.

When she got to the adjacent cabin, a robin's egg blue SAMARITANS, the curtain that had caught her attention stirred in a way the wind couldn't be responsible for. A foot stepped through, and then another. The body they were attached to twisted and a butt, a big one, followed slowly, feet reaching for a porch that was inconveniently low.

Now, Heather thought. She pivoted once, reassuring herself that she and the burglar were alone, and then she sprinted toward the candy-cane cabin. The burglar's feet found the porch and the rest of him came through the window, the curtain mussing his thick gray hair. The rest of him was as big as his tush, and she was disturbed to note that he had a pistol on his belt. At least it wasn't in his hands. Those were holding a stack of notebooks.

Heather threw herself the last few yards. He must have heard her coming because he started to turn as she joined him on the porch. She shoved the narrow end of the tube of pepper spray into the small of his back—not exactly the way it was intended to be used—and spoke with her most authoritative voice.

"Hands up or I'll blow your spine right through your belly button."

"Jesus! What's happened here?" It was Doc Jones. The sheriff hadn't heard him drive up again, though Doc's Buick was only a few yards away.

Dust from the grenades was still settling. The sheriff's ears rang and turned Doc's voice distant and tinny.

"It's Greer," the sheriff said. "He just tried a frontal assault that didn't work out real well."

"Doctor, you've got to help him," Neuhauser pleaded. He seemed on the verge of hysterics, so the sheriff reached over and took the gun out of his hand.

"I came over here as an MD, not a coroner, son." Doc didn't like to have his responsibilities explained to him. "Where's he hit?"

"God, man. Can't you see? Right there," Neuhauser pointed at Greer's bloody forehead.

"That's no bullet wound," Doc said. "He banged his head on something. Probably, whatever knocked him out." Doc joined the sheriff, who was already kneeling beside the lieutenant. "Bullet holes," Doc said, "that's my first concern."

"None on his torso," the sheriff said, unfastening and removing the bandolier with its collection of grenades. None of them were quite like what he'd used in Vietnam, and they weren't labeled in ways that meant anything to him.

"I don't see any bullet wounds at all," Doc said. "Just a gash on the tip of this steel-toed boot where it got grazed, maybe. And it looks like the heel got shot off, too, but no wounds."

"His jacket caught on the fence," the sheriff said, putting the grenades on the ground well out of Greer or Neuhauser's reach. English opened the cylinder and dropped the bullets out of Neuhauser's gun. "The steel bar that supported the top of the fence, that's probably what hit him, and then he didn't fall far. Not far enough for Chucky to have an angle on him from the back of the room."

"Lucky man." Doc peeled Greer's eyelids up and shone a flashlight into the lieutenant's pupils. "Mild concussion, probably, though I suppose I'd better get some x-rays and monitor him for brain swelling. But that can wait. I brought you a couple of volunteers, Englishman. And I brought my own gun, too."

The sheriff noticed two old farmers, one with a deer rifle, the other a shotgun, standing back by Doc's Buick.

"How can we help?" one of them asked.

The sheriff shook his head. "I don't know."

Doc had told the sheriff he owned a gun, but English hadn't seen the Luger before. He didn't think Doc had fired the thing since he'd moved to Benteen County. And those old men. One of them, the one with the deer rifle, wore a billed cap pulled down low enough to scrunch his ears. That was to hide his hairless head because he was undergoing chemotherapy. If Doc had brought him from the clinic, it was probably because this was one of his bad days. The guy with the shotgun was a lot stronger, but they'd had to take his driver's license away last year because his macular degeneration had gotten too bad. The man could probably still see well enough to point a shotgun at somebody, but he might not know who it was. And Neuhauser…. Greer's buddy had put a gun to the back of the sheriff's head. The sheriff needed help, but this was the stuff of desperation.

The sheriff went to the edge of the building. Preceded by his .38, he peered around the mangled fence at the shattered windows down in the stairwell.

"Chucky?"

No answer.

"Chucky. It's me, Sheriff English. Answer me, son."

Nothing.

"Anybody? Talk to me."

The silence was overwhelming.

"Shit," the sheriff said. "I think Greer flushed him. If he's got a key to that door, he can get anywhere in the building. Or out of it.

"You two," he said to the elderly farmers. "You know where the inside door to this basement is?"

They nodded.

"It was locked when I last checked. Go make sure it still is. If Chucky tries to come through after you're there, dissuade him. But remember, he's got hostages. Don't do anything foolish."

"We understand," the chemo patient said.

"And let me know anything that happens."

The two turned and headed for the front of the building.

"Doc," the sheriff said. "Neuhauser pulled a gun on me before. That's how Greer managed all this mayhem." Doc swung and covered the man with his old Luger. "Neuhauser might still be of some help if things go bad for me, but keep him in front of you." He gave Neuhauser his bullets back, but handed the oversized pistol to Doc.

"What are you planning?" Doc asked.

"I can't see that I have any choice but to go down there."

"Chucky could be waiting for that. You could be dead before you hit the bottom of those stairs."

"Then you'll know where he is and you can tell the professionals when they get here." He glanced at the parking lot, hoping to see a Kansas Highway Patrol car pulling in off of Main. Or a National Guard battalion might be nice—except they would all be in Iraq, or off patrolling the Mexican border.

"Chucky was talking to me. So was one of his hostages. Now nothing. And he hasn't fired any shots since Greer tried to take him single-handed. I think he's moving. And I'm afraid he knows there's more than one way out."

"But you've covered that." Doc was paying attention, but he was keeping an eye, and the Luger, on Neuhauser.

"There's another. The old furnace is down there. And a spider web of ducts with pipes that lead all through the building."

Including over the former girl's locker room, or so English had been told by a classmate who claimed to know. The boy had also said Michelle Nelson wasn't a natural blond and Becky Prichard had a tattoo on her right hip. The sheriff had thought the boy was bragging, his stories the stuff of adolescent fantasy. Then Becky Prichard overfilled a tractor tire down at the Texaco a few years later and got blown over into the Buffalo Burger Drive-In parking lot. The explosion killed her instantly, and tore most of her clothes off. The tattoo was right where it was supposed to be. That meant those heating ducts really were navigable.

"Can we cover you, or something?" Doc's voice made it clear he didn't like the idea of the sheriff going down there, but realized it had to be done.

"No. Just be ready to come treat any wounded. But stay out until I tell you it's safe."

Doc nodded and the sheriff realized there were no more excuses to put this off.

"Neuhauser," he asked, "you know which of those grenades does what?"

The man shook his head. "I was a private contractor in Iraq. We didn't do grenades."

The sheriff wondered if Neuhauser was lying, then shrugged and looked around the corner again. His guts churned. That's how he'd felt, going into the field in Vietnam. Every time. Apparently, it wasn't something you lost with age.

"Chucky," he called. "Sheriff English again. I'm coming down there. I'm bringing my gun, but it'll be in my holster."

Nothing. Just the wind, sighing down the alley behind the school, chasing a swirl of dead leaves toward Nebraska.

The sheriff made sure he didn't catch his own clothing on the jagged wire as he slipped inside the stairwell.

"Here I come," he said, "ready or not." That last part, he decided, probably applied to him at least as much as Chucky.

He lowered himself and sat on the concrete lip, dangling his feet in the well and diminishing the distance he'd have to drop. The bottom looked deeper than he remembered. He could hurt himself, jumping down there. The foolishness of that thought made him smile. He pushed off the edge.

It was Hailey.

Pam jumped back and Mad Dog swung around toward the door, expecting the embarrassment of being discovered *in flagrante delicto* by Galen. But Galen wasn't there. No one was. Just a smiling timber wolf. Hailey shook her head, as if surprised that Mad Dog could have gotten himself in so much mischief in so little time.

"How'd she do that?" Pam said. She beat Mad Dog to the door and hugged Hailey, then she bent and stuck her head out to make sure someone else hadn't opened the bin's door. It left Mad Dog with an interesting view, but he was relieved to discover blood flow was actually returning to his brain. It was needed there, to puzzle out what was going on, and get them somewhere Galen couldn't find them.

"I've never been able to keep her locked in or out of anyplace." Mad Dog hugged the wolf, too, being careful not to brush against Pam. No sense tempting blood flow again. Hailey covered his face with kisses, then slipped away from both of them and ran back into the dusky corridor. She stopped, just before it twisted out of sight, and looked back over her silver-tipped shoulder. Come on, she seemed to be urging them, we've got to get going.

"I think she wants us to follow her," Pam said. Mad Dog was sure of it. Pam crawled through the exit. More interesting views.

Mad Dog followed, glancing up and down the corridor. It weaved back and forth around a series of bins like theirs.

"Hey, what about your underwear?"

"Leave it," she said. "It's not very practical and it's not like it makes me presentable."

She was one hell of a distraction without it, but then he remembered how the cloth had seemed to emphasize what was underneath rather than hide anything.

"I chose that underwear for piano practice because the church is so self-righteous. A little invisible rebellion. I don't want you to think that's what I usually wear. So leave them, and close those doors behind you. If Galen comes back and can't find anything but my undies, maybe he'll think he missed the rapture."

He might, indeed. Mad Dog grinned and shut the doors. Galen hadn't left their clothes nearby. Nor had he left the pile from Mad Dog's pockets. And apparently he'd overcome his aversion to Pam's cooties enough to take her cell phone, too.

"Our clothes are probably in his office. But I noticed these hanging just inside the entrance to this corridor." She handed him a pair of coveralls. Not bib overalls, but the kind that enveloped you from neck to ankles and wrists. She stepped into the blue ones. He was a little disappointed and a lot relieved when her body disappeared under the heavy fabric.

His were white, or they had been. Now they were covered with a camouflage of stains. They weren't quite big enough for him. They ran out of material a couple of inches short on his arms and legs, but they'd been cut for someone with more weight around the middle and a broader posterior. Plenty of room for him, even after he relaxed the gut he suddenly realized he'd been sucking in ever since his clothes came off. He might be getting old, but apparently he wasn't too old to try and show a pretty girl his best profile.

"Now we just need shoes," she said. Hell, she still looked sexy, even in the most functional of work clothes, though knowing there was nothing but girl flesh under the fabric might have something to do with that.

"What's Hailey doing with that other bin?" Mad Dog turned to where Pam was pointing. Hailey was a couple of bins down on the opposite side. She'd jumped up and was pawing at the latch—probably the same way she'd opened the outer door on her way to rescue them. Only she didn't seem to be giving it her best effort. In fact, once she got Mad Dog's attention, she sat in front of the door, looking from it to him. She whined.

"She wants you to open that one," Pam said. "You don't suppose Galen's turned these things into prison cells, do you?"

Mad Dog couldn't think of any other reason Hailey would want in there. Not unless that was where their clothes and belongings had gone.

There was only one way to find out. He finished opening the outer door, then hauled up on the bar that unlocked the inner one. How had Hailey managed to do that one? The latch was tight and he had to plant his feet and grab the bar with both hands and put some muscle into it. But it gave, and since the inner door wasn't held in place by a few tons of grain, it swung open easily.

"Thank God," someone said. "I thought I was dead."

Mad Dog reached in and helped the young man out of his makeshift jail. The kid seemed dazed. He stumbled and practically fell into Pam's arms and she eased him to the floor.

Mad Dog didn't like the way she cuddled him to her and began making soothing noises, but now, at least, he knew what had happened to Mark Brown.

"Heather?" The burglar with the armful of notebooks and the pistol on his belt swung around and said in an accusing voice, "What are you doing here? You're supposed to be in school."

"Chairman Wynn." The former chairman of the Benteen County Board of Supervisors was pretty much the last person

Heather would have expected to find breaking into cabins at the Bible camp. Even if he had been recalled, along with the rest of his compatriots, for financial irregularities associated with the failed get-rich-quick-wind-farm scheme, he wasn't the criminal type. But that wasn't the only reason it surprised her. He was also the father of the perpetual screw-up, Deputy Wynn-Some Lose-Some, whose misadventures had begun the day's catastrophes.

"Why are you trying to scare an old man to death by pretending to stick a gun in his back?"

Heather flashed her badge as she pocketed the pepper spray. "I'm official, Mr. Chairman. Dad's shorthanded today. I came back to help him celebrate his re-election, so I'm helping out. But what about you? I thought you were in Wichita with your son."

"The doctors say he's better than 50/50 to make it. And they've decided to keep him in a coma for a few days. I figured I could pace the halls and worry with his mama, or I could hop back in the Beechcraft and come home. Maybe find out what he was up to this morning."

Heather felt a lot of sympathy for Wynn-Some's father. Deputy Wynn had been creating problems, or exacerbating them, for years. And the Senior Wynn and his fellow supervisors might have misused county funds, but they'd meant well. They'd been caught in a con-artist's scheme they thought might rescue the county from its continuing slide into insolvency. The senior Wynn had enough problems without being charged with burglarizing the Bible camp.

"You found this window already broken, right?"

It took him a moment to realize what she was offering. "Uh, right," he said.

"I understand why you'd be interested in looking around here," Heather said. "As soon as Dad and Mrs. Kraus told me about the accident, I wanted to come see why a bus load of kids would be coming here in the middle of the night."

"I think they were on their way from here, not coming here," he said. "I mean, you saw all those cars out in the lot."

Heather had.

"I think they gathered here before my boy ran into...." He paused, recognizing that might not be the best choice of words, considering. "...encountered the bus," he continued, "on its way somewhere else."

She nodded at the notebooks. "You find something that tells us where?"

"Not where," he said, "but maybe why."

She let her eyebrows ask the question.

"You should take a look in there." He gestured toward the candy-striped cabin. "That's no kid's camp infirmary. It's a high-tech medical lab. They've got more newfangled gizmos than Doc has down at the clinic."

She wanted to look and she trusted him, but she didn't think a good deputy would turn her back on a suspect until she was done questioning him.

Chairman Wynn knelt on the brightly painted porch and spread the notebooks out. He opened one as she bent to join him. "Look here."

He started flipping pages. Each one was headed by a first name and last initial—Butch B., Annie G., Mark G., Linda R., Chucky W. And lots more. Benteen County wasn't a big place. Maybe a quarter of the current students attending Buffalo Springs High were listed. Several of them had been aboard that bus this morning.

She said as much, and he pointed at the series of abbreviated categories beneath each name. "This is medical information. See, this first row. BT means blood type, I think. I mean, A, B, O, AB. What else could it be? Especially since the next row, RH, is all pluses and minuses."

"Makes sense," she said. "You know what the others are? BP, that's probably blood pressure. And BPM, pulse rate. But what are some of these others? HLA, for instance. That doesn't mean anything to me."

"Human leukocyte antigens," he said.

She turned to him, surprised.

"I wouldn't have known that," he said, "if the doctors hadn't run some tests on me this morning. They thought my son might need a liver transplant. HLA, that's one of the key factors."

"Oh." Heather didn't know what to say. A liver transplant, that was scary. But it struck her that all this might somehow link to the vials of supposed stem cells she'd left in the Gas – Food's refrigerator, next to a stack of beer. Link, maybe, but to what end?

"You have any idea what this is all about?"

He shook his head. "Medical experiments on those kids. Or maybe it's just a health study. But why conduct it out here? And why in secret? Who's funding all this? That equipment in there is expensive. Why would anyone put those kids on that bus this morning?"

Good questions. Heather didn't have answers, and didn't have to pretend she did, because her cell phone rang.

It was the other Heather. "You all right?"

"Fine," Deputy Heather said. "It's just Chairman Wynn."

"Not chairman anymore," he said. Heather didn't make the correction.

"Good," her sister said. "'Cause you may want to come out here. The Gustafsons just drove in with Annie to pick up her car. And Mr. Gustafson, he's real upset about where his daughter was last night. I think you'll want to talk to him."

Heather agreed. She snapped her phone shut. "Come on, Mr. Chairman. Let's go ask one of the kids on this list what it means."

A gust of wind tore across the porch carrying bright leaves and riffling the pages of the other notebooks. It left one opened to a page with the same list of names running down the left side. Across from them were numbers, percentages. Heather checked the heading at the top. "Match to Recipient," it said. Suddenly, she wanted to talk to Annie Gustafson real bad.

The sheriff didn't land quietly. There was no way to do that among the remains of broken window frames and shattered glass. But he was still alive and he stayed that way.

"Chucky?" he said. No answer.

Greer's shotgun lay at the sheriff's feet and he was tempted to pick it up. But a shotgun was the last weapon he wanted if he had to pull a trigger in a hostage situation. There wasn't time to unload it, so he kicked it aside and bent and peered through the windows.

It was dark in the old classroom. The lights might have been turned on, but it didn't matter. They'd been shot out. Broken fluorescent tubes and debris from ceiling tiles covered the floor.

All the desks had been cleared away from the door. No, not cleared, drawn up in front of the teacher's desk, near the green chalkboard on which a dark and illegible scrawl offered today's lesson. And the desks had been overturned, as if to make a sort of fortification that faced the stairwell.

What remained of the door at the bottom of the stairs was still locked, not that it made any difference, not with all those windows lying in splintered heaps. The sheriff stepped through one.

"Chucky?" he said again, still without response. "I'm coming in." He was pretty sure Chucky wasn't there anymore, but there was no sense surprising the boy if the sheriff turned out to be wrong.

It was quiet inside, but for the ringing in his ears from the shock of those grenades. He hoped that was why he couldn't hear the muffled breathing of the hostages or the wounded. He doubted it though. He had no trouble hearing the sounds his feet made, crunching debris as he advanced toward that fortress of desks.

"Chucky? Anybody?" One last try.

He pushed the first desk aside. Wood and metal complained as they scraped across ancient tiles. Two pair of unmoving feet lay in a pool of blood just beyond. The sheriff slipped through the gap and bent beside the bodies. Boys, but he couldn't tell who they were. Both faces had been blown away. Bits of bone and blood and brain matter were what covered that chalkboard. The eternal question—Why?—written up there as two Buffalo Springs teens perhaps learned the answer.

Another pair of feet protruded from behind the teacher's desk. There was nothing the sheriff could do for the faceless pair, so he proceeded to the third body. It was Mr. Gamble, would-be choir director and Darwin critic. He had been shot, too, but not in the face. Exit wounds had exploded from his belly and chest. He must have been trying to get away. The sheriff thought it was a waste of time, but he put his fingers to the man's throat. No pulse. The skin was already cooling. Gamble must have died before Greer tried to make his grand entrance.

Bad. Three bodies. The pair without faces… kids, not yet men, shot to pieces in a building that should have been absolutely safe for them. And their teacher…. But why had Gamble brought these kids down here? What were they doing in an abandoned basement? Could this secret "choir" have somehow caused Chucky Williams to begin his killing spree? No one in the room could answer. Chucky and his hostages were gone, leaving three bodies and an infinite quantity of spent brass and bullet holes.

"Englishman?" Doc's voice was made distant by the stairwell and the soft moan of the ever-present Kansas wind. "Need help?"

"No, Doc. Three here. All beyond your abilities, until you go back to being coroner. Otherwise, this room is empty. I'm going to check out the rest of the basement. Wait there in case he gets by me."

Getting by would probably mean the sheriff was dead, but he didn't mention that. Doing your duty…there were worse ways to go. He'd watched as cancer stole his wife. He'd rather let Chucky Williams empty a clip in him any day.

The sheriff stepped over to the classroom door, the one that led to the staircase where two old men had been sent to block an exit. He entered the dark hallway beyond.

"Chucky," the sheriff said, closing the door behind him. "I'm coming for you."

"Mark," Pam said. "What's wrong?"

"Water," Mark rasped. "No water since yesterday."

"I'll find some," Mad Dog said. There was a bathroom next to Galen's office. Besides, he needed to check whether Galen was still there. He didn't think so, because Hailey would have let him know. But maybe he'd find their clothes and cell phones and they could make contact with the outside world. Start to find out what was happening here.

Mad Dog glanced around. Where was Hailey, anyway? She'd been there to show them the grain bin Mark had been imprisoned in. Mad Dog had helped release Mark and now….Amazing, the way she kept appearing and disappearing, almost as if she could slip in and out of this world whenever she wanted.

Water. Galen Siegrist irrigated every acre he farmed. Water shouldn't be hard to find.

It was as dark in the warehouse as in the corridor at the base of the grain bins. None of the overhead lights were on and there weren't that many windows. None of the outside doors were open, either—the big ones for machinery or the little ones for people. Mad Dog examined the building from just inside the opening to the corridor, listening. The wind teased metal joints and rattled a loose panel somewhere. Otherwise, it was quiet. He couldn't see anyone. The lights were off in Galen's office. But Mad Dog's Mini Cooper had been moved in and parked behind Mark's truck. So it wouldn't be visible from the road, he supposed.

The Mini was closer than the office, so Mad Dog went there first. It was locked. There was nothing in it, anyway, except John Stewart CDs, and the new Neko Case he'd picked up the last time he was in Wichita.

Galen's office wasn't locked. Too bad. Mad Dog would have enjoyed breaking through one of its windows. Still, there could be an advantage to not making it obvious that they were on the loose again.

It was darker still in the office. Mad Dog was sure no one was in the warehouse. He took a chance and flipped the lights on. A computer sat, quietly powered down, on an inexpensive desk. Stacks of paper were neatly arranged and there was a lot of clear space on which to work. Compulsive, Mad Dog decided. He hadn't seen the top of his own desk in ages.

It was a thoroughly boring room—desk, file cabinets, a couple of cheap chairs for visitors, no ashtrays. The only decorations were a seed company calendar, displaying an ear of corn that reclined erotically, and two pictures that were all too familiar. They were duplicates of the watch-your-every-move Jesus and the scowling Aldus P. Goodfellow that hung in the room where he'd found Pam playing piano.

Mad Dog rifled the desk drawers and the file cabinets. Their clothes and his keys weren't in any of them. The closet didn't have a door and was empty except for another pair of coveralls. These had Galen's name embroidered on the pocket.

He didn't have to get water from the bathroom because the office contained a small refrigerator behind the desk. There were a couple of cans of generic cola and several bottles of designer water inside. Mad Dog filled his pockets. He was about to rush it all back to Pam and Mark when he realized there was something else of interest on the desk—a phone.

He picked it up, got a dial tone, and started punching buttons.

"Benteen County Sheriff's Office," Mrs. Kraus said, "please hold."

"Emergency," Mad Dog said, but she was gone before he got it out. He could hold or try his brother's cell. He held. Nothing ever happened in Benteen County. Mrs. Kraus would be right back.

Something clicked in his ear. Someone, somewhere, began pushing buttons. Time to hang up, Mad Dog decided, but then Mrs. Kraus was back on the line.

"Can I help you?" She didn't sound like she wanted to.

"Send the next donor," a man said.

"Beg pardon?" Mrs. Kraus replied. Her voice had gone beyond sounding male or female. It was more like listening to a steel girder under too much stress.

The other voice paused a moment. "With whom am I speaking?" he asked.

"Who are you?" Mrs. Kraus countered.

"I believe I have reached an incorrect number." The guy who wanted another donor spoke with the crisp perfection of someone whose native language wasn't English.

"You calling the Benteen County Sheriff's Office?"

"No, I am not."

"Then you're wasting your time and mine," Mrs. Kraus said. "Yours, I don't care about." There was another click when, Mad Dog was sure, she slammed down her phone.

More clicks followed, as the foreigner tried for a dial tone.

"Strange," the voice said to someone else. "How could I dial Gamble and get the sheriff's office?" The clicks started again and Mad Dog took advantage of them to put Galen's phone back in its receiver.

◇◇◇

Annie Gustafson didn't want to talk to anyone. But her father did.

"What do you think we elect your dad for?" he asked Heather English. "He's the law in Benteen County. We expect him and his deputies, you included I guess, to protect innocent children from bizarre situations like this."

Gus Gustafson was a retired Navy man. He claimed he'd wanted to get as far from the ocean as possible, and Benteen County qualified. The former seaman had gathered his retirement papers and his family and moved here to raise kids and organic vegetables. Their truck farm paid its way, with the help of his retirement checks, but the kids had all grown up and returned to coastlines—all but Annie, sixteen, the only one still too young to leave home.

"Dad's been kind of shorthanded," Deputy Heather said, "and I just got my badge this morning. But if you'll tell me what I need to protect Annie from, I'll do my best."

Gustafson sputtered a moment before confessing. "That's why Annie's grounded until she's thirty. She won't tell me why she was out here last night, or on that bus. She says she was doing God's work."

"Is that so, Annie?" The girl didn't answer or meet Heather's eyes.

Gustafson wasn't through, though. "Things haven't been the same since Goodfellow and these political Christians moved in over there across from the courthouse. If you ask me, the man's as wacky as his televangelist father."

That opened Annie's mouth. "Pastor Goodfellow was chosen by the Lord, Daddy, and his father's a living saint."

"What kind of God's work gets done by a pack of kids on a stolen school bus in the middle of the night?" Gus Gustafson was having none of it.

Annie opened her mouth and then shut it. "I can't say. I swore to Jesus I wouldn't tell."

"Why would you promise not to talk about taking medical examinations?" Heather asked. Chairman Wynn had come along with her and he'd brought the notebooks. Heather took one and opened it to a page on which *Annie G.* was prominently displayed.

That brought Mrs. Gustafson into the conversation. "Annie. You couldn't. We raised you to know and live according to the tenets of Christian Science. That's why we brought you right home from that hospital. God will take care of any healing you need. Doctors aren't necessary. You said so yourself, to the people in that emergency room. How could you betray your trust in God by seeing some other doctors?"

Heather's interrogation skills might need honing, but she knew when to keep her mouth shut and just listen.

Annie was on the verge of tears. "But Mom," she said. "I didn't do it for me. I just let them test me so I could be part of it, stay with the group. All I was going to do was pray for him. Sing for him."

"For who?" Mr. Gustafson demanded.

The tears were flowing now. Annie's voice broke when she answered. "I can't say," she hiccupped. "I swore I wouldn't tell."

"The people on that bus were just part of a choir?" Heather said.

Annie nodded.

Heather took the notebook from Chairman Wynn and flipped pages. "Look at this, Annie," she said. "This seems to be a list of people who would make the best transplant donors for someone. All the closest matches but Chucky seem to have been in your choir and on that bus this morning."

Annie was nearly hysterical. "Chucky was with us. He ran…." She stopped. "I can't say anything. I can't."

"They didn't tell you about maybe being a donor, did they?" Heather said.

Annie just sobbed.

"If they lied to you to get you to swear that oath, Jesus wouldn't want you to stay silent." Heather wasn't sure about that. She knew she was right, legally, but when you got to faith, that was another matter.

Annie wasn't sure either, though both her parents spoke up and agreed with Heather's interpretation. "I don't know what to do," the girl moaned.

Heather decided to explore escape clauses. "Did you promise not to tell where you were going?"

Annie nodded. That one wouldn't work. "How about who asked you to go?" Heather was getting desperate. "Or who was driving the bus?"

Annie seized on the last one. "The bus driver—that was Galen Siegrist."

Most of the basement of Buffalo Springs High had once been the floor of a gymnasium. When the new gym was built in the fifties, the old one had been converted into more classrooms and a theater that doubled for assemblies. The hall the sheriff followed led almost straight down what had once been center court. The doors on his right opened on what remained of the gym, a half court of scarred wood floor with a raised stage. On the left were the new classrooms, abandoned now, including the one where Chucky had taken three lives. Every door along the hall was locked, handles still covered with dust.

At the far end, behind the staircase, was the old furnace room. Chucky Williams was probably in there. There was no dust on that knob. Just in case, though, the sheriff climbed the stairs that led to the door the principal hadn't been able to open earlier. On the other side, presumably, two elderly make-do deputies guarded this exit. The door required a key from either side. It was still locked and dusty. Just as well, since the sheriff was likely to take a load of buckshot in the face if he stuck his head out to check on the farmers.

Back at the door to the furnace room, the sheriff paused. If he was wrong about access to those ducts, Chucky would be waiting for him in here. The sheriff put one hand on the knob, keeping his .38 in front of him. He allowed himself a couple of deep breaths, then threw open the door and stepped into the room.

It was dusky, though far brighter than in the hall. High, narrow, pebbled-glass windows proved it was still light outside, but that was about all.

The room was crowded with junk—stacks of old desks, boxes of files, antique band uniforms. Dust hung in the air, recently disturbed, and yet the floor was clean and shining. It shouldn't be shining. He slipped further into the room, got to the place where he could see around that stack of desks, and found the bodies.

It wasn't the floor that shone. It was the fresh blood on it.

Three girls lay in a circle. Their arms were bound with duct tape. Their mouths and eyes had been taped, too. Chucky must have brought them here, then realized he couldn't take them with him into the tunnels. Not three of them. And so he hadn't taken any. It appeared he'd made them kneel, each facing away from where he'd stood in their center. And then he'd used a knife. A hand in the hair to pull the head back, expose the neck, then one quick slash. None of them seemed to have struggled. The sheriff thought…hoped…they hadn't known what was happening to them.

Of course he knew them all. One of the girls looked a little like his beloved Judy. She had been about this age when he first noticed her at a basketball game in the adjacent gym, then married her shortly thereafter. The memories caused his eyes to tear up, although what he'd found here should have been enough. He'd been hiding his emotions, way down where no one knew about them, not even himself. He swiped a sleeve across his eyes, pushed his feelings aside again, and forced himself back to the business at hand.

Three bodies made for a lot of blood. He waded through it, checking each, knowing there would be no pulse to find. They were still warm, but the life had poured out of them and turned this room into an abattoir. Chucky's bloody footprints led toward the furnace. The sheriff's equally bloody boots followed.

He supposed he should have been wearing those silly little crime scene booties. Shouldn't have spoiled the scene at all, other than as necessary to determine whether they were alive. But the sheriff wasn't worrying about crime scenes anymore, or arrests—only meting out justice.

The furnace loomed like a huge sculpture of an alien god that might welcome sacrifices. It stood in the far corner, amidst a confusion of pipes and ducts. One pair of thick pipes rose to and entered the ceiling. Chucky's footprints led the sheriff to the wall beside those pipes. Metal rungs were set in that wall, spoiled by what Chucky's shoes had left on them. The sheriff kept his .38 in his right hand and followed, using care because the rungs were slippery now. He followed them to the ceiling. A trap door hung open there. Behind it, inside the ceiling, were those infamous ducts—tunnels to every room in this building. And somewhere, to Chucky.

At the top of the rungs, the sheriff had to stop and catch his breath. Not because of the effort it had taken him to get there. It was the tunnels. He'd done tunnels in Vietnam.

It was simple, really. You just followed your gun into the dark. And if you found the enemy, you killed him. Or he killed you.

"How is he?" Mad Dog asked, displaying his selection of sodas and water.

"Not bad," Pam said, though she was still sitting on the corridor's floor with Mark's head in her lap. She took a water bottle from Mad Dog and opened it for Mark, holding it to his lips. If he wasn't bad, Mad Dog wondered, why did Mark need to lie there and be waited on hand and foot?

"He tell you what happened to him?" Mad Dog might have asked Mark, but Mark was busy guzzling water.

"Not really. Just that Galen locked him in there Friday night, a few hours after you left. Galen brought him food and water twice a day until last night. Nothing today."

"Can I have some more?" Mark had drained the first bottle.

"Sure," Mad Dog said. "But talk to us first. What's going on out here? Why'd Galen stick you in that bin?"

"I don't know," Mark said. "I finished chores at your place, then I drove around some, trying to decide what to do about...." The words trailed off and he twisted his head back to gaze longingly up at Pam. He sighed and Pam ran her fingers through his hair.

"I always told you I would leave on my twenty-first birthday," she said. "But I was here Friday night. You could have called."

Mark sighed again, puppy-sad eyes locked on her face. Mad Dog couldn't take it anymore. He popped the tab on one of the sodas and offered it to Mark, holding it far enough away that the boy had to sit up and reach if he wanted it.

Mark sat and took it.

"So, what? Did you run into Galen somewhere? Did you come here?"

"I drove by." Mark paused to take a healthy swig of the soda. "When I saw the ambulance.... Well, naturally I stopped. I was afraid something had happened to Galen."

"Ambulance?" Mad Dog prompted.

"Actually, I don't remember that it had any markings, and there weren't any flashing lights, but it looked just like one of those emergency rescue vehicles. Besides, they had somebody on a wheeled gurney right by it. So I pulled in and asked who was hurt and one of the guys with the gurney pulled a gun on me."

Mark stopped to gulp more soda.

"And?" Mad Dog prompted.

"Galen came out. Then they brought me down here and put me in the bin. I asked Galen why, but he never said. Told me he'd explain later. And then he stopped bringing me food and water today and that was it, until you two came and let me out."

Mark smiled, but only at Pam. "Say, how'd you find me? And why are you wearing those Siegrist Grain Company overalls…and where are your shoes?"

Chairman Wynn wouldn't do it. Heather English had suggested he find the sheriff and show him the medical records, explain Annie Gustafson's story, and tell her dad what she'd left beside the beer at the Gas–Food.

"Honey," Wynn said. "I love your daddy, but this is my son we're talking about. If Galen Siegrist was driving that bus, I need to talk to him. Maybe Galen ran that stop sign. Maybe he knows something that'll prove the accident wasn't my boy's fault. If you think our sheriff should know all this stuff, you tell him. You're the deputy."

The two Heathers had already worked their cell phones in an effort to pass the information along. The sheriff's office phones remained stubbornly busy. Maybe a line was down.

It wasn't that windy today. If you lived somewhere other than Kansas you might call it windy, but not here. Phone and electric lines failed out in the middle of the prairie at all sorts of odd times. There weren't enough customers to justify much of a maintenance program on thousands of miles of wire. "Fix it when it breaks" seemed to be the usual approach.

The girls tried Englishman's cell, too. It was still on voice mail. They left another message.

"He's right, you know," Heather Lane said. "You *are* the deputy."

"What?" Heather English had been sure her sister would want to run the errand when the chairman refused. "I thought you were worried sick about Dad. Don't you want to see for yourself that he's all right?"

"That dream." Heather Two swept a hand at the sky, as if you only had to look at those cotton-ball clouds just right to understand her logic. "You had the dream, too. If yours was like mine, it wasn't so much that Dad isn't okay. It's that something terrible was going to happen to him unless I prevented it."

"So? Go see him, tell him what he needs to know, then stick with him and keep him safe."

"You can do that," Two said. "I have the feeling that bad something might happen at the Siegrist place. Maybe I need to go there to find out how to prevent it."

Deputy Heather felt the same. She wanted to solve this thing and keep her dad out of it. She already knew Englishman was safe back in Buffalo Springs. Now something told her she had to solve the mystery behind the school bus to keep him that way. But the Dodge station wagon and Wynn-Some's wreck were all linked to it. And Englishman was not only her dad. Thanks to that badge she'd accepted, he was her boss. Someone had to tell him what they'd discovered.

Apparently that someone was going to be her. She sighed. Maybe Heather and Chairman Wynn could solve this. If she stuck to Englishman's side once she found him, she could see that he stayed out of trouble. Maybe splitting up like this wasn't such a bad idea. Sooner or later, Englishman was going to find out about Siegrist. More kids from that bus were coming home. The sheriff could be talking to one of them right now, and then....

"Okay, I'll go tell Dad," Heather said. "But what are you two going to do? Just walk up and bang on the door and demand that Galen explain what he was doing with that bus last night?"

Two wouldn't meet her gaze, but the chairman did. "What's wrong with that?" he said. He put his hand on the butt of his revolver. "I can persuade him to talk if I have to."

"And get anything he tells you thrown out of court because you threatened him. You two need to be cautious. Anything Galen says can't be coerced. You should just go hide behind the nearest windrow and scout the place out. Then call me before you do anything. Promise?"

Two nodded. The chairman was more reluctant.

"You want to help your son, right?"

"Sure," Wynn agreed. "We'll take a look and report back to you. But if you're coming out or bringing Englishman, don't take too long. I got no patience today."

"We'll call," Heather Two said. "I swear."

It was true about the girls' locker room. Several holes in the tunnel had clearly been drilled with serious peeping in mind. Not that the angle was good, or that the peeper would have been close enough for the kind of scrutiny available, a click of the mouse away, on today's internet. But, back when this room and these peep holes were in use, it would have been far more thrilling to the person using them than any streaming video.

A few yards farther on, the tunnel passed over the boys' locker room. There were peep holes there, as well. That was a surprise. Had girls peeked at guys, too? Or guys at guys? Then the light filtering up though those holes illuminated the dried blood on the sheriff's hands, the inevitable result of following where Chucky's trail led, and the sheriff stopped caring who was looking or being looked at so long ago.

They'd gone far enough, now, that Chucky's trail was no longer so gruesomely fresh. But it was dusty in here. No one had followed these pipes, checking for leaks, lubricating valves, or spying on naked teenagers, for many years. Even in the gloom, Chucky's route was clearer than if he'd left breadcrumbs.

The sheriff took a moment to listen, again. He could hear lots of little noises now. Skittering sounds. Rats, maybe. Squirrels might have taken up residence in the attic and the walls. Or ghosts, perhaps, of all the students who survived the trauma of being imprisoned in this Guantanamo of the Plains. Or the joy of it. What a confused time high school was, your mind expanding and your body becoming adult, your consciousness caught between logic and the demands of hormones gone wild. How had they made it? How had all those students endured the psychopathology of being a teen? And, since the rest of them had, with varying degrees of success, why hadn't Chucky?

None of the sounds were of a human crawling. Nothing indicated Chucky was close by. Or that he wasn't. Chucky could be just around the next corner, waiting to unload a clip in the sheriff's face, or to thrust his blade in flesh one more time.

The sheriff began moving again. He turned a corner and found himself under the study hall. A pair of iron grates flooded the tunnel with light. Nothing held them in place except their weight. Why hadn't Chucky pushed one of them open and left this warren of twisting passages? Where was he going? What could he be planning to do to top what he'd already done?

The sheriff was under the biology room when the highway patrol arrived. Or he thought it was biology. The siren sounded distant. When it stopped, a loudspeaker crackled. The words were garbled as they echoed off stone and brick and found their way into the service tunnel. Something about putting down a gun. Was Chucky out there? Could the boy be that far ahead of him? No way to know. No way to get out there fast enough to make a difference. The sheriff considered using his cell to call Doc to find out, then decided against it. For now, he still had a trail to follow. And not much farther. He'd crawled and twisted to the opposite end of the building, or nearly so. If he was right about where he was, there was only one more corner ahead.

The sheriff rolled around it, behind his .38. This should be it. This should be the end of the tunnels.

It was…but it wasn't. A piece of metal he hadn't expected was lying next to where the last of the pipes rose through the floor. Once, they had made the history room the coldest in the building.

The sheriff scrambled across the final yards. When he was sure, he tore his cell out of his pocket, activated it, and dialed. It didn't matter, now, whether Chucky heard him, knew the sheriff was just behind. The metal plate had stood between passageways—a door from yesterday's heating system into today's.

Beyond it, the wide maw of the forced air vent from the new heating plant loomed. It was an avenue that could provide the sheriff, or Chucky ahead of him, with access to what was left of the Buffalo Springs student body. They were waiting in the false security of a lockdown, behind closed doors and windows, with never a moment's thought given to the ducts Chucky Williams might use as a route toward the elimination of an entire generation of Benteen County's youth.

The Kansas Highway Patrol cruiser came in from the east. It hadn't needed to slow down to pass through Buffalo Springs before it reached the high school. That was why it was going too fast, Doc decided, to make the turn into the parking lot. The turn wasn't paved, and since most folks entered from the opposite direction, gravel had gradually gotten banked the wrong way for a high-speed turn from the east. Siren wailing, light bar strobing, tires smoking (until they left the blacktop), the cruiser veered rather than turned as it came through the gate.

It didn't quite make it. The driver's side headlight exploded against the steel pole on the west side of the gate. The cruiser's rear end hopped off the ground, then spun around to leave the vehicle butt first to the school. A cloud of dust and steam enveloped the car as it began frantically backing across the lot. The driver tried to throw it into one of those dramatic about faces, but the left front tire had blown and come off the rim and he only managed to gouge up a lot of dirt and end up sideways to the building before the engine sputtered and died and the siren turned to a squeak before it stopped.

The driver's door opened and a trooper got out. He had a shotgun in one hand and a microphone in the other.

"Are you all right?" Doc called. He couldn't see any blood. Under normal circumstances, he would have been at the man's side as fast as he could get there, checking for injuries. Today, he'd promised Englishman he'd guard the stairwell and keep Chucky Williams from getting away if he somehow got by the sheriff.

The trooper didn't answer Doc. He raised the microphone to his lips as he pointed his scattergun Doc's way. "Toss your weapon aside," the amplified voice commanded, "then get down on the ground, face first."

It was a mistake. "No, wait. I'm the Benteen County coroner," Doc said, as if that explained why he was standing beside the local high school with an ancient Luger in his hand.

"I don't care if you're Jesus H. Christ," the trooper said. "Toss the gun or eat buckshot."

It wasn't supposed to happen like this. "There are dead kids in this building," Doc said. "I'm guarding an exit for the sheriff."

The trooper didn't care. Maybe he was angry, humiliated by what he'd done to his vehicle. Maybe he was on a power trip. Maybe he was just scared of what he was getting into. The officer dropped his microphone, racked the shotgun, and brought the weapon to his shoulder.

Doc stopped arguing. He tossed the Luger and dropped to the ground. He spent a brief moment, while the gun was airborne and before he was hugging dirt, wishing he'd had time to set the safety before he threw it. This cop was going to shoot if that gun went off when it hit the ground.

The Luger landed safely in a clump of grass and the trooper didn't kill him. "You've got to cover the back of this building in case the killer tries to get out," Doc said.

"I got to do nothing, old man," the officer replied. "Put your hands behind your back and shut up."

Doc's cell phone started ringing. He'd promised to keep the line open in case Englishman needed to talk to him. He started to reach for where he'd clipped it to his belt.

"Touch that and I'll blow your head off."

Doc stopped. "But that's probably the sheriff. If he's calling, it's important."

"Ask me if I care." The trooper was on top of him now. The shotgun touched the back of Doc's skull as the man kicked his arm, hard, and then bent and cuffed Doc tight enough to interfere with circulation. Doc decided not to complain. Apparently it wasn't Chucky Williams who was likely to kill him today. It was a Kansas Highway Patrolman with an attitude as bad as his driving skills.

"Careful, Officer," Neuhauser called from where he'd ducked behind a nearby tree. "The old guy's got a concealed weapon in his belt."

Doc had forgotten. He still had Neuhauser's gun there. Doc had a bad feeling the patrolman wasn't going to like that.

"D o you think it's safe to leave him here?" Mad Dog asked. He felt like he should give Pam an excuse to stay with Mark Brown.

They had found a hiding place for Mark in another warehouse, one that was farther from the house and, if the dust and cobwebs on the machinery were any indication, one that wasn't regularly used. They picked the cab of an old combine. It didn't look like it had been out for the last wheat harvest, back in June. The milo crop was mostly cut, though one field stood ripe and ready just east of Galen's house. Someone might show up to service this machine, but it was the best spot Mad Dog and Pam had been able to come up with.

Mark's opinion was that they should all get the hell out of there. The problem was, his keys had been confiscated, too. Mark's truck was old enough that Mad Dog thought he might be able to hotwire it, but he wasn't ready to try. His curiosity was up. He wanted to know what was going on out here before he ran from it. Besides, Mark's truck wouldn't be fast enough to outrun Galen's Dodge, or much of anything else. And Mad Dog didn't know where Hailey had gotten off to.

"Mark doesn't need a babysitter," Pam said. "And I'm just as curious about what's happening as you are."

For some reason, Mad Dog was inordinately pleased by her decision. Of course, it was probably just for the excitement and had nothing to do with which guy she'd rather be with.

The flip side of having her join him was that they'd already had a gun pulled on them. A warning shot had been fired. And they'd been locked in that grain bin. Those were pretty good indicators that further snooping wasn't the safest thing they could do. Still, he had the impression Galen hadn't wanted to hurt Pam. Not kill her, anyway. He wasn't so sure about himself. That was why he'd armed himself with a scoop shovel. It wouldn't be much use against Galen's pistol, but it made him feel better.

"What are we waiting for?" Pam stuck her face up against a dusty window that looked out on the back of the first warehouse they'd entered. "The coast is clear. Let's play spy."

"Hang on," Mad Dog said. "We've been inside three of these warehouses now. There's nothing interesting in them. I'm thinking we need to check the house, but there's no vegetation around it for us to hide behind. How do we get there and how do we get in...without Galen filling us with lead?"

"Follow me, mighty Cheyenne warrior." The smile in her voice matched the one on her face. She was enjoying this. He wondered if she was taking it seriously enough. He wondered if he was.

Pam led the way through an exit from this warehouse, then turned in a direction they hadn't explored yet. It kept them behind one of the long steel buildings. Pam hugged it, staying in its shadow. That was a good decision. They got to the far end without being discovered by anything more dangerous than an occasional Mexican sandbur. The thorns hurt like sin and reminded Mad Dog how nice it would be to find boots to go with their coveralls.

Pam stuck her head around the building's corner and invited him to join her. "See. We're on the garage side of the house now. No windows. And no one's out in the yard."

Clever girl. Mad Dog would have told her so, but she was already halfway across the farm yard to the side of the garage. He followed. At the wall, he asked her, "Now what?"

"I'm thinking we just let ourselves in the front door," she said.

That seemed too easy, but she was probably right. People in Benteen County didn't use their front doors except for formal events. Front doors opened on living rooms, and those didn't get much use either, except for entertaining.

"When I was over here with Mark, we'd leave his truck back by the kitchen and go in its door. Aside from a house tour, we were never in the front room."

"And I don't suppose the front door's more likely to be locked than the ones to the warehouses."

"I'd be surprised, but there's only one way to find out."

Mad Dog shouldered the shovel. "Let me lead."

She waved an arm. "You'll do anything to show off that cute butt, won't you?"

Had she really said that? Mad Dog shook his head and pretended she hadn't. He tiptoed to the front corner of the garage. No one was out front, either.

"All right," he whispered, though there was only the wind to hear them. "Here goes nothing."

The concrete drive was warm on their bare feet. As they were passing the second of the four doors, an electric motor whined to life and the door just behind them began rising. There was no place to hide. The front of the house was flat and empty of anything but driveway and that patch of grass in the front yard. They could dash past all manner of windows and try to get around the far corner of the house. Or to the front door, but by the time Mad Dog considered those options he knew they didn't have time. The door was open and a car was backing out. He grabbed Pam and swung her behind him and then edged up against the second door, shovel raised in a two-handed grip in case anyone came out with the car.

It was an anonymous white sedan, a Ford designed to look like all those imports that were selling better. There was one person inside. The man was a stranger to Mad Dog, and as surprised to see him as Mad Dog had been by the garage door.

"What are you doing?" the man said.

Mad Dog lowered the shovel back to his shoulder. They were on the wrong side of the car for it to be of any use. He smiled and tried to look innocent. He couldn't think of an answer.

"And what's with the shovel?"

"Ah, gophers," Mad Dog improvised. "We're supposed to dig the gophers out of the lawn."

"Oh," the man said. "Well, good luck."

Mad Dog and Pam smiled and waved at him as he backed down the drive. They were still smiling and waving when Galen came around the corner of the garage door with his pistol.

"I don't have gophers," he said.

The sheriff tried the high school's number. He got their automated system telling him no one could answer his call right now.

Stupid! He hadn't gotten the principal's cell number earlier. And he didn't know cell numbers for anyone else who might be in that locked-down gym.

Doc. He had Doc's cell on speed dial and Doc would be right out there with the law enforcement that had driven up behind that siren. But Doc's cell just rang, unanswered, until it rolled over to his message option.

Who else? He had to get someone who could either carry word to the gym or who knew the phone number of someone inside. Of course, Mrs. Kraus. He hit the speed dial number for his office and got a busy signal. Damn!

He started trying random numbers in the courthouse. No one answered. His own office was busy when he tried it again.

Somewhere, ahead of him in the labyrinth of air ducts that fed the school, Chucky Williams and an automatic rifle were making their way toward the gym. The sheriff couldn't just sit there continuing to waste time on his cell phone. He had to head for the gym, either through these air ducts—with a chance of catching Chucky before he started executing more children—or outside them—hoping to persuade those in the gym to open up for him, and then evacuate before Chucky got there.

It was a crap shoot. He had no idea how far he'd have to travel through the ducts. Not far, he guessed, but Chucky might ambush him on the way and still manage to pull off a massacre. The sheriff made a decision. Out. He was getting out. He turned and began retracing his path toward the grates under the study hall. That would be the fastest way.

He was just short of the first of them when his cell rang. He grabbed it out of his pocket and just said, "English," when he answered.

"Dad." It was Heather, his new deputy. "I thought I'd never get through to you."

"Just listen," he said, continuing a one-handed crawl toward the study hall. "I need you to get word to Mr. Juhnke. You can't call the regular school numbers because the whole school is locked down."

"What's going on?"

"One of the kids has gone on a rampage. Students have died here. A teacher. Tell Juhnke, or whoever you can get, that the shooter got out of the high school basement. He's in the air ducts on his way to the gym. They've got to get those kids out of there fast."

"Are you okay, Dad?"

"Do it now," he said, and disconnected as he began pushing on the air grate at the north end of the study hall. The thing wasn't as easy to lift as he'd expected. He managed to get one corner up when his cell rang again.

The sheriff clawed the thing back out of his pocket. He hit the answer button and said, "Heather, don't call me, call...."

But the voice on the other end of the line wasn't Heather's.

"Hi, Sheriff. Do you know who this is?"

The voice was little more than a whisper, but he knew.

"Chucky?"

"You asked me what I wanted," Chucky said. "Well, I think I've decided."

The sheriff shouldered another corner of the grate free and pushed the thing aside. "What's that?"

"New hostages, for a start."

The sheriff kept the phone to his ear as he sprinted across the study hall toward the staircase and the main exit. "After what you did to the last ones? No way. You'll get no replacements."

"I think I will," Chucky said. "'Cause I'm in the gym. You'll either give me the hostages I want or I start shooting. I don't think anyone can get out of here before I kill them all. What do you think, Sheriff?"

The sheriff thought Chucky might be right. "Okay," he said. "Don't shoot. Just tell me exactly what you want."

Heather English was at the intersection across from the Gas – Food beside the Buffalo Burger Drive In. She'd stopped at the four-way and there wasn't any traffic. It had seemed like a good time to try Englishman again. If she could finally reach him, he could tell her what to do with the "stem cells."

But what he said turned her heart to ice. All this time, while she'd been protecting him from the investigation by sneaking off to do it on her own, something bigger and more dangerous had been going on right here in Buffalo Springs. No wonder she hadn't been able to get through to him or get Mrs. Kraus at the sheriff's office. And she knew Englishman. He was right in the middle of it. If kids had been killed, if someone was trying to kill more, her dad was doing everything he could to stop it. Trying to put himself between a killer and those kids, probably.

It only took her a moment to decide. She didn't know any of the numbers Englishman wanted her to call. None, except his office. But the gym that needed to be warned was only half a mile away, just across town. She could be there, carry the warning herself, faster than she could contact someone to get it passed along.

The Civic burned rubber as it pivoted through the intersection. Fortunately, Main Street was empty, just the way it usually was, because she got the Honda up to eighty before she began slowing for the turn into the school. Her eyes flipped from cross-street to cross-street. The citizens of Buffalo Springs were unaccustomed to traffic. Many of them ignored the stop signs that should give her the right of way. She lucked out. The only moving car she saw was still a block south when she flashed across the intersection ahead of it.

She was so busy watching for traffic that she never saw the cluster of black walnuts she hit just before she got to the school. They exploded, like a string of firecrackers—or an automatic weapon—as she braked and downshifted and went through the gate to the school's parking lot like one of those daredevil drivers at the state fair.

She was surprised to find a wrecked Kansas Highway Patrol Vehicle blocking her way. She tapped the brakes, feathered the accelerator, and got past it by the slimmest of margins. Gravel from her tires ricocheted off its body work. She hadn't done the undamaged part of its paint any good.

Coming on the patrol car had been a shock, but it didn't begin to compare with the feeling she got when a trooper rose up from behind it, throwing a shotgun to his shoulder. She watched, fascinated, though her rearview mirror, until he disappeared in the cloud of dust she'd thrown at him. Then she couldn't see out her rear window because the officer had just shot it out.

She popped the clutch and drove past several lines of cars before ducking behind a row, stopping the Honda where it was temporarily out of the trooper's sight. What was this about? He was treating her like she was the school shooter. That didn't make any sense. Her dad had said the shooter was a student in the heat ducts on his way to the gym. She needed this guy's help. Instead, he and that shotgun could keep her from delivering her dad's message. The gym was just a hundred yards away, back across the parking lot and up a long sidewalk. But she'd never get there. Not on foot. She could already see the trooper's broad-brimmed hat bouncing toward her, threading between cars. She could surrender and explain, if he'd let her, or….

Heather hit the gas and released the clutch again. The Honda created another smoke screen—dust thick enough to sow with winter wheat. The Honda spun in a circle, tires digging through dirt and gravel to the solid earth a few inches down. She got herself aimed the right way and went barreling across the parking lot.

The gym's front doors were flanked by floor-to-ceiling glass panels. Just behind was the foyer with its ticket booth and concession stand. Thanks to all that glass, she could tell that the foyer was empty. She heard another explosion behind her—the trooper, doing his strange shoot-first, ask-later routine. He was too late.

She spent a brief moment wondering if an insurance company would ever cover another car for her. And then the Honda ran over a polling place sign and hurtled through the windows to the right of the door in a burst of sparkling shards. The car bounced off the counter in front of the concession stand and she spun it around and nosed it through the wide doors to the gym, barely moving as she did so in case there were kids behind those doors.

Juhnke had the students and teachers neatly arranged in the bleachers on either side of the basketball court. There were a few voters and poll workers with them. Perfect. She gunned the Honda to mid-court and spun it so it faced the emergency exit in the middle of the building.

Faces gaped at her, slack-jawed. She didn't blame them.

"Follow me," she shouted. "He's in the heating ducts with a gun. Dad says you have to get out of here now."

Juhnke tried to ask her something, but she didn't think they had time to discuss it. She hit the gas and hoped. Out wouldn't be as easy as in. The doors she planned to lead them through—they were steel.

"What's that? Who's shooting?" Chucky's voice went from menacing to panicky in an instant. The sheriff was moving before the echoes of the firecracker-like pops died. He kept the cell pressed to his ear with one hand and his .38 ready in the other. He went down the stairs and out the front doors of the high school as fast as when he'd taken that dare to flush a cherry bomb down the boys' toilet.

The sheriff was in time to see Heather's Honda make the turn into the parking lot. Damn! He hadn't wanted her to come here, into danger. He hadn't known she was so close.

A shotgun boomed.

"What?" Chucky's voice cracked into a terrified falsetto. "Who's out there? What are they shooting at?"

"Jesus!" the sheriff said. A state trooper was in the parking lot, firing at his daughter.

"Answer me?" Chucky sounded like he was about to cry, but the sheriff didn't have time to reassure him just now.

"Don't you shoot anybody," English told the boy. Then he broke the connection and sprinted into the parking lot. Heather's car was near the far side, but the trooper was sprinting toward her with that shotgun. And then Heather was moving and the guy was putting the shotgun to his shoulder again.

The sheriff screamed at the top of his lungs. "Hold your fire!" The trooper may not have heard him over the howl of Heather's engine. She launched the Honda toward the gym and the trooper pulled the trigger. The sheriff heard her go through the front windows, and knew she was all right, because the Honda's motor revved again and her tires squealed as she continued maneuvering the car. But he didn't see any of that. He was busy staring down the barrel of his .38...at the three bullet holes he'd just put into a Ford F150 right behind the trooper.

"Drop it or die." The sheriff meant it. Hell, he wasn't sure he hadn't tried to kill the guy with those first three rounds.

The trooper must have believed him. The shotgun dropped onto the gravel as the officer slowly turned to face English.

"There's gonna be a bunch more troopers here any minute," the man said. "Then we'll see who dies."

The sheriff was jogging across the lot, closing the distance. "Use your left hand and drop your belt," the sheriff said. The trooper had a service revolver against his right hip.

"You're going to do a lot of very hard time for this," the man said. "You might even get that chemical cocktail if any kids die because you interfered with the law."

Another, much louder crash came from the direction of the gym. The sheriff couldn't afford to look. And he couldn't afford to answer his cell phone, which had suddenly begun an insistent ringing again. The trooper did as he was told, though. His pistol dropped to his feet to lie beside the shotgun.

"Lean your face up against that truck and put your hands behind your back." The trooper did it, but not without continuing his litany of dire predictions for the sheriff's future. The sheriff slapped a set of cuffs on him, tight. Too tight, probably. Then he looked toward the gym. Heather's Honda, seriously battered, stood at the edge of the practice football field. Steam poured from under its hood as kids flowed around its sides. His daughter opened the driver's door and was immediately surrounded by teachers. But not before giving him a cocky little mission-accomplished salute. God, he was proud of her.

The sheriff's cell stopped, then immediately started ringing again. He took a breath. He hadn't heard any more shots. Chucky hadn't made good on his threat. Heather had saved the day, for now, at least. And this crazed Kansas State trooper wasn't trying to kill her anymore. The sheriff kept his gun on the man, who was continuing to sputter oaths and threats.

"Sheriff English," he answered his cell.

"Sheriff?" the trooper said. His square jaw dropped and he stopped running his mouth.

"Yeah," English told him. "Benteen County Sheriff. And that young lady you were shooting at may have just saved the lives of all those kids. She's one of my deputies, you imbecile. *Now* which of us do you think will do jail time?"

"Who's that you're talking to?" It was Chucky again, still panicky, but a little more in control. "Have they come for me?"

"Has who come for you, Chucky?"

Chucky paused. "You don't know, yet, do you? So maybe I've still got time to stop them before they get me."

"What…?" But that was all the sheriff managed to say before Chucky hung up on him.

"Who was that?" the trooper asked, more subdued now.

"That was our killer," the sheriff spat. "The one you may have just helped get away because you're out here firing on my deputy. He's gone, unless our coroner and my two volunteers manage to cut him off."

"That guy really is your coroner? Those two old farts, they were helping you?"

The sheriff swung his gun back into the trooper's face. "You haven't shot any more of my people, have you?"

"No, no," the man said, trying to back through the truck. "We've just had us a real failure to communicate, that's all."

"Where are they?"

"I cuffed them. They're in the back seat of my unit," the man said. "I'd be happy to let them go for you."

"Bet your ass," the sheriff said. But he was already wondering where Chucky was going and who "they" were. And most of all, how to get himself between Chucky and his next target.

Heather Lane found unobserved spying on the Siegrist farm wasn't that easy. Not with the way Galen had torn out the hedge trees that used to line the roads surrounding his place. Getting an unobstructed view was no problem. But not from anywhere close.

Windbreaks weren't as popular in central Kansas as they had once been. Corporate farmers, like Galen, made use of every inch of their acreage. And they weren't prepared to trade the water those Osage orange trees drank for the shelter they gave from the wind. The nearest line of trees to Galen's farm dead-ended half a mile north.

Chairman Wynn and Heather found a spot to pull their cars off the road and hiked to the end of the hedgerow. Galen's house, with its metal outbuildings and grain bins, shimmered in the distance across a plowed field. Of living things, including humans acting in a suspicious fashion, there were no signs.

The chairman was exasperated. "Now what?" He spread his hands in frustration and then rested them on his hips.

His holstered pistol was strapped to his belt on one of those hips, not that being armed was of much use under the circumstances.

Heather had brought her fanny pack along, the one she kept in the car for when she went hiking, exploring the country around Albuquerque for archaeological sites. She had a bottle of water in there, along with a Brunton compass, some New Mexico USGS maps, a notebook, a couple of high-energy snack bars, and a trowel. And something else. Something she thought might actually come in handy.

"Why are you wearing that gun?" she asked, digging through the pack's contents.

"It's legal," he said. "We've even got a concealed carry law now."

Heather remembered hearing Kansas had passed that legislation. Not that the law's absence had kept people she knew from packing heat when they wanted. This was the West, after all. Wyatt, Doc, Bat, and many other notorious gunmen were more than just historical figures. Locals knew you could never be sure whether you'd meet up with a Hickok or a Hickock—a Wild Bill or a Richard, the latter being one of the men who killed the Clutter family and played a prominent role in Truman Capote's *In Cold Blood*. Englishman always said people were more likely to shoot themselves or one of their family members with their guns. Few people believed him, but the statistics bore him out.

"Yeah," she said, "but you don't usually carry a gun. Not that I've seen."

"Well...." The chairman paused and thought about it. "I don't know," he admitted. "I was planning to search the Bible camp. And this whole thing feels like a life and death situation to me, especially after what happened in that accident and what could still happen to my son."

She didn't like guns, or knives, or violence. The last time she'd seen her real mom and dad, they'd been trying to kill each other...and willing to use her to help. But that was a long time ago. If the pistol made the chairman feel better, she didn't mind.

"Here," she said. She'd been pretty sure it was in there. She liked to get a better look at birds and wildlife sometimes.

"What is that? A monocular? Let me see."

She handed it over, ready to receive a little praise for having come better prepared than he was.

"This is only a five power scope," the chairman complained. He took it out of its case and put it to his eye. "Hardly helps at all."

"You're welcome," she said.

She reached out to snatch it back when he said, "Hey, wait. Something's happening over there."

"What? Let me look."

He kept a firm grip on the scope. "Garage door's opening," he said. "Car's backing out. Looks like there are a couple of people in uniform there beside it."

He wasn't going to give up the glass, so she looked for herself. She could see the open garage door, the car, and the figures, but not well enough to recognize a person or a make and model.

"Who are they? What are they doing?"

"Can't tell," he said. "This thing doesn't have enough magnification."

"Then let me try. Maybe I have better eyesight."

He wouldn't give it up. Another figure came out of the garage after the car continued backing out, turned, and took to the road.

"We gotta do something about this," the chairman said.

Yeah, Heather thought, like share the monocular. That made her all the more surprised when he handed it to her.

"You stay here and watch the house," he said. "I'm going to follow that car."

She wasn't sure that was a good idea, but he didn't stick around to argue. He was already trotting back up the road to where he'd left his Escalade. Rather than go after him, she took advantage of her chance to use the scope.

The chairman was right. It wasn't really powerful enough. And the car was already kicking up too much dust for her to tell anything about it except that it was white. The three people in front of the Siegrist place were heading for the garage, the two in uniform preceding the last to come out. She couldn't make out features from here, or even tell if those were really uniforms, but there was something about the big one, the one in what looked to be camouflage. Something about the way he moved. And his hair. He didn't have any.

She turned and tried to wave down Chairman Wynn as he sped by in his Cadillac SUV. He didn't slow at all. She put the glass back to her eye in time to see the garage door begin closing.

Only one man in Benteen County shaved his head like that, then left it uncovered for all the world to see.

So, what the hell was Uncle Mad Dog doing at Galen Siegrist's farm, today of all days? And that man behind Uncle Mad Dog…had that been a gun in his hand?

A million things to do and only one man to do them. That's how it felt to the sheriff. He stood in the parking lot next to the handcuffed patrolman and watched children, teens, and teachers mill around the field near Heather's battered Honda. He turned and glanced at the wrecked patrol car, where Doc and his two volunteers awaited rescue. He swung back and looked at the school and the ruined entry to the gym. Chucky was still in there somewhere, or nearby, and still armed. Too much, but all those people, that kid with the gun, they were all the sheriff's responsibility.

You had to start somewhere. He began with his cell phone. Heather had started walking in his direction. He watched her answer her own phone on the first ring.

"Tell Juhnke to get those kids out of here fast," he said.

She acknowledged him and turned back toward her car and the crowd in the football field.

"Chucky was in the gym," he told her, "in the heating vents. He's probably out by now. I think he's got another target, but get those kids away from the school."

"Where…?" she began.

"The courthouse," he decided. "Make sure nobody heads back toward the school or into the neighborhood behind it."

"Right," she said. He could see her talking to Juhnke and waving her arms and pointing in his direction. Juhnke soon had his students sprinting across the field, away from the gymnasium.

"Good girl," he told her and hit disconnect. He turned to the highway patrolman. The man was still leaning face first against an adjacent pickup. "I want my people out of your vehicle. Where are your keys?"

"Let me go and I can…." He stopped. Maybe he sensed the sheriff's rage. "My unit's back doors are only locked from the inside. And I cuffed them with plastic. There's a cutter on that belt you made me drop."

The sheriff had a razor-sharp pocket knife of his own. He grabbed the patrolman by the old-fashioned cuffs he'd applied and pulled him upright. "Let's go."

The two trotted across the lot to the wrecked cruiser, and the sheriff made the officer stand well back while he opened the door so the three prisoners could scramble out.

"Bastard saw me with a gun and assumed I was the problem," Doc explained.

"It was a mistake," the trooper protested. "Anybody could…."

"Wouldn't look at any of our IDs," Doc continued. "Wouldn't pay attention to the fact that we were all telling the same story. Then Neuhauser, he didn't help."

The sheriff pulled his pocket knife out of his jeans. It made short work of the plastic cuffs. All three men glared at the patrolman as they massaged circulation back into their wrists.

"What did he do with Neuhauser?"

"I thought he was an innocent civilian," the cop said. "I just told him to beat it."

"Better and better," the sheriff said. "Get your guns," he told the pair of farmers. Their guns were on the front seat of the cruiser, on the other side of the cage from where they and Doc had been held. "Go to the courthouse as quick as you can. I've sent the kids there. Guard the place. And take this asshole with you. Have Mrs. Kraus toss him in a cell until I can get around to him."

No one but the asshole argued. They rearmed themselves and prodded the patrolman into a battered crew-cab truck and headed into town while the sheriff told Doc about the six bodies in the basement. Heather trotted up and joined them in time to get the gist of it.

"Chucky?" she said. "I think I saw him run across the back of the school grounds and go through the fence into the neighborhood."

"Toward our house?" the sheriff asked.

There wasn't much of Buffalo Springs north of the school. The neighborhood where the girls had been raised was there.

"Yeah. Looked like he was carrying one of those guns like all the Iraqis have."

That would be an AK-47, the sheriff thought, weapon of choice for third-world militias.

Then she told them about seeing Chucky earlier that day, and how she'd thought she was rescuing him from Butch Bunker and Mark Goodfellow. Later, how he'd been lugging a trombone case into school. "You don't suppose…?" she said.

He did.

"Now what?" Doc asked, cutting to the heart of the problem.

Now he needed to go get Chucky, but how was he going to do that with almost no help and no idea where the kid was heading next? He didn't get time to answer. Heather's cell phone began ringing and, in the interval between rings, they heard sirens in the distance. The help he needed might not be a problem. Though getting it to cooperate, once the fate of the first officer into Buffalo Springs became known, could be.

"Hello," Heather said. She listened as the three of them turned toward the road. He could pick out the flashing lights now. Two cars, no, three.

"Stay where you are," Heather told the cell phone. "Dad," she said to him, "I need to tell you a bunch of stuff, but first off, Heather's out at Galen Siegrist's farm. She was watching the place because we learned Galen was driving that school bus this morning."

"Heather's here?" He couldn't quite get his head around that. First one daughter had driven home from KU. Now, it appeared, the other had come all the way from Albuquerque. Why? "And how'd you learn that," he asked, "about Galen?"

"Chairman Wynn broke into the Bible camp and found some medical records. It looks like someone's planning some sort of organ transplant. That might fit in with the stem cells I found in the Dodge and left in the refrigerator at the Gas – Food. But now Heather says Uncle Mad Dog's out at Galen's and she thinks maybe Galen was holding a gun on him."

"What?" the sheriff asked. Doc echoed him, but Heather didn't get a chance to answer and the sheriff didn't get a chance to sort out everything she'd told him because three Kansas Highway Patrol cars had swarmed through the gate to the school's parking lot and officers were tumbling out of them in bulletproof vests, wielding shotguns and demanding to know who was in charge here.

While the sheriff stood there feeling overwhelmed, Heather flipped open her jacket and showed them her badge. She nodded toward the sheriff. "He is."

It started out great. The Kansas Highway Patrol officers were pros. Heather could tell that by the way they got out of their cars, their weapons immediately covering everyone and everything without seeming to do so. And their officer, the guy who asked who was in charge, followed that with the perfect question.

"How can we help you, Sheriff?"

Her dad was equally professional. He explained the situation with as few words as possible. That resulted in a couple of troopers being sent toward the gym and the school's heating plant. Two more were sent in a car to protect the kids at the courthouse. But then, as it had to, the matter of the wrecked cruiser came up.

"Is my trooper all right? And where is he?"

"He's fine," Englishman said. "Now, we've still got a killer on the loose. There could be kids all over town after the way we had to clear the school. But only one of those kids has an AK-47 with him. We need to spread out, find him before he holes up or gets transportation. We need to...."

"We'll take care of that," the officer said. "But my trooper. His vehicle's pretty banged up. Is he getting medical help?"

"Not exactly," Doc said. The officer and Doc exchanged introductions and then Captain Miller asked for clarification.

"What does not exactly mean?"

Heather decided to be helpful. "He tried to kill me. Shot out the back window in my Honda."

The captain seemed to notice the bullet holes in the nearby Ford about then, and the trooper's belt lying on the ground beside it. "Where's my man? What have you done with him?" Captain Miller didn't sound friendly or helpful anymore.

"The troopers you sent to the courthouse can check on him," Englishman said. "I had a couple of my volunteers—the ones he disarmed and locked in the back of his vehicle with our coroner before he started shooting at my daughter—take him there. He should be in an eight-by-eight cell about now."

"What? You arrested someone sent to help you?"

"He lost control of his vehicle pulling into the parking lot," Doc explained. "After that, he lost control of everything. He started disarming those of us who were helping the sheriff. There was no reasoning with him. And when we heard shots just as Heather pulled into the lot, he assumed she was shooting at him. He fired his shotgun at her twice before...."

The officer swung on Heather. "Let me see your weapon, young lady."

Heather spread her hands. "I don't have a weapon. Just some pepper spray."

"There are bullet holes in that truck over there, right where it appears my trooper was standing. Who fired them?"

"I did," Englishman said.

The captain swung on him, face beginning to glow as his blood pressure rose. "You shot at one of my men?"

"Warning shots," Englishman said. "To prevent him from firing on my daughter again."

"Your daughter is your deputy?"

"Yes, sir." Englishman was getting a little hot under the collar himself. "You have a problem with that?"

"God save me from back country hicks," the captain muttered.

"He has," Doc interrupted. "Too bad he didn't save you from incompetent troopers as well."

Mad Dog and Pam were ushered into one of the first rooms off the garage. It was painted a generic beige with matching carpet. There was no furniture, but it was crowded all the same. Three men, in addition to Galen, joined them there. None of the three were locals. Mad Dog had only seen one of them before. He was the little guy with the bad hair who had had Mad Dog thrown out of the church. The other two were big guys, middle-aged, muscular, without excess flesh. They wore good suits with conspicuous bulges under their coats.

One of them drew a short-barreled semi-automatic with a muzzle wide enough to launch ICBMs while the other put Mad Dog and then Pam against the wall and frisked them. He did it professionally. His hands went everywhere, but they weren't copping feels, not even on Pam. The pair had deep tans and one of them wore sunglasses pushed up to rest on the short hair above his forehead. All of the men but Galen had some sort of communications device in one ear with tiny microphones curving down in front of their mouths. They reminded Mad Dog of the Secret Service agents assigned to protect the president.

"They're clean," the frisker said. "Nothing, not even clothes under their coveralls."

The guy from the church wore his hair long in a comb-over that emphasized his baldness. But his suit probably cost more than twice what the hired help wore. "What are these people doing here?" the little man demanded.

"This is the pair who came in the Mini Cooper," Galen said.
"I thought you took care of them."

Galen protested, "I did. I put them in a grain bin and locked it, like I told you."

"Like you did with that other young man? If these two are free, maybe you should check on him."

Before Galen could argue the point, or hurry to obey, the room got even more crowded. A tall man with thick silver hair pushed in. A doctor, maybe, because he was wearing scrubs and a stethoscope.

"Has our donor…?" he began. He had a peculiar accent. German, Mad Dog thought at first, then revised his opinion when the man continued.

"Must I remind you," he said. "We are rapidly running out of time. We have no more need of prayers from church folk." Mad Dog had heard his voice before—on the phone in Galen's warehouse office.

"These two are snoops," Comb-over said, "not church members."

"Expendable?"

The accent was Dutch, maybe, or more likely Afrikaans, Mad Dog thought. Then the word "expendable" registered.

"Expendable, yes," Comb-over nodded.

"So. Let us test them. Perhaps one of these will have to do if your substitute doesn't arrive soon."

"Test us for what?" Pam said, but no one paid her any attention.

"I will send the nurse. You will see that it is done."

The guy in the scrubs disappeared back into the hall. Galen started to follow him. "I'll go check on Mark. Make sure he's still in his bin."

"Go with him," Comb-over told the hired gun nearest the door. "Bring the boy back for testing, too. Or, if he's missing, hunt him down."

"He's long gone," Mad Dog said. "We let him out and sent him for help hours ago."

"You haven't been here for hours," Comb-over corrected, accurately enough. "Even if you did let him out, he can't have gone far, not without a car."

The little man turned back to the hired muscle. "Check it. Bring him in, or catch him if he's loose."

Galen looked a little pale. He followed the pro through the door just as a young man wearing scrubs entered. He was carrying a basket filled with needles and other paraphernalia. "Who shall be first?" he said. His accent was similar to the doctor's.

"I guess we shouldn't have snooped. We should have just run for it," Pam said. Mad Dog nodded.

"Roll up a sleeve," the male nurse said. "You should not worry. Liver donors have an extraordinarily high survival rate. Heart-lung, well, that's something else."

"So what do I do now?" Heather Lane couldn't know how many people in Benteen County had been asking themselves variations of that question today. Right now, she was asking it of her sister, Heather English, who seemed preoccupied and a bit put out at having to answer another call from the observation post just north of the Siegrist farm.

"Wait. Keep watching."

There was shouting in the background behind Heather One's voice. "What's going on there?" Two asked.

"There was a shooting at the school. Chucky Williams killed some classmates. He seems to have gotten away, but the highway patrol has arrived."

Two couldn't believe it. Not in Buffalo Springs. And not Chucky. She remembered him as kind of a wimpy kid.

"But Daddy's all right?"

"He's fine."

"Then what's all that yelling about?"

"He and the highway patrol captain are debating policing techniques."

"What?" That didn't sound reasonable, not under the circumstances.

"Look," the first Heather said. "I've kind of gotten involved in this and I need to explain some things to these officers. Just keep an eye on Galen's place, okay? Call me if anything happens. We'll be out there as soon as we can."

"But…" Heather began, only One wasn't on the other end of the connection anymore.

Heather Lane let herself feel a little righteous indignation, though she supposed things must be wild and confused in Buffalo Springs if the first part of her sister's story was accurate. Chucky Williams killing students? God, she wanted to know who had been hurt and what was happening now. But here she was, standing at the end of a tree row almost half a mile north of where her Uncle Mad Dog might have been taken hostage along with someone in a blue uniform. She suddenly wished Chairman Wynn had stuck around with his pistol so they could go over there and bang on the door, free Uncle Mad Dog, and demand some answers…if that was Mad Dog and he was a hostage and if Galen had really been driving that bus last night.

She put the glass back to her eye. The Siegrist farm looked pretty much the way she remembered it. Except—what was that? A man…no, two men were walking up to one of the metal outbuildings. They opened the door and went inside. Uncle Mad Dog wasn't one of them. Nothing suspicious about that, was there? Though something about it bothered her. Something nagged at a corner of her mind.

Then she realized what it was. One of them, the big one, was wearing a suit. No one in Benteen County wore suits. Oh, maybe for Sunday services or to attend a funeral, but that was all.

What should she do about it? Should she call her sister back? She hardly thought her message would be welcome. Keep watching, One of Two would say, and then hang up on her again.

Well, the adopted Heather wasn't any more inclined to sit around and wait on events than Englishman's natural daughter. She tossed her fanny pack over one shoulder, put the monocular to her eye and gave the farm and outbuildings one last careful look. Then she started back to her car.

Heather didn't know what she planned to do. A drive-by surveillance, at least. Maybe she could see more from up close or another angle. And then, if it seemed like Mad Dog was in need of immediate help she'd…. She'd…. Well, she'd figure that out when it happened.

"Look," the sheriff said. "Right now I don't care what you do with your trooper. I'll release him to your custody as long as you get him out of my county."

He was going to file charges later. Doc and his two volunteers, that was bad. But discharging a shotgun at his daughter—damn right he'd press charges.

"Right now, there's still a killer on the loose. I'm shorthanded. I need your help to find him."

Captain Miller looked like he wanted to add some disparaging adjectives to shorthanded. But the captain seemed to think he was getting what he wanted. He thought he'd freed his trooper and been given control of the investigation. "We'll find your killer, but we need a better description than just a kid with a gun."

"About five-two," Heather said.

Was he that tall now, the sheriff wondered? Kids always seemed smaller and younger in his memory than they actually were. Part of getting old, he supposed. He kept his mouth shut and let his daughter continue her description.

"Slight," she was saying, "but soft. Maybe one-ten, one-twenty at the outside. Medium-brown hair, neatly cut. Blue eyes. He's wearing blue jeans and a green corduroy shirt, long-sleeved but turned up at the wrists."

"That's a hell of a description, Deputy." Miller was obviously surprised to find competency in the Benteen Sheriff's office, especially from the sheriff's daughter. "You've seen him today, I assume."

"Several times. Last time, carrying the gun into the school, I think. He was toting a trombone case. I wondered about that because I thought he played the clarinet."

"Good job," Miller said. "You get that, men?" The officers who were still with him nodded their heads. "All right, I want two of you to take cruisers and start prowling the streets near the school. Work your way out. Hell, this town's not so big you can't cover all of it in short order. Sheriff, you and your deputy can ride along with them if you want."

"What about you?" the sheriff asked.

"I'm sending one man with your coroner to document the crime scenes and collect the bodies. I'll take the rest with me to check out the school and be sure it's really clear."

"Good," the sheriff said. "My deputy and I, we'll go check the kid's home. From what he said, I think he killed his parents before he started in here. He may have gone back home, or I may find something to tell me where he's headed next."

"Fine."

The sheriff could tell Miller was just glad to have him out of the way.

"But stay in touch with me." Miller gave the sheriff the radio frequency he and his men would be using as two patrol cars peeled out of the lot to begin prowling neighborhoods.

"I'm afraid the last mobile radio we had was destroyed with our black and white in an accident this morning." The sheriff hated to admit that, but….

"Ah. Yes. That deputy who ran into a school bus," Miller said.

"We're down to cell phones. Can we exchange numbers?"

"Sure," Miller said. "Better than smoke signals." He gave English his number. None of the other officers were carrying cells. Heather efficiently jotted the number down.

Miller was ignoring them now, giving his men instructions for how they'd go in and what they'd do once they got there.

The sheriff headed for his pickup. Heather followed.

When they got to his Chevy he asked her for Miller's phone number.

"Sure," she said, "but I could just program it into both our phones while we're on the way to the Williams place."

"You're not going," he said.

Her mouth dropped.

"I don't want you seeing what I expect to find over there."

"I can take it," she said.

The sheriff thought that was more bravado than an honest opinion. "And I don't want you with me if Chucky's there. I don't know if anywhere in Buffalo Springs is safe right now. The court-house is probably as good as it gets. You can walk there in a few minutes. Fill Mrs. Kraus in and help her contact parents. That's going to be a full-time job for the rest of the afternoon."

"But Dad...."

He got in the truck and started the engine. "No arguments. I'm not taking you with me."

He backed out, swung around the wrecked highway patrol car, and pulled onto Main. He looked over his shoulder before he made the turn toward the Williams place. She was still standing in the high school parking lot in the exact spot he'd left her.

The former chairman of the Benteen County Board of Supervisors had expected it to be difficult to trail the white Ford Fusion after it left the Siegrist place. It wasn't. The Ford's driver didn't seem to notice he was being tailed, or he didn't care.

They drove straight south to the blacktop, then followed it east into Buffalo Springs. The Ford led the chairman and his all-too-noticeable Escalade down Main Street, right to the school. It slowed as if it planned to turn in, then sped up and made a hasty right, south, away from the buildings. Wynn followed. He hardly glanced at the school, but he noticed a highway patrol car in the parking lot. Were they putting on some kind of driving clinic for students today? He hadn't heard about it. And why wasn't that cruiser parked normally? It looked like it had been in an accident. Then he was around the corner and concentrating on the Ford again, because it seemed to be in more of a hurry now. It turned right at the first opportunity, back into Buffalo Springs. He stayed on its tail, though not so close as to be obvious.

The Ford zigzagged through town. Was it trying to lose him? Another highway patrol car came toward them at one point and the Ford dropped south a couple of blocks before heading west again. Or was the guy avoiding those patrol cars? He certainly hadn't put any additional distance between himself and the Escalade.

They went north again, then, toward Main, crossed it, and turned west beside Bertha's Café. That put them next to Veteran's Memorial Park, and headed toward the courthouse. The Ford slowed. It had to. There was quite a crowd down near the courthouse. Amazing election turnout, he thought. But why was another highway patrol car there? And was that a uniformed trooper standing just inside the front doors?

The Ford turned left by the Church of Christ Risen and stopped next to the building. Wynn kind of pulled onto the edge of the park, for the first time feeling thankful that he hadn't managed to find the money for the curbs he'd wanted to put there to keep damn fools, such as himself, from driving on the grass.

The Ford's driver called to the group of men standing near the entry to the church. He must have asked to speak to Pastor Goodfellow, because someone went inside and returned with the man moments later.

Goodfellow and the guy in the Ford seemed upset about something. Goodfellow waved his arms about as if he were delivering one of his you're-all-doomed-to-eternity-in-hell sermons. Wynn couldn't hear them. Not over the babble of several conversations and the usual gusts of wind searching for leaves to usher through town.

Wynn did notice that two men had followed Goodfellow out of the church, though. One was Lieutenant Greer, Englishman's opponent in the race for sheriff. The guy with him was a friend of Greer's, but not a local man. New-something, Wynn thought. Neuhauser, that was it. Neuhauser was keeping an eye on the reverend and the fellow in the Ford. Greer was keeping an eye on everything. Wynn ducked down to avoid being noticed by the would-be sheriff. When he raised up to look again, the Ford and Goodfellow were moving. The Ford pulled into a parking place and the driver got out and joined the reverend. The two of them, still arguing, went into the church.

But it was Greer and Neuhauser who caught Wynn's attention. Greer had grabbed Neuhauser by the arm and was pointing back down the street to where several cars always parked around Bertha's Café. The Williams kid was getting in one of them. It looked a lot like Mrs. Kraus' car, but Chucky Williams wouldn't do that. An old farmer was standing alongside, saying something to Chucky, who nodded and seemed to thank him. And then Chucky settled the rifle he was carrying onto the seat beside him, started the car, and headed south toward Main.

Greer grabbed for his belt and then threw his arms open, as if surprised to discover he didn't have a gun strapped there. Neuhauser didn't have one either, though why they should need guns was beyond the ex-chairman, even if he was carrying one himself.

Greer was going to be a real pain in the ass if he got elected, and it seemed likely that would happen. The evangelicals had hit town well organized and well funded, as the former chairman knew personally from the results of his recall election. But he didn't care about Greer and Neuhauser. He cared about that Ford. He kind of snuggled down in his seat and prepared to wait for the driver to resurface.

Greer and Neuhauser came running his way. Wynn snuggled even lower. But they didn't notice him. They were focused on the car parked just a few feet away from his Escalade. It was a black Chevy SS. Neuhauser fumbled with his keys and threw open the trunk. The two men rummaged through the contents and came out with a series of weapons of the sort you'd expect to see them grab out of a Hummer in downtown Baghdad. They made selections, including ammunition, slammed the trunk and jumped in the car. A couple of citizens had to move fast to get out of their way as they tore out of the parking lot and headed south.

This was definitely not business as usual for the Benteen County seat. Wynn continued to watch the Ford, but he pulled his cell phone out of his pocket.

Now, who should he call, Englishman? Or one of the Englishdaughters?

Mrs. Kraus gazed longingly at the top drawer of her desk, the one where she kept her gun. She so wanted to draw the weapon and order everybody out of the sheriff's office. There was quite a crowd. Parents, mostly, who'd just begun learning there'd been a shooter loose at the school. They'd come to the courthouse to look for their kids and get information. Those who hadn't found their children yet were getting pretty upset. Several of them had commandeered the phones in the sheriff's office. At least she didn't have to answer calls anymore. Both lines were in the hands of citizens so determined that only her Glock might have discouraged them.

She was trying to maintain some sense of order in the office, but no one was paying her much attention, not since the highway patrol arrived and took charge. The troopers had pestered her, too, at first, wanting a fellow officer released. She didn't know a thing about that, but she'd shown them where the jail was. Now, the state's boys were surrounded by parents and taking the majority of their complaints. That was also a relief.

She was trying to keep an eye on the voting. She'd been doing that ever since the effort to stuff the ballot box this morning. She'd rounded up a couple of extra folks from each party to monitor voting here. And she'd passed the word so both parties could get more people out to keep an eye on other precincts throughout the county. But the elections officials had prevented her from seizing the ballot boxes and sticking them back in the jail. They would examine the contents and the voter count later, they promised her, with a special eye toward ballots that matched the fake ones Hailey had discovered.

She wished Englishman would check in, though there weren't any lines open. He'd probably call if she had a cell phone, but she refused to carry one of the fool things. She was sick of running into people who said hello while she was shopping in the Dillon's. She would respond and get a dirty look, as often as not, since they were talking to someone on their cell phones instead of her.

It was too bad that the department had stopped using their old walkie-talkies. Of course they hadn't reached halfway across the county, but today they would have given her another means of accessing the sheriff.

According to the troopers, the shooter was thought to have left the school. The kids and their teachers were here, or still coming. She would be just as glad to let those boys in their spiffy uniforms deal with that mess—hundreds of students and their hysterical parents reuniting at the courthouse.

It troubled her, though, to think that one of Benteen County's teens had gone on a shooting spree. A wounded boy had been taken over to the clinic, she'd heard, along with Lieutenant Greer, who'd been injured in a heroic assault on the high school. She was surprised and pleased that Greer and Englishman had set aside their differences on a day like this, cooperating for the good of the community. It made her feel warm inside.

She checked again, found both phones still in use, and wandered across the foyer to look out the front door and watch more folks from the school come flooding across the park. A sunburned old farmer who'd been sweet on her for years came up the stairs about the same time. "Howdy," he said, giving her a big smile.

"Howdy, yourself." She never gave him any encouragement because he had bad teeth and a potbelly of awesome proportions.

"That was nice of you," he said.

She had turned to go check on the phones again and his comment caught her by surprise. "What was nice?" That she'd turned her back on him? Was he being sarcastic, or had she just misunderstood?

"Loaning your car to that boy."

"I didn't loan my car to anybody." She elbowed past him so she could point it out, still parked over across from Bertha's Café, where she'd started her day with a wholesome breakfast of bacon, sausage, eggs, hash browns, and a short stack of pancakes. "See," she pointed, "it's right where I left it."

Only it wasn't.

"Lord!" she howled, hoping to get one of the troopers' attention. "Somebody stole my car."

The troopers ignored her. In fact, hardly anybody but the old farmer even glanced her way.

"Stole it? You sure you didn't just forget? He said he had your permission. And he's such a nice kid."

Mrs. Kraus got right in his face. "I am as sure as the day is long. I did not loan out my car."

"Oh dear," he said. "I don't suppose I should have told him you keep your spare keys in the glove box, then, should I?"

It was probably a good thing her Glock was back in the office. As it was, the look she gave him may have shortened his life expectancy by several years. "You damn fool," she said, "who'd you help steal my car?"

"What with all his family's problems, I figured if he needed to borrow your car it would be all right."

"Who?"

"Why, Chucky Williams."

Mrs. Kraus' jaw fell. "Chucky Williams. Don't you know that boy's been shooting up the school this morning?"

"You're joshing me," the old man said. "Things like that don't happen here." He smiled at her but she didn't smile back. "Though I did wonder," he admitted, "why he was carrying that AK-47."

Watching her dad drive off and leave her like that hurt. Deputy Heather thought she'd done a good job, getting word to the gym full of potential victims just in the nick of time and in spite of that rogue trooper. Not just good—kick ass. She deserved better than to be dumped in the parking lot with instructions to hike back to the courthouse and help with busy work.

She couldn't really blame Englishman for wanting to spare her what he was likely to find at the Williams place, though, or even for wanting to keep her away from the action where she was safe. After all, she'd come home today and gotten involved in all this because she'd been trying to keep him away from danger. She still wanted to do that, but a deputy on foot couldn't stay ahead of a sheriff in his truck.

After Englishman turned the corner and disappeared, she just stood there, staring mindlessly across the parking lot full of cars. Then it occurred to her that she was staring at one car in particular. It was an old gray Ford, a Taurus, slightly battered. There was something familiar about it. She'd noticed it earlier because.... Because that was the car Chucky had taken the trombone case out of as she drove away from the campus this morning.

She walked over for a closer look. It wasn't locked. She could see from here that both the driver's and passenger's windows were down. Some duly appointed law enforcement officer ought to check the vehicle out, she decided. She knew just the one for the job. Every other law enforcement officer had gone elsewhere. A couple to the courthouse. Two to patrol streets for Chucky. One, with Doc, to collect the bodies in the basement. And the others, with Captain Miller, to make sure Chucky wasn't still in the abandoned school.

The Taurus had experienced a close encounter with something that creased the left rear fender. Hood, trunk, and top were dimpled, like the surface of a golf ball—hail damage—a condition that wasn't uncommon in Benteen County. The interior was clean, though. Or mostly. A stack of books and a notebook lay on the front seat. She let herself in and checked. They were Chucky's. Nothing very interesting, until she found the bookmark in his English text. It was stuck in a section explaining gerunds—not something to uplift your spirits, but hardly likely to have started Chucky on his killing spree.

The bookmark, though, that was interesting. It was a plain business-sized envelope with Chucky's name neatly penned on the outside. No address or return address, no stamp—it hadn't been mailed.

Something else had been written on the reverse. This penmanship was tight and jerky and hard to read, but she managed to puzzle it out.

"We're so proud of you," it said. It was signed, "Mom & Dad."

The envelope had been neatly slit along the top. Heather wished she had some gloves, but she didn't, and she wasn't about to let that stop her now.

A single sheet of paper was within. It was folded exactly the way they told you professional communications should be.

She was disappointed, at first. There was no logo, no indication of who it was from. But this message was printed. Times New Roman, if she knew her fonts. Easy to read.

> Rejoice. You may help a man "take up his pallet and walk." You have been tested and found pure. At the hour of midnight on the 5th of November you will gather with the faithful in the selected place. From there, go forth unto the holy man. You are not the chosen, but you are first among the successors. You shall help "roll away the stone," should the chosen one prove unable. Come with great joy, for you are most righteous and you shall be rewarded on earth and, eternally, in Heaven.

Easy to read, maybe, but not easy to understand. She thought she got some of it. Chucky had scored high on those medical tests at the Bible camp. His name had ranked first among the best matches for a transplant. If she understood this Bible babble, someone else had been chosen to make the donation, but Chucky was being invited to come act as a backup. Jeez, talk about your unwanted honors. Well, she would feel that way about it. And maybe Chucky had, after the accident. Especially if the dead kid in the station wagon with the stem cells had been number one.

Had Chucky decided to decline the offer? Had people tried to force him? Was that why he'd gotten the gun and started shooting? Or was she misreading this and giving it more weight than it deserved?

Whatever, she was sure the "selected place" had been the Bible camp. Going forth to the holy man, that must be the journey that had been interrupted by this morning's accident. If she wanted the answer to the rest of her questions, she could ask Chucky. Or she could ask the driver of that bus, Galen Siegrist.

Doing either would be a problem, except that Chucky hadn't appeared to care what happened to his parents' car after he took the trombone case into the high school. That must be why he'd left the keys in the ignition and provided Heather with the transportation she had been lacking.

She got behind the wheel and turned the key and, in spite of the absence of any court orders, confiscated the evidence.

"I thought about staying home this morning, going down by the creek to practice singing," Pam said, "maybe take a dip."

"Would have been a better choice," Mad Dog said, rubbing his sore shoulder.

"Except I wouldn't have finally gotten to know you," she said, making him feel much better than the situation warranted.

They were alone now, in the same room where they'd been frisked and blood tested. The door was a solid core type with quality hardware that would resist being broken through. Oddly, all that hardware faced the wrong way. This was a room you locked people into, not out of. Besides, a professional gunman was nearby and, Mad Dog thought, prepared to do what was necessary to keep them from leaving. Before the guy locked them in, he'd told them not to bother trying to break out. He and the door would hold them, and the window, he said, was bulletproof glass. Mad Dog had tested the window, which faced on the front yard. He'd taken a running start and lowered the shoulder that was sore now. The window hadn't budged and he'd gotten a muffled "I told you so" from the guard in the hall.

Pam took over rubbing his shoulder and bent and whispered in his ear as she did so.

"Where's Hailey, now that we need her?"

Hailey had disappeared before they ran into Galen for the first time. Then she'd gone again, right after rescuing them from the bin and alerting them to Mark's presence. Where? What was she up to?

"She's my *nisimon*," he told Pam, also whispering. "That's a Cheyenne thing, kind of like a witch's familiar."

The girl nodded, as if she'd expected as much and ran into guys who had supernatural partnerships with their pets all the time.

"And you're right, actually. She might be able to help us get out of here."

Pam nodded again. "It would be nice if she could open that window the way she opened the door to the grain bin."

"Maybe she can, or maybe she'll help us another way, if I ask her."

"How?"

"Like this." Mad Dog sat on the carpet and folded his feet under him. It was similar to the lotus position he used to assume when he wanted to be one with the universe back in his Buddhist period. Fortunately, Cheyenne stopped short of that, since Mad Dog could no longer get both feet on top of his thighs these days.

"Would it help if I joined you?"

"Sure," Mad Dog said, "but maybe if you stay out of sight. Looking at you won't help me focus my thoughts where they're needed."

"How sweet," she said, and bent and kissed his ear before going around behind him and lowering herself to the floor. "Just tell me what to do," she said.

"No more of that." The ear thing had nearly made him forget why he was sitting there. "Uh, just think of Hailey," he said. "And the situation we're in. Close your eyes and try to find her and tell her we need help."

Mad Dog closed his eyes and thought of how Pam felt in his arms back in that grain bin. No, the kiss hadn't helped at all.

"Do I need to chant or anything?"

"Just try not to distract me."

She didn't say anything, but he glanced over his shoulder and watched as a grin spread across her face.

He closed his eyes and tried again. The look, the feel, the smell of her.... He slapped himself upside his spiritual head and started over. He was too old for this foolishness, to say nothing of being in the wrong circumstances for it. They'd stumbled onto some kind of secret medical activities. An organ transplant, or transplants, if the nurse was to be believed. Who for? There were sick people, dying people in Benteen County, of course. But none of them would be involved in using unwilling donors to prolong their lives. Well, maybe a couple of them. But who could afford it? And how did you go about importing a private surgeon with a personal army? No, this had to be about outsiders. Except Galen, though maybe this explained how Siegrist Farms had financed its aggressive expansion.

Getting his mind off Pam helped. Gradually, he managed to focus on the spirit world instead of his surroundings. He'd done this before in difficult circumstances. He'd contacted Hailey, and she'd helped him. He searched for the pure, sharp brilliance of her essence. White-hot, crystalline, burning...there. She was there.

Someone shouted from the hall. "That car's back!"

His eyes popped open and Pam was leaning over his shoulder, pointing.

It was a silver compact. Something Japanese and moving slow.

"Isn't that one of the Heathers?" Pam asked.

Sweet Jesus! It did look like Heather. And Heather Lane drove a silver Toyota Camry exactly like that. But Heather was in Albuquerque. Wasn't she?

Apparently not. The girl behind the wheel was his niece, Two of Two.

Someone on foot entered their field of vision. It was one of the gunmen in suits. Another one, actually, since this one was blond. That made three of them, at least. How many were there?

"Go, Heather, go," Pam said. And Mad Dog suddenly understood why. The new guy in the suit was holding a weapon in his hand, sort of masked from Heather and the road because he was half turned toward the house. The gun was much too big to fit in a shoulder holster, though the end of the barrel didn't hang much below his knee. What was really scary about it was the magazine, a shaft of dark metal nearly as long as the barrel. It was some kind of automatic weapon.

Mad Dog silently echoed Pam inside his head. Heather continued driving past, way too slowly, her head turned toward the house as if she were looking for something. She didn't seem concerned about the guy with the gun. And then she waved at him and started speeding up again, gradually, as if she'd been looking for someone and finally realized this was the wrong house.

Mad Dog and Pam had stepped up and pressed their faces to the window. Not that Heather would be able to see them. You couldn't see into the house from outside because the windows were covered with reflective film.

The guy with the gun waved back at Heather. Left handed. He kept the submachine gun down, pressed against his leg.

Mad Dog started to breathe again. "She's going to get away," he said.

Suddenly, another face pressed against their window. This time from outside. It left a nose print exactly opposite the one Mad Dog was making.

Hailey!

Bad timing, because Heather saw her. The Toyota's brake lights came on.

"Stop her," a voice in the hall said. The guy with the combover, Mad Dog thought. The man in the front yard brought his automatic weapon up. He had a device in his ear, too, and he'd heard. His weapon started chattering.

The Toyota accelerated, foot to the floor. A tire blew. The car wobbled and veered toward the ditch.

The man with the gun pivoted. He'd seen the wolf at the window. He aimed down the barrel.

"Duck!" Mad Dog yelled, throwing himself across Pam and away from the glass.

"Run, Hailey!" Pam screamed.

They hit the floor and the gunman fired.

The window glass might be reinforced, but it wasn't really bulletproof.

The bodies were in the family room. The scene was every bit as bloody as the sheriff had expected, but even though there were two corpses, it wasn't as horrible. Chucky Williams had killed his parents, but he'd done it from behind—a quick burst from that automatic weapon he was carrying. It appeared they'd never known what was coming. The sheriff had expected to find an execution here. Instead, it felt more like a mercy killing.

Chucky's parents faced a television displaying a blue menu screen waiting for instructions. Mrs. Williams had been on the sofa. There was knitting in her lap. Mr. Williams had been in his wheelchair, of course. It was parked beside a table containing his medications and a cup with a bent straw. The Lou Gehrig's disease had progressed to the point that Mrs. Williams or Chucky would have had to hold the cup for him.

The wall behind the TV was a mess, spoiled by bullets, blood, bone, and flesh. But the room was otherwise undisturbed.

It wasn't at all what the sheriff had expected. Rage—wasn't that what an act like this required? He had thought the house would be torn apart, terrible things done to Chucky's parents and the home they cherished. Instead, the place was undisturbed but for that single burst. The living room was neat as a pin. The kitchen, except for this morning's unwashed dishes, was equally clean. Beds had been made, clothing was neatly on hangers or in hampers. Even in Chucky's room. Aside from the bodies, the sheriff only found three things out of place. There was a gun cabinet down in the basement. It had been locked. If Chucky had known where the key was, he hadn't had the patience to go after it. The glass and wood of its door was broken. A screwdriver had been taken from the tools that lined the nearby wall and used to pry the bar that secured the weapons within. One gun was missing, replaced by a shiny trombone whose case had been needed for another purpose.

On the floor beside the gun cabinet, the sheriff found the TV remote, apparently the one that controlled the menu screen in the room above. That was curious. Why would Chucky have brought the remote down here?

The sheriff had thought the menu screen on the TV in the family room would wait a very long time for instructions. Now he wasn't so sure. He picked up the remote and went back upstairs. Everything was as he'd left it, neat, clean, and organized, with just a touch of gore.

He hated remotes. Fortunately, he didn't watch much TV. In fact, he didn't spend much time at home anymore.

He should have brought Heather after all. Either one of his daughters could make this thing work in a heartbeat. And then he found the rewind button, reversed to the start, and hit play.

Someone had made a recording in this very room. The camera was just behind the sheriff's head and to the left. He turned and found it on a bookshelf, almost unnoticeable amongst a profusion of gewgaws and bric-a-brac.

"Come talk to my husband."

He turned back to the screen in time to see Mrs. Williams lead a man into the room. It was eerie, hearing the dead talk while their wrecked bodies sat just in front of him.

Mrs. Williams took the seat she would continue to occupy until Doc Jones could come collect her. Mr. Williams, of course, stayed in his wheelchair. The room was unchanged but for the bloody disaster that had befallen it.

The man who followed Mrs. Williams was a stranger, a small man with a good suit and bad hair. Long wispy strands had been arranged in a hopeless effort to disguise an advanced state of baldness.

"You promised we'd have our stem cell therapy this morning," Mr. Williams said. His voice was soft, hoarse, and faintly slurred.

Stem cells. Hadn't Heather said something about finding stem cells? And storing them in the beer cooler over at the old Texaco?

"You'll get them," the little guy said. "Our shipment was lost in this morning's accident. More are on the way. Right now, I need your son."

"And the money. We haven't seen that, either."

"The money and the therapy were in exchange for your son's cooperation. Now, he's disappeared. He ran from the bus. Then a couple of Gamble's boys were going to bring him right from school. He ran from them, too. In God's name, Mr. Williams, we need your boy right now."

"You had him. He was on that bus this morning, just as we agreed. What happened after, we had no more control over that than you. You better deliver. We got insurance if you don't come through."

The little man ran his fingers through his oh-so-sparse hair. "Proof of what, that you sold your son? Where is Chucky, Mr. Williams?"

"We have been obedient to God's wishes. We did our part. Perhaps we did sell our son, but you promised to heal me and fix up my wife's Alzheimer's. And make it so's we could get out of debt. Where are our cures? Where's our money?"

The little man shook his head. "You'll get your therapies and we'll double your money if you give me Chucky right now."

"He's gone." Mrs. Williams finally entered the conversation.

"Gone?" The little man took a step forward and, for a moment, the sheriff thought he was going to strike her.

"I don't remember where," she said.

Mr. Williams laughed. "She don't remember nothing. But he is gone. We gave him to you people and you lost him. If he comes home or we hear from him, we'll let you know. But we're dead people here, both of us, if you don't keep your bargain."

"No Chucky, no deal. You don't have to die these awful deaths. We can still heal you, but the price is your son."

"I beg you, sir," Mr. Williams said. "I got no control over the boy, not since the accident bumped him to primary. He's scared, and I don't blame him, but I'd give him to you in a heartbeat for those cures—if I knew where he was."

"Then I'm afraid you'll continue to rot away, Mr. Williams, your body weakening along with your wife's mind. Find the boy and salvation is still available. If not…."

Mrs. Williams looked up at the man and extended her hand. "I don't believe we've met," she said. "Would you care for a cup of coffee?"

"You know where to call," the man with the bad hair said.

Mr. Williams whispered something. It sounded like "Siegrist's," but the other man had turned and stormed from the room. The sheriff heard him slam the door on his way out. And then Chucky entered the room from somewhere behind the camera. He had the AK-47 and he appeared to be crying.

Mrs. Williams saw him. "Let me fix you some breakfast," she said, but she turned around and took up her knitting.

Chucky, tears streaming down his face, turned toward the camera and the TV screen went back to its menu. The sheriff was glad Chucky had turned the camera off. His imagination was more than adequate to show him what happened next.

Mad Dog hit the window with the same shoulder he'd used before. It didn't hurt as much this time because the window gave. The line of holes the automatic weapon had made hadn't shattered it, but they hadn't done its structural integrity any good. The pane folded along the line of holes and collapsed into the neat row of dwarf evergreens just below, with Mad Dog sandwiched in the middle.

He landed and rolled and the glass gave without splinter-ing—safety glass, no sharp edges—and he was free. Free, except that a large man with an automatic weapon was standing in the yard, undecided. His eyes were skipping from Heather, who was scrambling out of her Toyota where it had gone head first into the south-side ditch some fifty yards down the road, the corner of the building where Hailey must have disappeared (unless she'd simply vanished into thin air), and the fellow who'd just come out the window he'd perforated. That last was Mad Dog, who had no way to get to the gunman without giving him ample opportunities to empty his clip into Benteen County's only Cheyenne shaman. Lacking options, Mad Dog just gave the man a thumbs up and then waded back, barefoot through glass and decorative vegetation, to see about Pam. She was on the far side of the room, against the door, trying to hold it closed. The guy who wanted it open was Mad Dog's size, or bigger, so it opened.

"Run!" Pam yelled as the guy grabbed her with one hand and leveled a pistol at Mad Dog with the other.

"Hold it!" The guy offered contrary advice.

Mad Dog took Pam's suggestion and no one shot him. The man with Pam didn't manage to get a shot off because she'd kneed him in a very tender place as Mad Dog bolted. The one in the yard had apparently accepted Mad Dog's gesture at face value. He was sprinting toward Heather, or where Heather had been before she ducked into the milo field just east of the Siegrist house.

The problem was where Mad Dog should run. He didn't want to leave Pam behind and he needed to help Heather. He didn't have shoes, or car keys, or even a sharp stick with which to take on all these armed men. Whatever, getting out of sight seemed to be his first order of business. Especially when the blond guy changed his mind and opened up with his machine gun again. At first, Mad Dog was afraid the guy was trying to gun down Heather. Then a row of explosions threw dust and broken masonry up from the driveway and wall of the house in front of him. Galen wasn't going to like this. But that was nothing to how Mad Dog would feel about it when the guy fired a more accurate burst.

That burst didn't come. Mad Dog risked a glance over his shoulder. The blond was yanking a clip out of his weapon and reaching for a replacement. Mad Dog had a moment. Not long enough to get around the corner of the building, but just enough, if he and Pam had been right earlier.

His hand found the front door, twisted the knob....

No one locked their doors in Benteen County.

◇◇◇

It was Heather Lane's second pass by the Siegrist place that got her in trouble. She'd known once might be risky and twice could be stupid. But she hadn't seen anything on her first drive by. Not until she was looking in her rearview mirror and caught a glimpse of Hailey, sitting by the corner of the house.

She'd turned around at the next mile and come back, slower this time. No Hailey. But there was a guy in a suit standing in the front yard, giving her the evil eye. Still, she'd tried to maximize her chance for a close-up look. With nothing to show for it, she played stupid, smiling at the man in the yard and waving as she began to accelerate away. And then, there was Hailey again, in her rearview mirror. Her uncle's wolf was standing with her front feet on a window sill, her nose right to that damn reflective glass. Heather had a pretty good idea who was on the other side. Without a thought, she hit the brakes, planning to go back and demand an explanation. Only then the guy was shooting at her and she began madly trying to get away. The back end of the Toyota went all wobbly as she did so and the next thing she knew she was in the ditch.

Heather threw her door open, grabbed her fanny pack, and scrambled out of the car. It was just registering on her that the man had shot at her. And with some kind of automatic weapon on top of that. She wanted to rush back and tell him he was going to pay for any damage he'd done to her beloved first car, but she was angry, not nuts. She used the front of the car for cover. The gun opened up again, but it wasn't shooting at her this time. She risked a glance.

Hailey. The bastard was shooting at Hailey. But missing, because the wolf disappeared around the far corner of the house while the gunman's stream of bullets was still three feet behind.

Heather took advantage of his diverted attention and ducked into the field of milo. Galen's crop was late this year, but ripe. Rows of red-headed sorghum stretched for at least half a mile, easily thick enough to hide her from the house. But unlike corn, which milo resembles except for the distinctive red clump of grain at the top of each stem, the plants in this field were no more than four feet high. That meant she would have to keep down and move slower. The guy with the gun wouldn't have that disadvantage if he came after her instead of Hailey.

More shots. She didn't hear them hit anywhere nearby, but they prompted her to move a lot faster than she'd thought she could.

She dove a couple of dozen yards deeper into the field, then popped her head up, just high enough to check on him. The guy in the suit was trotting down the road, nearly to her car now. He'd find out she wasn't there and would begin checking this field any minute. She had to get away, but there wasn't really any good hiding place because Galen, damn him, had planted these rows arrow straight. The gunman would have to check every row, but when he looked down the one she was in, she wouldn't stand a chance of losing him again.

She could probably get to the corner before him. The north-south road at the next mile wasn't far. Half a mile north on it and she'd be at the spot where she and Chairman Wynn had begun their surveillance. But she wouldn't get across the east-west road without being seen. Not that there was anything to hide in if she did. Just a plowed field all the way to that distant windbreak. And nothing on the other side of the other road either. Those fields had also been recently tilled. There weren't even clumps of weeds to hide behind. There would be weeds along the ditches, but not enough. And culverts under the road, but they were really just a good place to get caught in. All that was the direction he'd expect her to go. Away, just as her first panicky reaction had demanded.

Toward the house, now that was something else. He wouldn't go back and check the rows of grain for some ditzy spy stupid enough to drive by twice and wave. He'd follow the ditch her Toyota had ended up in and he'd check rows from there to the corner. He wouldn't check the others until he didn't find her where he expected.

She wiggled through the first row, slithered though the second. Getting past him, getting past the car, that was the trick.

The seventh row showed her the Toyota's front bumper. She went slower now. And there he was, but he had his head down as he bent to look inside the car. She took a chance and popped up and sprinted half a dozen rows before diving back below the top of the copper berries.

No rain of bullets followed, nor any shouts to halt and come out with her hands up. She thought that was a good sign.

Just to be safe, she did the wiggle and slither number for a dozen more rows, doing her best not to jostle the plants. Thanks to the Kansas wind, he wasn't likely to notice her move them. It wasn't gusting, but it was steady, forceful enough to keep the sorghum waving in interesting patterns all its own.

As she continued, she began putting more distance between herself and the road, as well. She wanted to get around behind the house and the outbuildings. Once she was there, she was going to be awfully hard to find.

Crawling across a field, though, was taking too much time. If whoever was in that house was desperate enough to start shooting at curious drivers and nosey wolves, Uncle Mad Dog's safety had to be at risk. She pulled out her cell phone and dialed her sister.

"Yeah." The other Heather didn't usually answer that way. She must be busy.

"They shot at me," Heather Two said.

"Hello," the original Heather said.

"I said they shot at me. Can you hear me? I need help."

One of Two evidently wasn't getting her signal. "Anybody there?" One asked it another time and then hung up.

Heather Lane pulled the cell away from her face and noticed the fresh scar across the front of the phone, right at the mouthpiece. At least one of those bullets had come a lot closer to her than she liked to think about. Maybe that was why her sister hadn't been able to hear her.

"*Hola.*" The voice came from immediately behind her and she dropped the phone and only just managed to stop herself from screaming. She turned, very slowly.

He was short and dark and a little scruffy. But he wasn't the man in the suit. He hadn't been shooting at her.

He had a heavy accent. "Jew wan' help?" That's what it sounded like he asked. Like he was starting a discussion on the troubles in the Middle East.

"I help. Jew follow me. *Vamanos*, okay?"

Jew. You. He might speak Spanish better than English, but he was offering assistance.

"Okay," she said. He began twisting through the rows of grain and she followed.

No one locked their front doors in Benteen County. Or not until Mad Dog locked Galen's behind him. Let blondie and his submachine gun waste a lot of bullets getting in, if he wanted.

The living room was big, but traditional. It wasn't an extended part of the kitchen. More important, the room was empty, unless you counted the sofa and pair of armchairs on that generic beige carpet, all facing a lonely fireplace from twenty feet away. Those three pieces of furniture, and the empty coffee table in front of them, were filler. It looked like Galen had bought them to take up space, not use them. All of which was fine by Mad Dog, especially at the moment. The only person he wanted to run into in here was the guy who'd grabbed Pam. And he wanted that to come as a complete surprise.

He checked the mirrored windows on either side of the front door. The blond gunman had changed clips, but he wasn't following Mad Dog. Instead, he was hoofing it down the road toward Heather's Toyota. Of Heather, there was no longer any sign.

Mad Dog couldn't think of anything he could do for Heather right now, so he'd start with Pam. That meant he wanted to go east. That was where the hall to the garage was, and the room in which he and Pam had been held. But he thought it might be best to take a circuitous route. Scout out the rest of the house and determine where the big guys with the guns were so he could avoid them. Maybe put them out of commission along the way, if he was very lucky. When he got to Pam, if he got to Pam, he wanted to know exactly where to take her to keep her safe.

Mad Dog zigged around the lonely furniture and zagged through the arched entry to a formal dining area. Big table, uncomfortable-looking chairs, all showroom new and as virginal in appearance as the stuff in the living room.

There was a swinging door near the end of the dining room. Kitchen, he guessed. He slowed down for this one. Pam had said she and Mark came in the kitchen door when they visited Galen. Living room and formal dining area, those might not get used in a house that was way too big for the bachelor who lived here. Too big for his well-armed guests, as well. But the kitchen, that was another matter.

Mad Dog put his ear to the door. He could hear voices, but they sounded far away. He edged it open with his shoulder, just enough to use one eye. There was no one in the part of the kitchen he could see. But this was a room that was being used. A pile of dirty dishes was stacked on a counter next to the sink and dishwasher. Mad Dog kept a steady pressure on the door and it gradually swung farther into the room. A breakfast bar and stools and more dirty dishes indicated still heavier use, and sloppy guests. So did the table near the back door and a set of windows that looked over the farm yard with its stunning array of metal warehouses and grain bins.

The kitchen was empty. Mad Dog started to let himself in just as empty ceased to be the right word. Fortunately for him, Pam led the way, stumbling, pushed from behind by the big guy Mad Dog wanted to meet up with, but not while he had that heavy caliber pistol that followed Pam into the room.

She saw him. Her eyes got big and her mouth told him to run again, though she never made a sound. Mad Dog managed to get the door back down to a crack just big enough for his eye as the gunman followed his weapon into the kitchen. The little guy with the bad comb-over brought up the tail end of the parade.

"What do you mean you can't find her?" the little man was saying. It didn't make much sense until Mad Dog realized the man was speaking into the electronic device that extended in a thin tube to a microphone near his mouth. He must be talking to the blond guy who'd gone off chasing Heather.

"Lord," the little man said, confirming Mad Dog's suspicions. "Bravo checked the registration and the car belongs to Heather Lane. That's the sheriff's adopted daughter. What's she doing, snooping around here?"

None of these armed men were going to have an answer for that, not if Mad Dog himself didn't have a clue. Both the Heathers were supposed to be in school. Until moments ago, he'd been sure Heather Two was in Albuquerque.

"Find her quick." The little man turned to Pam's escort. "Lock this one up and go help Bravo look for the girl from that car out front," he said.

The big guy nodded. "Where should I put her?"

"Basement, I suppose. Just keep her out of the doctor's way."

The big guy didn't say anything, but he prodded Pam again, this time toward another opening off the kitchen. Mad Dog was getting damn tired of watching Pam being shoved around, but the room was too big and he wasn't close enough to get to the guy before he could use the gun. And the little balding guy might be armed as well.

The gunman went through the opening and he and Pam obviously began descending stairs. The little guy continued his conversation, this time with the gunman who had accompanied Galen. Apparently they hadn't found Mark yet.

This might be a good time to take out one of the opposition, Mad Dog thought. He felt a lot more confident of being able to overpower this dweeb, and, if so, he might arrange an ambush for Pam's prodder when he came back up those stairs.

Before he could do anything, though, the nurse appeared on the basement steps and began asking when the doctor could expect his "subjects."

In a house of this size, surely there was another entry to the basement. The kitchen seemed to have become a sort of headquarters for the army of occupation. Mad Dog decided to go exploring.

There was another wing on the west side of the house. Mad Dog found the hall and, just inside, another set of stairs. Sounds rose from below—whispers that weren't voices and some kind of chime. He went down, slow and quiet, emulating the select few of his ancestors who had been American Indians. There was a big, softly lit room down there. Something large, a pool table maybe, with a sheet over it, stood in the middle of the floor beneath faint blinking lights. It was surrounded by indistinct shadows. What were those lights? What were those noises?

From the bottom of the steps, he peered to either side. One was a dark hall, the other, just more strange shapes he couldn't recognize in the dim and flickering light. No people, though he thought he heard someone breathing.

He took a couple of steps into the room. It wasn't a pool table and there was something on it.

A little closer. The something became a shape, a person. Someone hooked to wires and tubes and suddenly the things around it made sense. Monitors, drips, oxygen. Jesus, had he found the intended recipient of those organ donations the nurse had hinted at?

He leaned in closer. There was a tube down the man's throat. The breathing he'd heard was being done by a machine on the other side of the hospital bed Mad Dog had thought was a pool table. The man was covered to the waist by a light sheet. He was old, pigeon-chested, wrinkled, familiar somehow. And then Mad Dog had it. The face was softer in unconsciousness, but no less severe. What the hell was Reverend Aldus P. Goodfellow doing in a makeshift surgical ward in a basement in Benteen County, Kansas?

Something stung Mad Dog on the shoulder. He started to swing around and defend himself but his muscles stopped working about halfway there. A pair of hands grabbed him and eased him to the floor, face down. Mad Dog couldn't see who it was. But he recognized the doctor's voice.

"Ah. I'm so glad you have reappeared. It seems you are nearly as perfect a match as the ones we've lost."

The Spanish-speaking man led Heather down into a low place, part of a drainage she hadn't suspected but that must once have run across this field. There wasn't much evidence of it anymore. Galen had done his best to fill it and make it match the rest of this half-mile long strip of grain. The remains of this streamlet, though, were lower than the surrounding field. Enough so the two of them could stand and proceed in a crouch and make some real progress. They could run, as the little guy demonstrated, if they stayed low. That was fine with Heather. The farther she got from the guy with the automatic weapon, the better she'd like it.

"*Aquí*," he told her. "Here."

Her Spanish wasn't bad. She'd spent a lot of her youth in New Mexico, as well as several recent years of college. "I'm right behind you," she said, using that Spanish.

He glanced over his shoulder and smiled and said, "*Bueno.*"

He led her toward the farm yard, but the back of it, away from the house, toward the third warehouse over. By the time they reached it, the other warehouses blocked her from being able to see her car or the corner of the milo field where the gunman had been searching for her.

This man led her to a little building built against the side of the warehouse. A couple of fifty-five gallon drums stood near one wall. He slipped between them and pulled back a piece of siding and gestured for her to go in. It probably wasn't the best thing to do with a strange man she'd met while sneaking across a milo field, but he'd helped her once and might again. She needed a safe place to consider her predicament and what to do about it and she needed allies. She went inside.

From the big electric motor and all the pipes, she thought this must be a pump house—irrigation, probably. Whatever, it was closed off from the rest of the warehouse by metal walls. It wasn't very big, but a couple of lamps made it comfortably bright. The power came from an orange drop cord that had been patched into the pump's wiring. The little TV the room's occupants were watching was attached to the cord as well. A man and two women huddled around a softly playing soap opera. One of the women was patting out tortillas. The other was keeping an eye on something in a crock pot. Heather got a whiff that smelled delicious when the woman opened it to add some seasonings. And then it was closed and the pump house smelled of machinery and oil again, with only a hint of chili.

"Wow," Heather said. "All the comforts of home."

"This is our home," her guide said. "I am Xavier." Then he proceeded to introduce the others, his wife, his wife's sister, and the sister's husband. They all welcomed her profusely.

"You work for Galen?"

"*Sí.* Us, and some others. Or we did until a few days ago. When the ambulance came, he told us to go home and not to come back for two weeks."

"But you stayed."

"Yes and no," Xavier grinned. "We went home, but Mr. Galen, he doesn't know our home is so near."

"So Galen Siegrist is staffing his farm with illegal workers."

She'd muttered that aloud, but in English, and her only intended audience was herself.

"No, no," Xavier protested. "We citizens, like jew." He pulled out his wallet and showed her his driver's license and a social security card. She'd heard of bad driver's license photos, but if this one was Xavier, it made him look twenty years older and a hundred pounds heavier. It also suggested Xavier spelled his name with a "G", as in Gilbert Hernandez.

"Look, I don't care whether you're here legally or not. You just saved me. Why were you out in that field, anyway?"

Xavier, or Gilbert, shrugged. "I was going shopping."

It was almost ten miles to the nearest store. "You were going to walk?"

"Oh no, we have a car parked in an abandoned barn a little south of here."

The car might come in handy. But what about Uncle Mad Dog and Hailey? They might need help sooner than she could hike and then drive to get it. Besides, that guy with the gun was probably still searching the field for her.

"You amaze me," she said. "You have everything you need here. I think this is probably better furnished than my dorm room. But you don't have the one thing I need."

"No, I'm sorry," Xavier said. "We don't have a computer."

"Not a computer," she said. "A phone."

All four of them reached for pockets and each produced a cell phone.

"Or I have a BlackBerry," Xavier said, "if you need to check your email."

For reasons she couldn't explain, Heather English decided to approach the Siegrist farm from the long way round. Maybe it was because she had appropriated the Williams' car. Maybe it was because her sister was keeping the place under surveillance. Or it might be because she'd started this day with a premonition and she wasn't about to stop listening to her feelings now.

She turned north by the Gas–Food. This route would be slightly slower, a couple of extra miles of dirt road instead of blacktop. She turned again a mile north of the road that led by the Siegrist place. She had decided she didn't even want to pass the place before she and Heather could talk. She needed to get a look at it and come up with some way to find out what was going on in there, and without getting themselves or Uncle Mad Dog killed.

Her cell rang just as she pulled off the blacktop. She flipped it open and answered, but there was no one there. She disconnected, then out of curiosity checked to see who had tried to reach her. Heather, the read-out told her. That was curious. Well, she'd meet her sister at her observation post in just a couple of minutes.

She had just put the phone on the seat beside her when it rang again. "Heather?" she said. She hadn't checked to see who was calling. She'd just assumed. And, besides, you had to pay some attention to your driving. Using a cell at the wheel was something Englishman had promised his girls would get them grounded when they first started driving. He wouldn't be thrilled about it now, even if her deputy's badge and the demands of what was going on gave her some good excuses.

It wasn't Heather, though, it was Chairman Wynn. "I hate to bother your daddy in the middle of all this," he said. "So I figured I'd report to his deputy instead."

"Report what?"

"Well, first, that Ford I followed from the Siegrist place. It's at Christ Risen here in Buffalo Springs. Fellow driving it came to talk to Pastor Goodfellow. They've gone inside, but it looked like they were arguing."

"Interesting," Heather said, though she had no idea what it meant. "But you said first. There's something else?"

"Yeah. Real peculiar. Your daddy's opponent and that friend of his, Neuhauser, they just left the church in a big hurry. Armed themselves with everything short of cruise missiles and then tore out of here in a black Chevy SS."

"What's that about?"

"Seemed like they were following Chucky Williams."

"Chucky? You've seen Chucky?"

"Yeah. And that was odd, too, 'cause it looked like he was toting a gun and I think the car he drove off in belongs to Mrs. Kraus."

"You don't know about the school, do you?"

"Well, I know they seem to have dismissed classes for a hike to the courthouse. There're kids and teachers all over, and lots of parents gathering, too. But I've been keeping a low profile so I can track that Ford when it moves again."

Heather told him. She kept it short and simple and left out lots of gruesome details. As she did so, she turned the car south and began following the shelterbelt toward her sister's surveillance spot. "Maybe you should call Englishman about Chucky and Lieutenant Greer." Better if he did it. Then she wouldn't have to tell her dad where she was and what she was doing here. Chairman Wynn could pass that information along, if he did the calling, and Englishman wouldn't be able to read her the riot act. Except by phoning her. Maybe she should start screening her incoming calls. She'd rather explain after this was over, after she and Heather succeeded in solving this and keeping Englishman safe.

"I'll tell Mrs. Kraus," he said. "Here she comes, looking mad as a freshly shampooed cat. And I'll stay on this Ford."

Heather decided that would work. She agreed, and hung up. Her sister's car ought to be parked along here, but she didn't see it. And then she was at the end of the windrow. She pulled over to the edge of the road and stuck her head out. "Heather? Where are you?"

No answer. She stepped out of the car and shouted again. Still nothing. She looked across the field, half expecting to discover she'd counted the miles wrong and the Siegrist place was maybe another mile south. But there it was, right where she'd thought.

Now where would Heather have gone? One had told Two to lay back and wait. But that phone call…. Maybe something had happened and Two felt like she had to go do something about it. One climbed up on the jamb of the Taurus' open door. It gave her a little more elevation. Just enough to see a glint of sun off the roof of a car a couple of hundred yards east of Siegrist's driveway. Could it be…?

She got back in the Taurus and drove south. It was a Toyota, all right, the same model and color, and it was in a ditch. She turned west. The driver's door was open. It was obviously her sister's car. But no one was in it. In fact, there was no sign of her sister at all. Just, oddly enough, a man with short blond hair and wrap-around sunglasses and a good suit, standing a hundred yards deep in the adjacent milo field.

It wasn't until she passed Heather's Toyota that she noticed the bullet holes in the trunk.

To Lieutenant Greer's surprise, Chucky Williams was difficult to chase down. Okay, impossible to chase down, and damn hard to follow.

First, Chucky didn't take Main Street out of town. By the time Greer and Neuhauser spotted the boy's car, he had a huge lead and was headed in a direction they hadn't anticipated. The Chevy couldn't make up the difference. And Chucky's route slithered around a long curve lined with trees so when they emerged, Chucky was no longer visible. There was only a column of dust to show which road Chucky had taken. Greer followed the dust.

Earlier, the nurse practitioner at the Buffalo Springs clinic had suggested Greer stick around and take it easy and let them monitor him for the afternoon. Greer treated the suggestion the way he'd treated similar ones in Iraq. If he wasn't dead or crippled, there was no reason he shouldn't be out there killing the enemy. Over there, it was hard to tell who the enemy was. Here, it was just some stupid teenager who'd blown apart Greer's favorite boots and made him drop his shotgun and lose some of his best grenades. The kid should be easy to take down. And doing it should make the lieutenant enough of a local hero to get him virtually every vote that hadn't already been cast today. Of course he expected to win anyway, but taking out the little bastard ought to cap his victory and send a message to anyone planning to mess with the future sheriff of Benteen County. And, hell, the kid had made it personal by embarrassing him over at the school. That, and the resulting double vision that made it harder for Greer to see the kid's car or keep Neuhauser's Chevy on the road, were reasons enough for the boy to go down.

The dust led them to Galen Siegrist's farm. Greer didn't think much of Siegrist, but he was important to Pastor Goodfellow and the Buffalo Springs Church of Christ Risen, and they were the funnel for the PAC money that was going to get Greer elected.

He didn't wonder why Chucky went to Siegrist's. Greer didn't care. He was hunting prey, not solving crime.

"There," Neuhauser said, pointing between a couple of the Siegrist warehouses. It was the car the Williams kid had made off with. Greer should have seen it. He shook his head to clear his vision and then wished he hadn't. His head still throbbed like insurgents were setting off IEDs every time his heart beat. Greer knew he should have let Neuhauser drive, but the lieutenant liked to be in control.

There were a couple of other cars around the place, too. A silver Toyota in the ditch with…shit, with a row of bullet holes stitched across its trunk. And in between another pair of warehouses, an old Ford Taurus.

"What's going on here?" Neuhauser asked. "They having a convention or a war?"

Greer and Neuhauser were well equipped for the latter.

"How we gonna do this?" Neuhauser wondered.

From the streets of Fallujah to the plains of Kansas, Greer couldn't think of anyone he'd rather have covering his butt. Newt was a natural follower, Greer's perfect wing man. "When in doubt," Greer said, "bust down the front door and go in shooting."

They'd have to be a little more discriminating than that, but maybe not much. He turned into the driveway and his double vision betrayed him. He dumped one tire off into the edge of the ditch and saw stars—nothing but stars—for a moment. And then they were parked just off the road and Neuhauser was out and covering the west side of the car, including the front of the house. Greer did the same for the field of grain and the road toward that shot-up Toyota.

A man came jogging out of the field. He was big and blond and he was carrying what Greer's impaired vision took to be a weapon.

"Bogey," he said.

Neuhauser confirmed that the man was carrying a high powered submachine gun. With the suit, Greer was thinking FBI or some other federal agency. That didn't stop him from whipping the M-4 he wasn't supposed to have, complete with grenade launcher, to his shoulder and shouting, "Drop the weapon and show me empty hands."

The guy in the suit didn't comply. He just shouted back.

"Lieutenant Greer. Newt Neuhauser. Haven't seen you guys since Ramadi. Good to have you aboard. Go inside and report to Delta. I've got an intruder to neutralize."

The blond loped off toward the metal warehouses and left Greer and Neuhauser standing by the Chevy.

"What the hell is a private security contractor from Iraq doing in the middle of Kansas?" Neuhauser asked, even if the question might be asked of him as well. "And who's Delta?

Greer shook his head and wished he hadn't. "One way to find out," he said.

Deputy Heather almost climbed through the roof when her cell rang. Vibrated, actually, since she'd had the good sense to turn off the ringer before entering one of Galen Siegrist's metal warehouses. The bullet holes in her sister's trunk, and the fact that the man in the field had aimed some kind of weapon at her, had persuaded her to duck the Taurus between warehouses, well out of view of the man with the gun. Then she'd abandoned the car in search of an inconspicuous spot from which a girl with a badge and handcuffs and a can of pepper spray could decide how to take on gunmen in suits, rescue her sister and her uncle, keep Dad safe, and otherwise save the day.

She fumbled the phone out of her pocket without taking time to see who was calling.

"Hello," she whispered, ducking between a dump truck and a small tractor.

"Something really weird is going on at the Siegrist place." It was Heather, Two of Two.

"You're all right? I saw your car."

"You saw my car? Where are you?"

Heather explained, then the other Heather did the same.

"Maybe you should call that highway patrol captain," Heather Lane suggested.

Heather English, with recent memories of having her own car shot at by one of those highway patrolmen, wasn't so sure. But Englishman would hear about Mad Dog and the Siegrist place very soon. He was almost certain to put in an appearance right after that. Englishman would come armed, but he'd be seriously outgunned by the guy in that field. Heather One told her sister she'd make the call.

Heather Two, sounding more like an identical twin instead of an adopted one, read One's mind. "You're going to look around, first, aren't you? Maybe I should slip out of here and help."

It was hard to suggest that what was good for One would be stupid for Two. "You're right," Deputy Heather said. "I'll hole up and call the captain and we'll let the professionals take care of this."

"That's smart," Two said.

One guessed her sister wasn't planning to stay put any more than she was. "I'll get back to you as soon as I talk to the troopers," she said, "and then call Daddy and try to make sure he gets here *after* they do."

The girls promised each other they'd stay someplace safe until the state officers arrived. Then they disconnected. Heather English stuck the phone back in her pocket and pulled out her pepper spray and peeked around the dump truck.

She was near the middle of the warehouse, a big, dusky expanse of parked machinery with occasional work benches and tool boxes where things got repaired.

She wanted to get nearer to the house. Actually, she wanted to get inside the house to search for Uncle Mad Dog and figure out what was going on here, so she'd know if outside help was really needed. A blown-out rear window and the news that Chucky Williams was still armed and had stolen Mrs. Kraus' car didn't do much for her confidence in the state boys. Maybe she could find out where these guys in the suits kept their armaments, get the drop on them, and have everything nicely sewn up before Englishman or the troopers got here.

She found Mad Dog's Mini Cooper in the warehouse. She recognized the license number, not that there were any other Minis in the county, especially red ones with bumper stickers that read, "It's a good day to be Indigenous," and "Jesus would use his turn signals." So, Two was right. That was Mad Dog she'd seen being led into the house at gunpoint.

Deputy Heather angled for the window across the building, the one nearest the house. Her path took her past a small office. She thought about investigating it, then decided to put it off until later. She had just passed the door when it opened and the blond guy with the suit and the gun came out.

"How'd you get out of that field and into that Taurus?" He seemed more puzzled about that than concerned she might be a threat. The pepper spray was already in her hand and he was close enough for it to be effective.

The mist caught him by surprise and square in the face. And then she realized he was wearing wrap-around sunglasses and thought she maybe should have called the highway patrol after all.

◇◇◇

"Don't be alarmed," the doctor said. "You've just received a dose of an extraordinarily effective neuromuscular blocking agent. A little something I developed myself. The drug causes paralysis without interfering with your level of consciousness."

And I shouldn't be alarmed, Mad Dog thought. He was lying on the floor and he couldn't move. Paralysis seemed to be an accurate description. Hell, he couldn't even make his eyes look at anything but the tiles immediately in front of his face.

"You're not a young man," the doctor continued. "But you're quite large and I was disinclined to join you in a wrestling match. Besides, if we get back on schedule, you're due for surgery before long."

This wasn't any more reassuring than the first statement. If he could have done anything other than quietly drool on the floor, he would have asked for more details about that surgery. Was he to be a liver donor the way the nurse had hinted? Or heart and lungs? Either way, he'd really like the chance to do a little wrestling with this man. Or pummeling, maybe. Or just plain beating the fellow to death.

"I'm afraid I'm going to have to leave you on the floor for now. You've got our security team running in circles looking for you and that girl, and now I understand we have some other visitors."

Mad Dog felt hands on his right shoulder. His view of the world shifted as the doctor turned him face up. Well, face sideways, since his head lolled in the direction from which it had come.

Out of the corner of the eyes he couldn't move, he saw the man attaching a plastic bag to one of the stands beside Reverend Goodfellow's bed. Mad Dog felt a prick in his right arm as the doctor started a drip.

"This should preserve you in your current state until we're ready to get on with things."

Hands took hold of Mad Dog's face and turned it and he was suddenly looking straight into the surgeon's eyes. The doctor produced a light and examined them. He made small humming sounds as he applied a stethoscope and then a blood-pressure cuff.

The man chatted quietly while he worked. "Did you recognize our famous guest? You should feel honored. In your small way, you may help me keep this man alive forever. How, you may ask? By aiding my personal innovations in gene and stem-cell therapies, of course."

He opened Mad Dog's mouth and explored it with his flashlight. Mad Dog desperately willed his jaw to snap shut and bite those fingers off. Nothing happened.

"Perhaps you're concerned with the ethics of this endeavor. You will be pleased to know that I have come to my own accommodation with that question. Until now, everyone died. If a few more have to die sooner than they might have in order to make immortality available for those who deserve it—or, I will admit, those who can afford it—oh well. There is a saying. One cannot make an egg without breaking omelets.

"You have an athlete's pulse, and excellent blood pressure. You will make a superb subject for this afternoon's procedure."

He patted Mad Dog affectionately on the cheek. "You must excuse me now. I have other preparations to make. I promise to get back to you as soon as possible. I hope you won't find the floor too uncomfortable."

The man's hands reached for Mad Dog's eyes and gently closed them. "There, now. We can't have your lovely eyes drying out, can we?"

Mad Dog wanted to grab those hands and break them. Smash that smiling face. Bash that aquiline nose until it was flat. He couldn't move. He couldn't even scream.

Except inside his head....

"Can you believe it? Somebody stole my damn car." Mrs. Kraus was steaming. When she'd noticed Ex-Chairman Wynn, she must have decided he was the perfect target to dump on. "I can't even report it because we got no deputies and all my phone lines have been appropriated 'cause of this shooting over at the high school. And those state boys won't pay me no attention. Then there was that voter fraud this morning and...I swear. It makes you wonder what the world's coming to."

The former chairman was slumped in the front seat of his Cadillac SUV, trying to pretend that would make him invisible even though his Escalade was the only one of its kind in Benteen County. People picking up their kids at the courthouse kept honking and waving to him.

"I'm sorry," Mrs. Kraus said, getting closer to his window and forcing him to look her in the eye. "That was thoughtless of me, that comment about us having no deputies. What's the news on your boy? Is he much improved? Is that why you're back in Benteen County? But why are you all scrunched down in your seat like that?"

He flushed and sat up a little and told her how Deputy Wynn was in an induced coma and likely to stay that way for a few days. He told her, too, how he hadn't been able to sit around and pace the halls under those circumstances, so he'd come home to try to solve the mystery of this morning's bus wreck.

"The reason I'm keeping a low profile here is because I'm trying not to be obvious while I follow that white Ford over by the church. I think the guy who came to town in it had something to do with the school bus being out there this morning."

Mrs. Kraus turned and looked and asked, "Which guy?"

He sat up real straight now, peering over her shoulder. A truck went by, further blocking his view for a minute, and then he saw it. The Ford had backed out while Mrs. Kraus was at his window and now it was heading down the street toward Main. The driver wasn't alone in there anymore, either. He had two passengers.

"Who's in there with him?" the chairman asked, reaching down and starting the Cadillac.

"Don't know. Never got me a good look at 'em."

"You got to excuse me," Wynn said. "I need to follow that car."

"Then you'll need to get out of this park," Mrs. Kraus said. "Can you run me back over to the courthouse so I can get my Glock?"

He just wanted her out of his way. And he needed the parade of cars that were suddenly coming and going to the courthouse to pause long enough for him to back into the street.

"I don't have time to wait for you," he said. "Or for all this damn traffic. They're getting away."

Mrs. Kraus yanked his door open and shoved him toward the passenger seat. "You let me behind the wheel. I'll get us clear."

He could sit there and argue with her while the Ford disappeared, or he could do what she asked and let her drive. Neither one seemed to offer much of a chance, but talking Mrs. Kraus out of anything was likely to take longer. He crawled into the passenger's seat as she slammed the door behind her.

"How are you gonna break into that traffic?" he said.

She put the Cadillac in drive and floored it, throwing up chunks of sod from Veteran's Memorial Park and bouncing over any shrubs and bushes that happened to be in the way. She tore a giant circular divot in the park's grass and came barreling back toward the line of cars and trucks, horn blaring. They made room for her, though only just.

The chairman thought he might be the second member of the Wynn family to be in a vehicle that injured the county's citizens today. Even after they managed to get across the street, a cluster of pedestrians had to flush like a covey of quail to clear the way for Mrs. Kraus.

He closed his eyes to avoid seeing people get plastered to his grill like summer's grasshoppers. When there were no sickening thuds, he risked peeking. He was just in time to confirm Mrs. Kraus' observation.

"Damn," she said. "Now where's that Ford got to?"

In all his years in Benteen County, Doc had never brought a load of six bodies back to Klausen's funeral parlor at one time. A trooper had helped him load them. He was getting too old for toting bodies out of basements. Hell, he was getting too old for carting in murder victims by the half-dozen. Maybe it was time to retire. He'd only taken the coroner's job in the first place because Benteen County never had violent deaths other than traffic accidents, or farmers who forgot the uncaring power of the machinery they used every day.

Doc glanced over his shoulder as he maneuvered the Buick into Klausen's parking lot and backed it up near the "delivery" entrance. The stack of body bags was in the way, so he had to use the rearview mirrors on his doors. There was a white Ford near where he wanted to be, but it got out of his way before he began swinging his Buick into place. A car full, maybe relatives who'd come to begin making arrangements before their children's bodies had even arrived. He didn't pay attention. He was focused on the grim task ahead, six autopsies. More, if what he'd heard about Chucky's parents was true. And Chucky was still out there.

He felt the weight of his years as he let himself out of the Buick—his occasional ambulance and current meat wagon. It was all he could do to drag himself to the back door. He punched the buzzer that would alert a Klausen brother, or one of their employees, that he needed help. He opened the door and trudged down that sterile white hallway, leaving what had started as a perfect autumn day far behind. For him, its perfection had been ruined by that first body he'd brought in earlier this morning.

He passed his office and proceeded straight to the work room. There were two stainless steel surfaces inside. He'd have to find something to do with the other four while they waited their turns. Then it occurred to him that the refrigerator, where they would end up after his indelicate attentions, might not hold as many bodies as he was going to need to store in there.

He sighed and slumped across the room to have a look and consider how to arrange them so they would all fit. There was more room in the converted meat locker than he'd expected. And not because it was bigger than his memory told him.

"Hey, Doc." It was the youngest Klausen. "I hear you've been out drumming up business."

Normally, Doc would have laughed. To survive in this business, or Klausen's, you had to develop a macabre sense of humor. But not today, not under these circumstances.

"Where's the boy?" Doc asked.

Klausen's brows furrowed. "What boy?"

"The kid who died in the accident this morning," Doc said. "Isn't he in there?"

He wasn't. Neither were the containers into which Doc had placed his vital organs, after careful removal, measurement, and recording. "No," Doc said. "He's gone. Everything is gone."

The blond guy in the suit was quick to back out of the cloud of pepper spray. "What did you want to go and do that for?" he coughed.

Deputy Heather considered a mad dash for safety, but he had already swept the sunglasses aside and centered his weapon on her chest. His watering eyes were in the open for her pepper spray now, but she'd never get the can close to his face again.

"Drop it," he said, as if he were reading her mind. "I don't want to shoot you. I'm just supposed to bring you in for questioning."

The pepper spray can rang as it hit the floor and rolled behind her.

"Why?" It seemed like a reasonable thing to ask. Your sister's car didn't get shot up in Benteen County every day, and guys with suits and guns and, damn it, sunglasses, didn't hunt you down. "What do you want with me?"

He shook his head. When he spoke, his voice was a little hoarse from the spray. "Hey, missy. I'm just hired muscle. You'll have to ask the boss. Or he'll have to ask you."

"Who's the boss? This is Galen Siegrist's place. Galen doesn't hire armed security to patrol his farm. He's raising seed crops here, not cocaine."

"Galen? That wimpy kid. He's not my boss. And this sure ain't about drugs. It's about maintaining security. You kept driving by, checking the place out. I'm guessing they want to know if you're just a nosey neighbor or if we've got a security breach."

Driving by. Ah, he thought she was her sister. The good side of that was they wouldn't be looking for Two anymore. The bad side was they had her. And she didn't like the sound of that last part. Breached security? What, was the government holding secret prisoners here for questioning? Was some sort of terror cell in the county about to get busted? This was so over the top for Benteen County, and Galen Siegrist, that it boggled the mind.

Galen was a smart, ambitious, and obnoxious kid from a few classes ahead of hers. She'd pretty much known him all her life, and disliked but not despised him. He'd always been a religious fanatic and a bigot and he had a way of looking at girls that made her uncomfortable, no matter how often he preached about the evils of the flesh. He'd asked her out a couple of times, but she'd found excuses. So had her sister. They both agreed the human race would simply have to end if Galen should turn out to be the last man on earth.

But Galen was small-minded and greedy, not evil. And he'd rushed off and finished his agronomy degree in three years so he could take over this farm. He wasn't political, or no more so than any of the rest of the zealots in the neighborhood. She had to admit there were a few. She could picture Galen plotting to make abortions illegal, replace evolution with creationism, even working to install Christianity as America's official religion. But not getting involved with secret medical operations and a private army. Heather had always thought Galen would opt for profits over prophecy if he had to make a choice.

"Yeah, I got her," the blond guy said. No one had joined them. He was talking into a little microphone attached to something in his ear that she hadn't noticed before.

He gestured with his weapon toward a door across from the office. "Come on, girly. They want you at the house."

She was pretty sure she didn't want to go there with him, but like, what were her choices?

"Is this some kind of government thing?" She started backing away, going slow, delaying the inevitable. "Are you Homeland Security?"

That brought a smile to his face. "Oh yeah," he said. "We're anxious to talk to you about your liberal outlook. Unless the CIA has decided to pull a rendition and ship you to a black site for questioning."

He was teasing her, and he thought she was a dweeb. But that could be useful.

She let her eyes get wide. "Oh yeah. Really. 'Cause I'm no liberal." Actually, she supposed she was, though mostly because it was liberals who so outraged the neoconservatives she thought were madly rushing about destroying the world. "You're in Kansas, after all."

"As if I hadn't noticed." So, *he* was the dweeb, too feeble to realize there were Democrats and liberals and even the occasional pacifist among the white Christians right here in the heartland's heart.

"I mean, like, I'd vote for Mr. Bush today if I were old enough." She was old enough, but this was a mid-term election and the younger Mr. Bush would be constitutionally ineligible to run again. But a little Kansas hayseed wouldn't know that.

She sidestepped a little and gave him a big smile. "So are you like CIA?"

The pepper spray can was just off to the side a little, just short of a stack of seed bags. She edged toward it.

"Licensed to kill. Double-Oh number and all." That was James Bond and a fictional British secret service. He must think the turnip truck had dumped its load right here. She felt for the spray can with her foot, found it, stepped on it and went over backward into the bags of grain. He reached for her and she rebounded off the sacks and put all her weight into the kick she aimed at his groin.

His face turned pasty and she grabbed his gun with one hand and ripped his communications device out of his ear with the other. She put a hand over the mouthpiece and kicked the less than efficient pepper spray across the building. He slowly folded onto the floor, holding himself more tenderly than Elvis had suggested in that song her mother used to love.

She pointed the gun at him, though she had not the slightest clue whether it had a safety or if it was on, and said, "I'm licensed to kill, too. But I'm just Benteen County Deputy Heather English. Now, I expect you know this part. You have the right to remain silent...."

◇◇◇

The sheriff answered his cell, "English." He'd been surprised, but hardly disappointed, that his phone remained quiet while he investigated the Williams place, then drove across the county. He'd been hoping to hear that the state troopers had rounded up Chucky, though he wasn't surprised they hadn't. And he'd been expecting updates from his daughters and his office, or maybe from Doc.

"That you, Sheriff?" It was Mrs. Kraus. No one else had such a whiskey-and-cigarettes voice. It didn't matter that she only had a little wine on special occasions these days, or that she'd given up her multi-pack-a-day habit nearly a decade ago. She sounded more like she should be welcoming you to a New Orleans bordello than a central Kansas sheriff's office.

"How are things at the courthouse, Mrs. Kraus?"

"Damned if I know," she said.

Her answer shocked him. Mrs. Kraus was not someone who would abandon her post.

"Things are insane over there, what with parents picking up kids and confiscating my phones and those troopers treating everybody like terror suspects. Then my damn car got stole. By your murderer, no less, Chucky Williams himself."

"Chucky stole your car? You know where he is?"

"Nah. He was long gone by the time I got over to where I'd parked. That's when I ran into Chairman Wynn. He and Heather, that would be Two if you're keeping score, were scouting out Galen Siegrist's place, where, by the way, they think Mad Dog might have got taken hostage."

"So, Heather and the chairman, they're with you now? Where are you, Mrs. Kraus? Is my other daughter keeping an eye on the office for you?"

"I'm at Klausen's. The chairman, he left Two to watch the farm while he followed a car to town. Then lost the car when it left the church. We were driving around, trying to find it, when we saw Doc pacing up and down on the sidewalk in front of the funeral parlor like he misplaced something. Which, it turns out, he has. In a manner of speaking. That boy. The one who died in the accident this morning. Doc says someone stole his body."

"You're kidding." The sheriff knew she wasn't, but this thing was getting weirder by the minute. Still, the missing body made a kind of terrible sense if what he'd learned from that video at the Williams place was for real. Maybe there really was an organ transplant waiting to happen. And, with Chucky on the rampage, maybe someone had decided to go back for the original donor. Unreal. This was like some bad horror movie. Where would you do an organ transplant? The county didn't even have a hospital.

"Doc with you?"

"He's here."

"Ask him if that boy's organs would still be good to transplant."

A whitetail deer came bounding out of one pasture, crossed the road, and leaped the fence into another. Hell of a time to look for greener grass, the sheriff thought. He barely managed to keep his truck out of a ditch. Doc's voice was on the phone when he got it back to his ear. "…not my area of expertise," he was saying.

"Sorry, Doc. I missed that. Any part of that kid still useful for a transplant?"

"I said I don't know, Englishman. Some of him, probably. But I didn't harvest his organs the way they do for transplants. And it's been half a day now since he died. His heart won't restart. Lungs, kidneys, liver—hell, I can't imagine any of them would still be good."

"Do you know who stole him? Or when?"

"He don't know jack shit." Mrs. Kraus' rasping voice cut into his ear as gently as a chainsaw. "But the chairman and I, we think it was probably that car from Galen's farm. And them men from the church he picked up. Even Doc thinks he might of saw it when he pulled in with his load from the school."

The sheriff was getting close to Galen's place. The kid had poured a lot of money into that farm since he came home from college. It was clear he had outside backing. Could he have built a transplant clinic into that new house of his?

"What kind of car?"

The sheriff took his foot off the accelerator and let the Chevy slow as it approached the last intersection where he could choose, unseen from Galen's farm, a different approach to the Siegrist homestead. It proved a lucky decision. A car plowed around the corner, throwing dirt and dust and narrowly avoiding the ditch as well as the sheriff's pickup.

"White Ford Fusion," the sheriff said, in tandem with Mrs. Kraus.

"How'd you know that?" she said.

"All of a sudden, I'm right behind it."

He got back on the throttle and stayed there, though he didn't close the gap. The Ford was producing rooster tails of dust. He thought about trying to catch it and force it off the road, see if the corpse Doc was missing might not be in there. And see who was doing the transporting. But he didn't have any backup. If he stopped them, what was he going to do with them while he went to see what was going on at Galen's?

"Call Heather Two. Tell her to stay where she's at. Not to get any nearer the Siegrist place, no matter what."

"Ah, well...." He could tell Mrs. Kraus had bad news for him. "Chairman says he's tried calling her. She's stopped answering. And, you asked me if Heather One was covering the office for me. Well, she ain't. I've not seen her since she was trying to break Lieutenant Greer's finger this morning. And Chairman Wynn, he says he had the impression she planned to drive out and join her sister. We just tried her number and didn't get an answer from her either."

"Shit. I told her to...."

"Course you did," Mrs. Kraus said. "And of course she didn't. Girls that age, even with what happened to their mother, they think they're immortal."

The sheriff disconnected. There was nothing more to say. And he wanted his .38 in his hand, not his cell phone.

Immortal, huh. They better be right.

Heather English felt her cell phone buzz, but she was a little busy. She had arrested the guy. That meant she couldn't just go off and leave him. She had to secure him somehow. And that was beginning to look like it might not be easy. He was still in a lot of pain, but he was getting angrier by the minute. It wasn't going to be long before he was willing to let go of the family jewels and start looking for a suitable way to kill her, even though she'd already slapped the handcuffs on him.

She needed to tie him up somehow. Secure his legs or attach him to something. Baling wire would be ideal, but nobody used it anymore. When she was growing up, old baling wire was still the fix-all for every emergency farm repair. These days, it was duct tape. But neither was handy in Galen's warehouse. Finally, she checked his office and found what she needed in his closet. Clothes hangers. Those, and the fencing pliers she'd seen hanging on a nearby wall.

He was mixing curses with moans, now. She stuck the barrel of the gun she didn't know how to shoot in his face and told him to lie down on his stomach. That meant he'd have to put pressure on a tender area. She had some trouble persuading him it would hurt less than getting shot. And then, securing his legs meant she had to put the gun down and use both hands.

She was twisting the wire around his left ankle when he lunged for her. Even handcuffed, he got hold of one of her arms and might have torn it out of its socket except the effort strained his groin. He let go of her and huddled on the floor again, retching. She finished trussing his feet and then tossed the pliers on the far side of the nearest tractor. He'd have to do a lot of squirming across the floor to get to it. She was guessing it would be a while before he felt up to that.

His communications device turned out to be on his belt. A wire ran up inside his jacket to where it had connected to his earpiece and microphone. She removed them while he suggested some things he'd like to do to her, none of which involved improving social relations. She reconnected the pieces, turned it on, and put the thing to her ear.

"...receiving me? Able? Speak to me, Able. What's going on?"

She switched the thing off again and asked him, "Are you Able?"

"Fuck you," he said.

She reminded him that he was in no condition to do that and she was responsible. She suggested she might be able to make it worse. He still wouldn't tell her who he was.

She patted him down, looking for a wallet or some other ID. He wasn't carrying any. She turned on the radio again.

"...check on Able," a voice said. "And see if there's trouble with our new visitors."

"No trouble, Delta, I've got them," another voice said. "Bravo, find Able, then come back to the house."

She didn't like the sound of that. Someone was coming to look for Able, and she was betting that "Fuck you" was actually Able. What she should do, she supposed, was disarm this next one, too, then go take on the voice in the house. But she couldn't count on the next one taking her so lightly, especially not if he got a look at Able. And if there was an Able, a Bravo, and a Delta, there had to be a Charlie around here somewhere, as well.

She thought about trying to hide him, but he was too big for her to drag anywhere, at least in the time frame she was probably dealing with. Instead, she decided not to do anything before she figured out how this gun worked.

She flipped Able a mock salute and faded into the warehouse, passing a window that let her look out on the yard. An Able look-alike, but for the blond hair, was trotting across the gravel from the house, sweeping his machine gun back and forth in case he spotted someone along the way. He was going to hit the front door in under a minute. She thought it would be a good idea if she took another exit. The sooner the better. She headed back toward the door she'd used to come in.

"Delta," a third voice whispered in her ear. "I'm almost back. I got cargo and passengers. Also a truck on my tail."

"Truck?" the second voice said.

"My passengers think it's the sheriff," the last voice said. "Let Able wait. Neutralize the truck."

Heather felt her heart flip. If it was Englishman, he was driving into an armed camp and he hadn't a clue. God! This could be exactly the situation she'd been so terrified of all day. She had to learn whether she could make this gun work and she had to do it now. She blew through the back door and saw someone with a gun duck around the south corner of the building. She pointed the weapon that way and squeezed the trigger and nearly fell over.

A line of holes appeared in the metal wall not far from where she'd aimed. They started about ground level and climbed fast. This thing had a hell of a kick.

"Able's gun," the first voice said. "Either Able's on to that girl or…."

Heather switched on her mic and said, "Or Able's dead. Special agent Starling, FBI. Your operation is surrounded. You will put down your weapons and come out of the house into the front yard with your hands up. And I mean now."

There was a pause, then one of the voices answered. "Is that you, Clarice?"

Shit. She should have come up with a better alias than Starling, but Jodie Foster's version of the FBI agent in *The Silence of the Lambs* was exactly who she wanted to be right now. Too bad the bastard had seen the movie or read the book.

"That's no Fed," he continued, "but our intruder has neutralized Able. Commence fallback one. I repeat, fallback one. Radio silence begins now."

Heather sprinted for the nearest corner of the building, threw herself around it, and spotted the Able look-alike running for the front of the house. He was the one who was supposed to take Englishman out. She pulled the trigger again and tried to hold the muzzle down until she landed on her backside. The guy wasn't there anymore, but there were all kind of holes in the window nearest the corner he had probably gone around. And a white car was turning her way down at the corner, a blue pickup right behind it. An old Chevy pickup. It was Englishman. It was Daddy.

The other Heather had been spending an altogether different afternoon. Her hosts had insisted she stay for lunch—chicken and beans and tortillas and salsa. She'd been raised to be polite and she and her sister had agreed to stay put and wait for the pros, so she accepted and discovered she was a lot hungrier than she'd thought. Not that she really intended to just hunker down and wait. But it seemed like a good idea to give the man with the gun a few minutes to stop searching for her. She ate quickly, though. Uncle Mad Dog was still a prisoner in that house, as far as she knew, and while the Highway Patrol might be on the way, she guessed her sister was out there, trying to save the day on her own. Heather Lane thought she could help.

"*Muchas gracias*," she told them. "That was wonderful. But I have to go."

Her announcement met with a chorus of protests. "Not now, *señorita*. That man, he could shoot you. He could shoot all of us, if he sees you leave here."

She hadn't thought of that. It was one thing to put herself at risk. Something else, again, to bring danger to the people who'd rescued her.

"Look," she said. "My sister's out there. And my uncle." They would understand family obligations. "Isn't there a way to sneak out of here?"

They looked sheepish and tried to pretend they didn't understand her, but she knew she was onto something.

"You've got a way into this adjacent warehouse, don't you?"

Well, they did, but that wasn't safe either. Who knew where the man with the gun might have gone?

She wheedled and cajoled and they finally agreed to let her out that way. It was a matter of clearing away some blankets they'd hung like tapestries, and some lumber they'd used to block a door. Heather wasn't concerned about how they'd rearranged things. She just wanted back out where she could size up the situation and decide what to do before her dad, inevitably, arrived.

"I will go with you," Xavier said. "Just in case. But we must be careful. And very quiet. You understand?"

She tried to talk him out of it, but he was insistent. He'd saved her once, she supposed. Now she was his responsibility.

"I understand," she said. "I will follow you."

On Xavier's instructions, his extended family turned off the lights and the TV and he spent an inordinate amount of time listening carefully after he cracked the door into the warehouse.

"Please?" she pleaded.

He put a finger to his lips. "Listen," he whispered. "Someone is in there."

Just the wind, she thought, putting her own ear near the door. But then she heard metal scraping against metal in a way the wind wasn't likely responsible for. And a voice. Not close, yet, but maybe coming this way.

"Mark?" it said. "Where are you? The bin. That was just a joke."

It wasn't the man with the gun. Not that she would recognize his voice. He hadn't even shouted at her, just pulled the trigger and chased her. But this voice she knew—Galen.

She didn't understand what he meant about Mark or a bin, but Galen didn't scare her all that much. Oh, she remembered he'd appeared to have a gun with which he'd forced Uncle Mad Dog into the house. But she thought she could handle Galen, if she had to.

Before Xavier could protest, she pushed the door open just far enough to slip through and ducked into the dusky warehouse. Xavier wasn't quick enough to catch her. That was good. She didn't want to put him in danger. She melted into the twilight before he could find her and she watched him shrug his shoulders and return to his family's home.

She almost turned around and followed him when a burst of machine-gun fire tore through the afternoon's stillness.

God! What did she think she was doing?

◇◇◇

They had found the front door to the house locked, so Greer just kicked it in.

He and Neuhauser had swung their guns to cover the big, mostly empty living room, then Dunbar, his campaign manager, came through a door and started shouting at them. The little man with the bad hair was not pleased to find them there. "I told you to stick around town. You need to get out of here. Go campaign or something."

The lieutenant hated being spoken down to. But Dunbar was the man who had persuaded him to run for sheriff, then organized the campaign and provided an endless channel of funding. That meant he had to be put up with.

Dunbar's shouting and the effort to hold his temper made Greer's head spin worse than before. He had to wait for the little man to run down before Greer could get a word in.

"Don't you know what's been happening in town?" Greer said.

"Of course I know. And it was good that you helped stop the shooting. People are calling you a hero. That's great PR. Go back and capitalize on it. You shouldn't be here."

Hero? It felt more like he'd made an ass of himself.

Dunbar put a hand to his ear, flipped a switch, and then spoke into his microphone. "No trouble, Delta, I've got them. Bravo, find Able, then come back to the house."

Dunbar went back to shooing them toward the door as he listened to the device in his ear. Another big man with a suit, sunglasses, and a machine gun went jogging past the front of the house.

"What's going on here?" Greer demanded.

"We've got an intruder," Dunbar said.

"That's what I've been trying to tell you," Greer said. "We're not the only ones you don't want here."

"You criticizing our security?" Dunbar sputtered. "After you're elected, maybe we'll consult you on matters like that. Today, it's not your business. Now be a good soldier and go back to town. Shake some hands or kiss some babies or catch that kid who shot up the school. Just go."

"That's why we're here, damn it! We followed the boy who hit the school to this farm."

Dunbar's jaw dropped. "You're kidding."

"I don't kid. That boy's here and he brought an AK-47 with him."

"No way," Dunbar said. "Our security would have...."

Before he finished, someone let loose a burst from an automatic weapon. Inside the living room, it was hard to tell where the shots had come from, but it was close. Dunbar looked shocked.

"That was no AK," Neuhauser said. "Maybe your security got him."

"There's someone else here, claiming to be an FBI agent," Dunbar said. The little man paled, then relaxed a little. "She's not for real, but one of our men isn't reporting. We don't know who fired those rounds."

"Let's take a look," Greer said. They turned toward the door.

"No, no!" Dunbar said. "You really have to leave this place."

"After I get Chucky Williams," Greer said, over his shoulder. That was a mistake, because it cost him his balance and he literally fell through the front door. Just as well, perhaps, since it kept him from shooting the armed man in the suit who came flying around the corner of the building. And it kept him from getting hit by the stream of bullets that followed.

The sheriff did a power slide that only lost a little ground to the Fusion at the corner east of Galen's. With the turn, the dust that had kept him from a clear view of the car he was following was carried away by the south wind. The Fusion continued to make fresh streams, but these blew across the road out over a plowed field.

The sheriff finally had a clear view of the Siegrist farm, too. There were people in Galen's front yard. Two hitting the ground.

A third, throwing himself toward the front door. Armed men. And he recognized the chatter of an automatic weapon.

He didn't recognize the men. He didn't have time because he had to maneuver around a silver Toyota that had gone nose first into the south ditch. Heather Two's Toyota. The doors were open and he managed to get a look inside as he flew by. She wasn't there. Nor was there any blood. But those were sure as hell bullet holes in her trunk.

One of the guys in the front yard rolled, trying to bring his gun to bear on the sheriff's truck. Or maybe on the Fusion. The sheriff couldn't tell. The Fusion slowed and made the turn into Galen's driveway. It went through an open garage door too fast, probably doing no good to the back wall or anything stored against it. The door started closing and the sheriff concentrated on getting the Chevy in the same driveway. He didn't aim for the garage, though. He went for where the gunmen were. Or had been. The three of them dove for the front door, went through as the sheriff's left front fender tried to follow. The fender was a bad fit, though it had been a convincing argument against staying in the yard and drawing a bead on him.

The sheriff slammed a shoulder into his door as he pulled the handle and rolled out onto the concrete, .38 up and ready to return fire from the house. None came, but he didn't like all those mirrored windows reflecting images of himself and giving no clue of who might be watching or aiming from the other side. The front door was not the place to go. Not with three well-armed suspects having just preceded him there. The garage was out, too, because all the doors were down and closed and there were likely armed men piling out of the Fusion just as he'd piled out of his Chevy. The front of the house didn't offer many options. There was only one other entrance, a window that had been broken out. He scrambled to his feet and made for it, expecting a line of bullets to climb his spine any second. They never came. He got a hand on the sill, leaped, dived, and landed rolling, ready to take on whoever was inside the room. It was empty.

Move fast, he told himself. You're seriously outnumbered. That means you've got to use the element of surprise. They probably knew this window was out. Though they might not have seen him come in here, they'd soon realize this was the most likely place for him to get in. So he had to move someplace else. Maybe find some of them before they got organized—start thinning the opposition.

It wasn't much of a plan, but you worked with what you had. He grabbed the door handle to start implementing it and discovered it was locked. And when he took a good look, he knew it was time for that backup plan he hadn't gotten around to yet. All the hardware, including a deadbolt, was on the other side. He hadn't found the perfect entry to Galen's house. He'd found the perfect trap.

Pam felt helpless. She was in a big, square, empty room. She'd gotten a brief glimpse of it before they slammed the door on her and left her in the dark. And it really was dark. The door sealed tight, even against the concrete floor. Maybe they'd shut off the light out in the basement hall, but there'd been a casement window at the end and it was daylight outside. She should be able to see something around the door frame. She couldn't.

It was because there was a rubber seal. She had to use her hands to find it. It was a good one. She couldn't get a decent hold on it to pull it loose. She couldn't even get a grip on it to pull it aside and let in a little light. Well, a little, once, when she got a fingernail under there, but long nails were inconvenient when you played a lot of piano and a little guitar. One brief glimmer, and then her nail had slipped before she'd been able to turn around and try to make out any weaknesses in her cell. No matter how hard she'd tried, she hadn't managed to get a nail under there again.

Cell, that was the right word for the room. It was like it had been prepared to hold someone—similar to that room where she and Mad Dog had been taken upstairs, only better.

There was nothing in here. She'd felt around for light switches or furniture or anything. Nothing. Just flat, smooth walls. And there didn't seem to be any casement windows in here. Only concrete or plaster where windows might have been.

Had Galen converted this room into a prison? She supposed it was possible. She'd always thought he was freaky. A religious fanatic who didn't like girls as people but lusted for their bodies. Were these rooms for...? No. There weren't any girls who'd gone missing in the county. Or nearby. She hadn't heard about anyone who'd been kidnapped and abused, then released. Besides, this room had a new feel to it. As if it had been prepared for something that hadn't happened yet. Was she that something?

She shook her head and tried to shut down her imagination. It didn't work. Not with all the spooky things that were going on. Maybe Galen hadn't built this room to imprison *her*, specifically, but it appeared he *had* built a prison.

She tried kicking the door. She tried shouting. She tried scraping at the plaster with her fingernails. None of it accomplished a thing. Not even when she jumped up and pounded her fists on the ceiling. Well, she did manage to crumble a little plaster and get particles in her hair and eyes.

Where was Mad Dog? He'd gotten away through that window. Then he'd sneaked back into this house. Why? Because they were still holding her, that's why. Had they caught him? Was he still looking for her?

Waiting here in the dark, both mentally and physically, was taking a toll. She wanted to scream, but what good would that do? If they heard her, it might make her captors smile. Or it might remind Galen of how helpless she was, and how desperate to escape. No, she wouldn't scream.

What would Mad Dog do? Well, she knew that. She'd seen him do it. He'd communicated with Hailey, asked for his wolf's help. And he'd gotten it. Sort of. Hailey had found them. She'd seen Hailey's nose appear on the glass exactly opposite Mad Dog's. Maybe Hailey really did have some kind magical abilities. And it wasn't like Pam had anything better to do.

She sat on the floor and assumed the lotus position. Wasn't that what Mad Dog had done? Remembering made her smile, because he'd had so much trouble getting her out of his head in order to concentrate. She had the same difficulty with him. He had wrinkles and scars and a bit of a belly, but more muscles than any of the guys she'd dated recently. And such a cute butt to go with his fascinating outlook on life. Did he like the way she looked as much as she admired him? Judging from his reaction in the grain bin, she thought so.

But this wasn't the way to contact a spirit. Not considering how Mad Dog had struggled to get her out of his mind when he tried for a connection with Hailey. She cleared her mind and tried to focus. She wished she'd paid more attention in those yoga classes she'd taken while she was at Ft. Hays State.

She made herself concentrate on a spot inside the middle of her head. She forced it to glow. That was her, Pam Epperson. That was her essence. Now where was Mad Dog's essence? She was surprised when she thought she recognized it. And not far away. She was pretty sure he was frightened about something. For her? For himself? She couldn't tell. She wasn't very good at this.

Where was Hailey? Mad Dog had told her Hailey's spirit was blinding, fiery. It burned in the psychic darkness like the comet whose name the wolf almost shared. Like, like something she suddenly thought she perceived. Right there. Just a few feet away.

Her eyes shot open and found only darkness. Darkness and disappointment. And a scratching sound. Right where she was looking.

She climbed to her feet and felt her way across the room. The scratching came from the wall opposite the door, up near the ceiling.

She reached up and found more concrete there. No. The consistency was different. And she could feel a vibration, as if something was scraping against it on the other side. She tried banging a fist on the spot. It was softer than concrete. It gave a little, and showered her with dust and particles—more plaster.

She banged again. And again. And the scratching on the other side got more frantic. And then there was a hole. Light. A wolf's muzzle. The upper half of Hailey's mouth came through, snatched plaster, and tore a hole that revealed dirt and fur and what had once been a casement window. And, with only a little more work, a path to Pam's freedom.

In retrospect, Deputy Heather thought she should have come up with a better strategy. Well, any strategy, really. What she'd done had simply been a reaction to events.

She'd come around the corner of the warehouse and seen the gunman she knew had been ordered to stop her father from getting to Galen Siegrist's house. And he was running in that direction. Englishman's truck, hard on the heels of a white Ford, was coming down the road, heading her way. And so she'd shot. And missed. And ended up on her butt in time to watch the Ford tear into the driveway and disappear in the vicinity of the garage. Her dad followed it, a bit wider through the curve, so he seemed headed for the front of the house. Englishman's Chevy disappeared to the accompaniment of a metallic crump that made her think he'd rammed something. Her angle was wrong to know for sure. She couldn't see around the west side of the building to know what might be happening in the front yard. And so she scrambled to her feet and ran, as hard as she could, to the northwest corner of the house. It was only after she got there that she realized she'd been a wide-open target if anyone inside had been doing sentry duty on the stretch of gravel she'd crossed.

There was a lot to see from the corner. A black Chevrolet was parked just short of the front door. Its doors were open but no one was inside.

Her dad's battered blue pickup was just beyond that, only inches short of filling the doorway. Judging from the way its front end was freshly crumpled, it had made contact before bouncing back. One of its doors was open and her dad wasn't in the pickup. He was sprinting along the front of the house toward that window where the glass was missing. She watched, relieved, as he dived in. No one shot at him on the way. No one shot at him after he was inside. In fact, it was eerily quiet at the edge of Galen's house, considering all the firepower she had reason to believe was guarding the place.

What now? It was a question she was becoming all too familiar with. There were too many windows in the front of the Siegrist place for her to cross the yard and join her father without getting caught or shot. Actually, there were too many windows on the side that faced the warehouse she'd just come from, but apparently no one had been looking out of them. Or no one had wanted to shoot her just then. That didn't mean they might not change their minds.

The nearest window had some holes in it. Ones she'd put there a few minutes before. She was willing to bet no one was behind it. Or, if they were, they'd be keeping a very low profile. Besides, she was short on options.

The window with the holes had the same reflective film as the rest of the glass in the Siegrist house. But one of the holes was down close to the corner nearest her. She took a deep breath and stuck her eye to the hole and tried to make sense of what was inside. Dark, mostly. Especially after the cheerful autumn sunshine on her side of the window. Then shadowy shapes began to make sense. That was a bed. And there was a dresser. And over against the far wall—that had been a TV before one of the bullets she'd put into the room turned it into hazardous waste. There didn't seem to be any people in there.

She stepped back and slammed the butt of her submachine gun against the glass. One of the cracks radiating from the nearest hole lengthened a few inches. The shock of the blow numbed her hands a little. Nobody shot at her, but it was going to take a lot of pounding to get in that room. That or a few more shots focused on that weakened corner. That would make a lot of noise and tell them she was coming.

Heather considered her cell phone. It was probably time to get those troopers on their way here. She flipped it open and began to punch numbers. And stopped, because there was a strange noise from back among the warehouses. A kind of rumbling sound, heavy and metallic, with an underlying hum that sounded like a big engine working.

She flattened herself against the wall and checked the warehouses she could see. Nothing moved out there. Nothing but a tumbleweed out for an afternoon stroll. And then metal screamed and the wall of one of those long metal buildings buckled, deformed, and collapsed. A monstrous metal blade appeared in its place, followed by a Caterpillar tractor. She hardly had time to take that in before the thing swung on its nearest set of treads and pointed itself and its blade straight at the house. The blade was raised a couple of feet off the ground, just far enough to make it impossible to see who was piloting the thing. She thought she knew, though. She'd seen that green corduroy shirt up close several times today. Chucky, it seemed, had found a surer way to get into the house than she had.

Mad Dog lay in the timeless dark. He was no longer on the floor. The nurse had assisted the doctor in lifting him onto some kind of gurney. Then they'd raised it and wheeled him somewhere more convenient. Some place well lit, if the glow on the other side of Mad Dog's eyelids was an indication.

"You want me to cut him out of these grubby clothes," the nurse asked. "Scrub him? Get him ready for surgery?"

"Yes," the doctor said. "Let's clean him up in case our other donors fail to arrive. He's not a good match for our primary patient, but we'll make do if we have to."

Mad Dog heard a snipping sound. Felt cool air wash across his leg, his hip, his side. The nurse was cutting him out of the coveralls.

"Catheter?" the nurse asked, as the last of the fabric was pulled away.

"Shouldn't be necessary."

A cool, damp cloth touched Mad Dog's face. His pre-surgical scrubbing had begun.

"Don't neglect his eyes," the doctor said.

Something chattered far away. An automatic weapon, maybe. After a few moments, he heard it again, slightly louder. That was followed by a thump, also distant, but somewhere in the house. Then a second thump, louder, nearer.

"I hope that's our donor," the doctor said. "I'll go check. Put our guest on a monitor. Make it look good." The man didn't seem to have noticed the gunfire. Had it been gunfire? Mad Dog wasn't sure, but he suspected he was more attuned to strange noises than his companions, considering the other sensory limitations he was experiencing.

Footsteps left the room. The respirator attached to Aldus P. Goodfellow whispered. The nurse continued his ministrations.

"Big fellow, aren't you?" the male nurse said. "I can see you've taken care of yourself. That's a benefit, though I suppose not for you anymore."

He washed everything, coolly, impersonally. It was about as pleasant as undergoing a major physical exam. Not that Mad Dog had trusted himself to western medicine in recent years. Not even to his friend Doc Jones.

While it went on, Mad Dog tried to take himself somewhere else. He'd managed, in that room upstairs, to establish some sort of contact with Hailey. He looked for her again. The touch of the damp cloth made the effort difficult. He fought for it, though. Not that he wanted Hailey to come for him again. There were too many guns in this house and, even if she managed to find him now, he couldn't move. There was no way she could get him out of this. But Pam....Pam was in danger because he'd brought her here. Maybe Hailey could rescue Pam. And for just a moment, he thought he touched both of them. The fire that was Hailey, the fresh vitality that was Pam. And then they were gone and he was just a helpless old man lying on a gurney as a nurse scrubbed him from head to toe.

After swabbing Mad Dog's feet, the man slid something soft and, no doubt, absorbent under Mad Dog's rear and up between his legs, then velcroed it on both sides.

"You may survive this," the nurse said as he attached leads to Mad Dog's torso and wrapped a cuff around an arm. "With a great deal of luck."

Light flashed in Mad Dog's right eye. He caught a glimpse of some kind of lamp and a shadowy figure hovering over him, and then eye drops spoiled his vision before his lid was closed again. He was ready when the procedure was repeated on the left eye, but ready didn't allow him to adjust to the light or focus before it was completed.

"Looks like you'll keep your heart and lungs. Liver and kidneys, too." Mad Dog was glad to hear that. But not what came next.

"Having your eyes harvested, though," the nurse said, "that will not be fun."

The sheriff was at a moment of indecision. He had lots of them, every day, but most didn't come with quite such deadly consequences. Should he go back out that window into what could easily be a killing zone? Or should he waste some of the precious few bullets he had in his .38, blowing the locks off that door separating him from what could be an equally hazardous area inside the house?

His mind was made up for him when someone released the dead bolt and a voice he recognized spoke from the other side of the door. "Don't shoot, Sheriff, it's only us."

He recognized their faces, too. Two old men in baseball caps, one pulled low to mask the hairlessness of advanced chemotherapy, the other, because that was the fashion for Kansas farmers these days. They were the blind man and the dying one, the pair Doc had rustled up for him when he desperately needed help covering exits so he could go into the high school after Chucky Williams. Lord, had that been just this morning? With all that had happened since, it seemed like years ago.

"What are you two doing here?" the sheriff asked.

"Come in that Ford you was following," the blind one said. He must not be able to see worth a damn, because he was pointing his shotgun at the sheriff's belly. English tried to edge aside, but the old man and the shotgun swiveled right along with him.

"How? I mean, I thought there were more bad guys in that Ford, not help for me."

"Bad guys depends which side you're on," the cancer patient said. "And it troubles me to tell you this, Sheriff, but you've made a mistake."

The sheriff didn't like the way this conversation was progressing. "But you two came the minute Doc found you. Risked your lives to help me stop Chucky. Why would you do that if…?" Hell, he didn't know what "if" was.

"It shames us, Sheriff, but there's this miracle worker here. A doctor who don't follow the rules. He's promised to give me my sight back."

"And cure my cancer," the other old-timer said. "We paid pretty near every cent we've got for this, then your crazy deputy ran that car off the road before he hit the bus this morning and spoiled everything."

"We was over to Klausen's to recover the body," the blind one said, "the one from the wreck. See if anything could still be salvaged. Doc come by there to get his gun. Told us you was looking for Chucky, so we come along 'cause…."

It was starting to make sense. "'Cause Chucky was the back up," the sheriff said. "The donor who would stand in, just in case."

The cancer patient raised his deer rifle until it was centered on the sheriff's chest. "I always said you're a lot sharper lawman than this county deserves. I told these folks we're working with not to underestimate you. Well, now we need to relieve you of that pistol. Take you downstairs for some tests. See if you maybe match up with his eyes or my bone marrow."

A terrible metallic shriek penetrated the room. It was a distant noise, but so unnatural that they all reacted to it. The old man with the deer rifle started to swing toward the open window. The sheriff dropped his pistol and stepped in and got one hand on the rifle and the other on the shotgun and managed to put his body inside the reach of either weapon's muzzle.

"Drop your guns," someone yelled.

The blind man discharged his shotgun, instead, tearing a hole in the plaster.

Another gun answered. Two shots.

The blind man's face exploded. He would need more than eyes, now. And the sheriff needed something to wipe the results off his face.

Both the shotgun and the rifle came free in the sheriff's hand. He swung toward the cancer patient only to discover the man had suffered similar damage. There was a hole leaking blood just in front of one ear. The other side of his face was splattered over the door they'd come through.

The sheriff turned toward the window, the only place the shots could have come from. He was still trying to grasp what had happened. How could two old farmers have turned so desperate that they were willing to kill for a chance at health? And how could their lives have ended so suddenly, just as he was about to disarm them?

A big man, back-lit, stood in the window, weapon still to his shoulder. The sheriff recognized him before he spoke.

"That's right, English. The next sheriff of Benteen County just saved your ass."

"You didn't have to…," the sheriff began. He'd planned to continue that with *kill them*.

"I owed you one from that fiasco over at the school," Greer said, climbing in the window. He pulled a bandana out of a pocket and wiped the sheriff's face. "And for playing this whole campaign so nasty. But that's just politics. Come on. Let's clear this house. Chucky Williams is around here somewhere. As well as a bunch of hired killers."

Someone had filled the casement window with dirt, replaced the glass with plywood, and plastered it over from the inside.

How had Hailey managed to find it, let alone move all that earth and tear the wood away? All Pam had needed to do to help the wolf was shatter a little plaster, something Hailey could have quickly accomplished by herself.

It only took a couple of minutes to open the hole wide enough for Pam to crawl through, though it took a lot of twisting and wiggling to get out.

She hugged the wolf and thanked her and received a big sloppy kiss in return. But Hailey wasn't interested in being hugged. And that made sense. They were under a series of windows that looked out across the yard toward the bins and warehouses. Easily spotted if someone happened to look out and down.

Hailey whined and grabbed the sleeve of Pam's overalls, pulling her along the side of the building. Mad Dog's wolf seemed to have more of a plan than she did. Pam followed. After no more than a few feet, she understood why. Steps led down to another hole in the ground. This one had been dug by the people who built this house, an outside entrance to the basement.

Pam followed Hailey down concrete stairs to the thick steel door at the base. There were scratches around the handle and along the bottom. Hailey had been here before. The big silver-tipped wolf dug at the corner of the door for a moment. Then she put her mouth on the handle and twisted. The door didn't budge and Hailey turned and looked back at Pam and whined.

"I don't know if I can help you with this one," Pam said. If the wonder wolf couldn't get in, what chance did a would-be Vegas lounge-act have? Still, she tried the handle. Locked, of course. She examined the door for weaknesses. She didn't see any.

Hailey scratched at the door again, impatient, as if to say, *Why did I bother rescuing you if you can't be of more help than this?*

Something shrieked in the yard behind them. Hailey continued to worry at the door, unconcerned. But Pam knew that sound wasn't caused by anything natural. She climbed back up enough steps to peer into the farm yard. A wall was missing from one of the metal warehouses, and a Caterpillar was slowly crawling across the yard toward the house, blade raised so she couldn't see who was driving. If that thing kept coming, she and Hailey would soon have another opportunity for getting inside.

Someone else must have realized that. The kitchen door slammed open, only a few feet to her right. A couple of muzzles emerged and she ducked just as several hundred rounds went singing off toward the metallic monster advancing on the house. She heard bullets ricochet off steel even over the racket of the weapons. Pam raised her head again, just far enough to see that the bulldozer was still coming. Its blade not only hid and protected whoever was driving it, but hid and protected the radiator and engine block as well. The only moving parts she could see were the tracks. Those weren't going to be troubled by anything smaller than an artillery round. Maybe not even that.

The shooting from the house stopped. The men inside must have realized the same thing. They were going to have to find a better way to stop that thing. And then she saw a flash of something just over the top of the bulldozer's blade. The driver had an automatic weapon of his own. Chips of brick, wood, glass and concrete exploded from around the kitchen door. A second batch tore up dirt in front of her face and convinced her to stop peeking and get back down and concentrate on that door with Hailey.

The guy on the bulldozer had seen her. Whatever chance she and Hailey might have had to make a run from this entry to the cellar was gone. And now, the guy on the bulldozer might come after them here. Or, when he got close enough, be able to shoot down into the stairwell and remove wonder wolf and friend from his list of problems.

Why wasn't there a mat down here? People always kept keys hidden under the mat, didn't they? Instead, the bottom of this stairwell was a steel grate over some kind of drainage so the first hard rain didn't turn the well into a miniature lap pool.

What about the grate? She got down on her hands and knees and examined it. No, it was solidly implanted in the concrete that surrounded it. But there was one peculiarity. A bent paper clip was hooked over one of the steel bars. She grabbed it and lifted and found exactly what was supposed to be under a mat.

"Voila," she told Hailey, and inserted the key in the lock and turned it. Another round of gunfire erupted from the kitchen. Return fire from the bulldozer whined off the top of the door as Pam opened it and followed Hailey into the dark room beyond.

Heather Number Two had never imagined modern farming required the kinds of machinery she discovered in the warehouse. Not that she made those discoveries very quickly. She'd just slipped away from Xavier and his friends when a burst of machine-gun fire sent her diving under the nearest piece of equipment—a backhoe with a bucket that looked big enough to trench your way to China. Actually, she spent most of her first few minutes under it studying one of the tires up close, because that first burst of gunfire had been followed, moments later, by a second. It hadn't sounded close, though. Not as close as the first rounds. And there weren't any more immediately after.

She thought she heard some cars, but it could easily have been the wind trying to slip breezy fingers under the metal panels of the building. The place groaned and creaked and when she thought she heard footsteps on the other side of the backhoe, she didn't believe they were real. Not until she noticed the feet that accompanied them.

Heather scooted a little to the right and kept the tire between her and whoever those feet belonged to. It might be Xavier, though she thought he would be coming from the other direction if he'd been foolish enough to follow her out here.

More likely, it was Galen. But it could be the guy with the gun, too, so she took her time and risked a peek only after he was moving away from her.

It was Galen, sure enough, and headed toward a dusty window, likely as curious as she was about that gunfire. There was a tall metal cabinet up against the side of the window. He kept most of his body behind it while he craned his head around to see out toward the back of his house and the farm yard in between. She rolled over to the other side of the backhoe and moved behind another colossal tire that was closer to Galen. He had pulled a bandana out of his pocket and was using it to scrub at the window. He had a pistol in the other hand. Even if the gun had been temporarily out of play, she wasn't sure she could take him bare-handed. He was bigger than she was and, damn it, guys were just naturally stronger. She was probably better trained, though she hadn't ever been as good as her sister at martial arts. It had been more than a year since she'd taken a class or done anything but exchange a few playful kicks with One.

A shotgun would be nice, since she didn't like guns and wasn't much good with them. Englishman had made sure both his daughters could shoot, but he hadn't forced either of them to do more than understand the basics. One was better than she was with guns, too.

Of course, there weren't any shotguns lying around. A broom and a shovel lay nearby, however, just a few yards from the wall where Galen was peering into the yard. Someone might have planned to use them to clean out the clods of earth that still clung to the backhoe's bucket. The broom wouldn't do her much good, but the shovel might.

"Heather," Galen said.

Oh shit, she thought, flattening herself back behind that tire. He'd seen her. Caught her reflection in the window somehow. But he didn't say anything else, like come out of there with your hands up. When she got her nerve back enough, she peeked around the tire. He was fumbling a cell phone out of his pocket, not looking in her direction.

Maybe he'd seen her sister out there somewhere. If so, he was planning to tell someone.

A starter turned over not far away. It froze both of them for a moment, and then Galen was moving along the wall, ducking past the cab of a semi truck parked on the other side of the backhoe. He folded the phone and put it back in a pocket. Heather darted to the wall, got the shovel and followed.

An engine fired up. Something big, but she'd expected that from the sound the starter made. Galen passed several more machines and then ducked around a dump truck big enough to handle ore instead of grain.

The big engine revved a couple of times. It wasn't as close as she'd thought. At the far end of the warehouse, most likely. She sprinted after Galen. He wasn't paying any attention to what was behind him, but he was sprinting now, too.

She followed him around the back of the first of a row of shiny new combines, just as the pitch of the engine changed yet again. Lower, throatier, it was taking on a load. She heard metal grate on concrete and then metal on metal, shrieking, as some of that metal tore.

Heather saw it then. Big and yellow and moving not much faster than she could trot. It was a Caterpillar, and someone had just decided to drive it through the wall of the warehouse.

Galen stopped. His gun hand came up, but too late. The cab followed the rest of that hulking machine out into the farm yard.

Heather slowed, swung the shovel back. She wanted to hit Galen's gun arm. She didn't want to bean him. That might kill him.

She was ready to swing when he started sprinting again. It took her a moment to follow.

Galen ran straight to the middle of the hole in the wall. He brought the gun up again. He was going to shoot whoever was driving that Caterpillar in the back. She went full out, bringing the shovel off her shoulder in a sweeping blow. He realized she was there at the last instant and jumped and the flat of the shovel slammed into his shoulder instead of his arm because he'd tried to aim the gun at her instead. It didn't matter. He howled as the gun went skittering across the building's concrete floor. And then a hail of bullets came screaming through the opening the Cat had torn as it exited. Someone was shooting at it, from the house, and that put Galen and her in the line of fire.

She hadn't even noticed the other Caterpillar until she turned around to run. Another, smaller one, with its blade resting on the floor. The perfect shield, and she dove for it. Something slapped her on the hip before she got there and sent her rolling into the treads instead of fully behind the blade. Her leg went numb and she felt something moist running down her hip and thought she was hit. But she couldn't make herself check her own wound. Her eyes were locked on Galen, now doubled over on the concrete, holding his belly with his one good hand. The hand wasn't enough. Something wet and ropy oozed around it and spoiled the floor. So did Two's lunch.

Greer went through the door, low, covering the hall leading into the house, but swiveling to look back toward the garage. English might have shot Greer if the sheriff hadn't dropped his pistol to grab guns from the two men who lay on the floor at his feet and stained the carpet.

If he had, it only would have been to wound. And even that was just something he liked to imagine. He needed help, as usual. Also, as usual, the kind he'd get wasn't what he'd had in mind. For the moment, it seemed, he'd have to put up with Greer's cowboy, shoot-first style.

The sheriff dropped the long arms on their recently deceased owners and recovered his pistol. Then he followed Greer into the hall.

"Check the garage," Greer said.

"Check it yourself," the sheriff nearly answered. But Greer was the expert on house-to-house combat, so English nodded and said something else. "Several innocent and unarmed civilians may be here. Don't shoot anyone unless you absolutely have to."

Greer grinned. "You either. Neuhauser's in there with these hired guns. He'll back our play when we get to them."

Oh good, the sheriff thought. The guy who'd pulled a gun on him earlier this afternoon was going to have the opportunity to do it again. But he didn't say anything. He ducked down the hall and went into the garage. There were three vehicles in it. The white Ford he'd followed here hadn't quite managed to stop before it flattened its front end against the back wall. Its trunk was open. There was a dead body in there, and a trussed up and angry highway patrolman. Englishman recognized them both, the boy from the accident and the asshole who'd taken pot shots at his daughter in the school parking lot. He left them both where they were.

Next was a Dodge station wagon, similar to the one Deputy Wynn had chased across the county until he ran into that school bus. And last, an emergency medical services truck, the kind city fire departments use to respond to 911 calls. This one was marked AMBULANCE, though with no indication of a jurisdiction.

The ambulance took longer because he had to open the back and make sure no one was inside. Greer was at the door between the house and the garage when the sheriff finished his sweep.

"I was beginning to think you ran into problems…or just ran."

"Garage is clear," the sheriff told him. "You want to take the left side of the hall and leave the right to me, or you want back-up at each room?"

"Let's each work doors. I think everybody's in the kitchen where the action is, but when we go in there we need to know our backs are clear."

The first door on the sheriff's right was the one with the two dead farmers in it. With the window out, someone else could have entered, so he gave it a quick look again.

The next room held a pair of single beds with personal items scattered about. Two people were using the room, if the pair of duffel bags was an indication.

Next, a bathroom, surprisingly feminine. In it, four tooth brushes and shaving kits were neatly laid out military style. The men guarding this house weren't mobsters. They were professionals. Government? Military? Mercenaries? He waved Greer over. "Pros," he said.

"Yeah," Greer said. "We knew one of them in Iraq. A hired gun."

They each had one more room to sweep. The sheriff's had a small bathroom of its own. Someone had gotten preferential treatment, but not a squad leader. There were suitcases in this room, enough clothes to last a month. The double bed wasn't made and the bathroom was messy. This guy might have hired the others, but he wasn't their equal.

"Three people living in the rooms on my side," the sheriff said. "Five toothbrushes in two bathrooms, though."

"Two sharing one room on my side. The other rooms were empty."

"So five, anyway, and Galen Siegrist," the sheriff said.

Greer shrugged. "There's another wing."

They were at the spot where the hall opened out onto the living room, which was also empty. There was one more door, the kitchen most likely. That's where the shooting had been coming from. It was quiet now, except for the throaty rumble of a big motor.

Greer offered a grenade to the sheriff. "Flash-bang?" he said.

The sheriff declined.

"Okay, then. Follow me."

Greer put a shoulder to the door. The sheriff followed, but Greer didn't clear the doorway.

"Damn," the lieutenant said. "You again?" And then, "What's with the bulldozer?"

With so many other weapons going off, Deputy Heather decided a quick burst into the window she'd already damaged wasn't likely to be noticed. She pointed the gun at the bottom edge of the glass and tapped the trigger. The tap resulted in four shots, and a new series of holes radiating spider-web cracks more or less where she wanted them. She used the gun's butt to turn the cracks and holes into an opening big enough for her, then followed the gun into the room.

It was a master bedroom, complete with a pretty fancy bath containing a custom shower and a whirlpool tub. The bed was neatly made, but there was nothing to personalize the room. It had all the mandatory furniture, but the only things that told her Galen Siegrist slept here were pictures of his parents and a pair of portraits on the wall. One was a Jesus whose features appeared more Nordic than Semitic. The other was an angry old man she thought she should recognize but didn't. She wasted no time on drawers or closets. She had one thing to do—make sure nothing bad happened to her father.

The bedroom door opened onto an empty hall and across from it, an office—unused. Galen must prefer the one in the warehouse. It was a big office, though, with windows facing west and south. The bulldozer was walking across the farm yard behind the house, slowly closing the distance between itself and the people who were spraying it with machine-gun fire. She slipped back into the long hall, down which the sound of that gunfire echoed. She followed it, checking the rooms on either side as she went. A second master suite, also occupied, though from the look of the suitcase, temporarily, and another, smaller bedroom with its own bath. More suitcases, so it was also being used by someone passing through. There were stairs to the basement, as well, and then a formal dining area off which a vast and empty living room opened on a door to the front yard and the nose of her father's pickup. No people, though, so she focused on the swinging door she thought must lead to the kitchen.

She paused there. When she went through, she needed to do it right. She moved her badge from inside her jacket and pinned it over her heart. She checked her weapon. She didn't know much about it. She knew it used bullets in a big hurry and that she would inevitably run out before long if she continued pressing that trigger. It seemed to have a pretty large magazine, though, and all the automatics she knew about always locked the breech open when they'd fired their last shell. This one's breech was just the way it had been before she'd hosed a couple of buildings and blown out a window. What was still in there would have to be enough. Especially since she didn't intend to shoot anyone.

Heather took a deep breath, put her foot in the middle of the door, and kicked. She followed her foot into the room—it was the kitchen—and she arrived at a particularly opportune moment. One of the gunmen was in the middle of exchanging clips. He was kneeling beside the back door with an empty gun in one hand and a full magazine in another. When he saw her, he dropped them both. Another gunman had his back to the wall by a kitchen window, his head turned away from her and toward his comrade. When he saw his friend drop his weapon, he did the same.

There were three other men in the room. One of them was Lieutenant Greer's buddy, Neuhauser. Another looked faintly familiar—a little, middle-aged guy who was balding and had one of those haircuts designed to hide the fact, though it simply looked silly. The third was a stranger, a big guy like the two she'd just disarmed by appearing where and when she had.

Neuhauser was on the other side of a counter that extended into the room like a peninsula. He surprised her by swinging his weapon to cover the two who were still armed. The little bald guy froze, but the big one moved like a cat. He snaked an arm out and grabbed the little guy and pulled him back into the opening of a stairwell. She had plenty of time to shoot them, and Neuhauser looked to be on the verge of it when a burst of return fire from the bulldozer tore through the already ruined windows and turned part of the kitchen cabinets into wood chips. The big one and the bald one were gone down the steps when she managed to refocus on them. And one of the other big guys was trying to sneak a hand inside his coat. She let her gun slide over to point directly at him and shook her head. At that moment, Lieutenant Greer burst into the room from another door in the far wall.

"Damn," the lieutenant said when he saw her. "You again?" And then he looked out the back windows and added, "What's with the bulldozer?"

A timely question, since the thing was only a few yards away now, and headed straight for them.

Greer stood in the door and blocked the sheriff from entering the kitchen. The lieutenant couldn't believe it. The English girl had beaten him again. Was she that good, or just that lucky?

"Get their guns," he told Neuhauser. "Then herd them out front." He nodded toward the bulldozer. "We need to be out of here when that thing arrives."

"What's going on in there?" the sheriff said from directly behind him.

"Two more, still armed, went into the basement," Neuhauser said, kicking guns aside, and putting the two big guys up against the wall while he patted them down and confiscated a pair of pistols and knives. He ripped out their radio equipment and battery packs, too. And by the time Neuhauser shoved them toward the living room, the English girl had slipped back through the swinging door on the other side of the room just before her father bulled his way in.

"Leave the ones in the basement, for now," the sheriff said the moment he saw the Caterpillar. "If that thing comes through the wall, the floor in here won't hold it."

Greer hadn't thought of that. He'd planned on letting Neuhauser and the sheriff take these two out front and put them in custody somehow, while he went after the ones downstairs. The sheriff's observation changed his mind. Besides, he didn't especially care about this private little army. Chucky Williams was who he wanted. And Chucky wasn't one of those who'd just gone where the bulldozer might soon be following. In fact, if he had to guess, Chucky was most likely driving the thing.

"You heard the sheriff," he told Neuhauser and the prisoners. "Out front, now."

Greer led the way, backing across the front room and then scrambling over the hood of the sheriff's truck, all the while keeping the pair of hired gunmen covered. They came next in the little parade, followed by Neuhauser and finally the sheriff.

"Where you want 'em?" Greer asked, as the sheriff's head emerged over the hood of his truck.

"In the ditch, other side of the road," the sheriff said. "You guys have any grenades that'll stop that thing if it does get through the house?"

Greer didn't answer. He'd used the sheriff's distraction at climbing over the hood to signal Neuhauser and sprint toward the nearest corner of the house.

Newt got the message. "Probably can't stop it," Neuhauser said, occupying the sheriff's attention, "but we can sure make things unpleasant for whoever's driving it."

The Cat hit the building as Greer went around the back corner. The earth shook and the building moaned and things started collapsing. The lieutenant found the open window on the Caterpillar's cab over the sight of his M-4. He fired a grenade. The explosion and shrapnel cleansed the interior. The machine rocked when the grenade blew, but kept moving, and the back wall of the Siegrist place collapsed in a heap of bricks and mortar.

Greer swiveled his gun, looking for a target. Chucky Williams hadn't been in the smoking ruin that had once been the Cat's cab. The machine was on its own.

When the doctor came back down into the basement, Mad Dog thought his voice was shriller and he was breathing too fast.

"Customers are here," the man said. "But the place is under assault. Law enforcement, maybe. We must be ready in case we have to leave suddenly."

"Our security," the nurse said, "those men are professionals." It sounded like he was trying to convince himself.

"Yes," the doctor agreed. "Maybe," then he laughed. "Look what they brought me." Mad Dog heard him open something. Plastic on plastic.

"My God," the nurse said. "Are those…?"

"Autopsied organs," the doctor agreed. "From our primary donor. The rest of him is upstairs in the trunk of a car."

"Good thing we're in Kansas," the nurse said. "You could never pull this off anywhere else."

"I don't know," the doctor replied. "When lives are at stake, most people are prepared to suspend disbelief."

The two stopped talking after that, though they moved around a lot and Mad Dog could hear cases opening and closing, metal things, surgical tools, he suspected, being placed on cloth-draped trays. His gurney was moved, pushed nearer to where the reverend lay. The hiss of the breathing machine got closer and he could tell, even through closed lids, that he was under very bright lights now.

Mad Dog could hear gunfire from all over. And something big was moving, shaking the ground. He couldn't imagine what that might be. It must have felt like this when the great buffalo herds stampeded—like Maheo, the Cheyenne All-Father, was striding the earth.

Feet came rushing down a set of stairs. A door slammed. A bolt was thrown. A new voice spoke.

"Law just took down Bravo and Delta. At least three cops, up in the kitchen. My guess is they got your customers, too."

"Good thing we collect a large down payment," the nurse said.

The doctor was concerned about other things. "Are we safe down here?"

"Doubt it," the new voice said. "I recommend a withdrawal."

"No. You can't do that." Yet another voice, but Mad Dog had heard this one before. It belonged to the rude little man with bad hair who'd evicted him from Christ Risen that morning.

"The Reverend Goodfellow needs a new heart and lungs. Isn't that right, doctor?"

"Well, yes. Kidneys and liver, too. But...."

"And you," the guy with the bad hair said. "We hired you to get the reverend and this medical team in and out of here and to maintain security while the surgeries take place."

"Yes, sir. You did."

"Then I expect you to see that the doctor is undisturbed while the operation proceeds."

"I can't operate under circumstances like this," the doctor said.

"Why not? You're all set up. You have a donor."

"Well, this man was suitable for the eyes and bone marrow for my other two patients. He is not a match for your good reverend."

"Why's that?" The bad hair guy was getting hysterical. And it was increasingly hard to hear over a noise that sounded like metal striking stone. The house groaned and Mad Dog barely heard the doctor's reply.

"He's a kaffir."

Bricks were falling nearby. The earth was shaking, literally. Mad Dog felt dust sifting onto his face.

"Kaffir?"

"He's not racially pure."

Beams cracked. Ceiling plaster fell.

Someone screamed, "Run!"

An avalanche cascaded into the basement. Something massive and metallic and sharp sliced its way through the ceiling like a gigantic guillotine. It landed only a few feet away, then began inching toward the gurney where Mad Dog lay.

Run. That sounded like good advice. But Mad Dog was still paralyzed. He couldn't even open his eyes to see what was coming to kill him.

Hailey led Pam into a storage room. Its walls were lined with shelves, still empty, since Galen hadn't filled the rest of his oversized house. Pam slammed the metal door behind them and closed them in inky blackness. But this time, she'd noticed light switches on the wall beside her. And, this time, they worked. Bullets pinged off the door behind her but failed to penetrate. Still, with the floor under her feet beginning to vibrate as the Caterpillar drew closer, the room hardly felt safe.

Another door stood in the wall across the room. It should open onto the hall at the base of the stairs she had been brought down. She thought she remembered seeing it before they locked her in the blacked-out prison room.

Pam started for it, but Hailey blocked her path.

"Mad Dog's out there," she told the wolf. "He needs us."

Hailey didn't move, or she didn't move out of the way. Instead, she crowded against Pam's legs and forced her back toward the corner east of the door they'd entered.

"What are you doing?" Pam complained, but there was no getting around the hundred-pound timber wolf. Pam felt like a sheep being herded into a pen. Hailey pushed and Pam stumbled until her back rested against the shelves. "Hailey, stop it," she demanded.

The shelves vibrated, jumped. She felt the bulldozer hit the building. The lights went out and they were back in darkness and things were collapsing around them. A huge beam slammed to the floor next to them, followed by all manner of debris—broken two-by-fours, plasterboard, carpeted flooring, even pieces of roof. And she could see all of it because sunlight was pouring in from where the ceiling used to be. Someone—she thought it looked like that Williams kid, but with all the dust she wasn't sure—walked through the hole where the south wall had been and clambered over the debris to the door she'd planned on using to search for Mad Dog.

It opened and two men in suits were just beyond.

Hailey grabbed Pam's arm in her mouth and pulled, hard enough to hurt. Pam went down, banging her head against the broken beam. She couldn't believe Hailey was doing this to her, but then the shelves above her head exploded as someone emptied a clip into the spot she'd just occupied. Another gun was speaking, too, in a different voice. Someone screamed in pain or terror and Pam was surprised it wasn't her.

The second gun, the one that hadn't been aimed toward her, spoke again, short and terse. And then the guns were quiet, but the bulldozer wasn't. It was still moving. Pam couldn't see it, but she could feel its treads clawing at the floor as its blade bit the same surface. That thing had to be stopped. It could bring the whole house down.

"Mad Dog's still in there," she told Hailey, as she began trying to crawl out of the hole in which they'd nearly been buried. She scrambled up onto the beam and felt it give a little and turned back to help Hailey up the pile. The hole was empty. Hailey was already gone.

Deputy Heather lay on the staircase and tried to remember where she was and how she'd gotten there. She'd left her prisoners in the care of Greer and his buddy in the kitchen. She'd ducked back through the dining room and made for the staircase at the entrance to the hall, planning to go down and find Uncle Mad Dog and deal with the pair of armed men who'd taken the other stairs. And she'd intended to do all that before Englishman got there.

She was on the stairs—she remembered now—when the earth moved. And not the way Hemingway described it.

The bulldozer must have collided with the house, and closer than she'd expected. The lights flickered and died and things had begun falling. Including her, apparently.

Her head hurt. When she put her hand to her scalp she found a swollen place back near her crown that was leaking a little blood.

How long had she been out? Not long. At least not long enough for any of the people running around this farm with guns to find her. And not long enough for the dust to settle, or the bulldozer to finish making its way through the house. She could hear it, just the other side of a plaster wall that hadn't been open to the sky when she started down here.

She scrambled to her feet, felt her knees go wobbly, and braced herself against a banister. She didn't have time for this. She stepped over a pile of rubble and around the end of a wall and found herself next to the machine's blade.

Sunlight flooded the basement, but she couldn't see anyone. The big Cat had gouged a hole in the basement floor from which the rest of the blade protruded high enough to block her view of everything beyond.

A pair of guns erupted nearby and she remembered that she'd had one of her own when she started down here. She looked back and found it protruding from under a clump of bricks. She went back and bent to retrieve it and the woozy returned, but not as bad as before. Just as well. She had things to do down here.

Heather had to squeeze past the splintered dining room table at the bottom of the stairs. She could see things now. A bed…no, a bed and a gurney, with two pair of feet, one on each of them, just beyond the edge of the Caterpillar's blade. She slipped forward, gun ready. Someone else down here was armed. And then she heard voices. Clear, loud, in the sudden silence as the bulldozer's engine died.

"Throw your gun down or I'll slit the Reverend Goodfellow's throat." The voice had a little bit of an accent. Not one she recognized.

The one that answered, though, belonged to Chucky Williams.

"You'll be doing me a favor. He's on my list."

Two more steps and she could see the man with the accent. He was tall and aristocratic and surprised. Adaptable, though, because he shifted his scalpel to the neck of the figure on the gurney. "This man, then. Do you care if I kill him?"

It took her a moment to recognize that the man's second choice was Uncle Mad Dog. Too many tubes and wires, and she wasn't used to seeing him stretched out utterly still, naked but for some kind of glorified diaper.

"That's your decision. I plan to kill you either way."

The man with the scalpel didn't get a chance to make good on his threat. Hailey exploded from the staircase behind Heather. The wolf dropped something from her mouth—an electrical relay and a clump of broken wires. Could that be why the bulldozer stopped? Hailey crossed the room and leaped onto Mad Dog's gurney. Her jaws closed around the wrist holding the blade. Heather heard bones snap. The man fell back onto the bed with his other patient, frantically kicking and trying to fend off the timber wolf. His scalpel rang as it hit the floor and bounced under the bed. Hailey was just as suddenly off him and tearing at the tubes and wires connected to Mad Dog. They fared even worse than the man's arm. She held one end of a tube in her mouth while it dribbled clear liquid onto the floor. Her hackles were raised and her eyes swung back and forth between the man she'd attacked and Chucky. And then her legs splayed out from under her and she sprawled on Mad Dog's chest.

"My God," the man whose arm Hailey had broken said. "What was that?"

"A wolf," Chucky said. "The man whose throat you were about to cut, Doctor—he's her person. She wasn't going to let you do that. It looks like whatever was in the IV may keep her from killing you if you try again. So I guess that's up to me."

There was a panicky quality to the doctor's voice now. "Why kill me? I can make it worth your while to let me go."

"What I want, you can't give me," Chucky said. Heather edged farther into the room. She'd spotted the big man who'd run down the stairs from the kitchen. Someone, Chucky probably, had run a row of bullets across his chest and turned it to pulp. And, beside him, whimpering quietly, was the little man with the bad hair. He'd been shot, too, but just in the legs. Well, considering the way they twisted now, maybe "just" wasn't the right word. Both those men's guns lay on the floor, but well beyond their reach. Not that either of them was capable of the effort. The guns were a long way from the man who'd had the scalpel, too.

"I have access to great quantities of money, and I'm a surgeon. I can perform miracles."

"Miracles?" Chucky seemed to consider that. "Can you raise the dead?" Heather had reached a spot where she could see Chucky now. He waved the muzzle of his automatic rifle over toward the big man with the holes in his chest. "Start with him. If you can bring him back, and all the others I've left behind me today, we may have something to discuss."

Heather had the drop on him. It seemed like a good moment.

"Put the gun down, Chucky," Heather said. "He isn't bringing anybody back and you aren't adding any more."

"Hi, Heather." He didn't seem surprised by her presence. He didn't seem inclined to obey her, either.

"I mean it. Drop your gun."

"I'm sorry, Heather. I'd like to. But you won't shoot me if I don't. Even though you'd be doing me a favor. I've got nothing to live for once I take care of the doctor, here, and the Reverend Goodfellow. Except for maybe finishing off the little guy over there, and going to make sure of Galen."

"Shoot him, officer." The doctor had seen the badge on her lapel. "You heard him. Otherwise he'll kill me."

Would he? Heather never would have believed it. But Chucky had left a trail of bodies behind him this morning.

"Shoot him now," the doctor squealed.

Chucky was right. She couldn't do it. He was still the little boy she'd babysat for. The one who'd made her check his closet and under his bed for the demons he was sure were going to get him. After this morning, she wondered if they finally had. She tried to see the evil in his eyes. All she could find was the frightened little boy she remembered.

"See," Chucky told her. "You can't."

"Maybe she can't." The voice came from just behind Heather's shoulder. "But I can."

◇◇◇

Sheriff English wormed his way out onto the precipice that used to be the living room floor. He hadn't noticed how alarmingly it creaked until the motor died on the Caterpillar. Then the conversation between Chucky and the doctor, and his daughter's intervention, overwhelmed any concerns he had about a cave-in.

He'd just gotten to a spot where he could peer down into the ruin below. He could see Mad Dog and Hailey on a gurney. He could see part of the doctor and the foot of a hospital bed. He could see Heather. He didn't need to see the guy who'd spoken, though. He knew his would-be replacement's voice all too well.

"I expect that's true, Lieutenant Greer." Chucky sounded sincere, but unafraid. The boy might be almost ready to die. But the sheriff didn't think Chucky intended to let it happen until the old evangelist and the doctor preceded him.

"I'd rather take you alive," Greer said, stepping out from behind the sheriff's daughter.

"Why?" Chucky seemed honestly puzzled.

"I don't know," Greer admitted. "Maybe a live prisoner will get me a few more votes than a corpse."

Chucky smiled. "At least you're honest," he said. "Let's bargain. How about you let me kill the doctor and the Reverend Aldus P. Goodfellow first? Then I'll give myself up?"

"You've got nothing to bargain with," Greer said.

"Actually," Chucky said, "I do." The sheriff wondered what with. Chucky's gun was aimed just in front of his feet. No way he'd be able to get it up to take Greer, or anyone else, before the lieutenant blew him all over the basement. "I've got this."

There was something about the rubble in front of Chucky. Something the sheriff should recognize.

"Don't kill me," another voice said. Chucky's hand, the one that wasn't holding the gun, yanked something up off the floor in front of him. Not something, someone—a pale man in scrubs. Another doctor? A male nurse? Whoever he was, he was suddenly between Chucky and the lieutenant.

"Please don't hurt me," the man whined.

Chucky twisted his AK-47, putting the barrel under the small man's chin.

"Damn!" Greer whispered.

Three feet to the left, four maybe, and the sheriff would be right above Chucky. He would only have to drop into the basement and he could knock Chucky's gun aside. Probably take Chucky down, too, and then he was a lot bigger and stronger than the high school sophomore. A few feet and this would all be over.

"Maybe I don't care about him," Greer said. He could kill Chucky, easy, but only through the second guy in scrubs.

The lieutenant aimed and Chucky made a small target of himself behind his hostage.

"Let him go or I'll shoot you both," Greer said.

Did he mean it? If the sheriff dropped, would he get shot by his opponent, too? It didn't matter. This was his county. At least until after the election. That made Chucky his responsibility. And Heather. He was responsible for her, too. The changing situation, though, had changed his angle. He had to go another couple of feet and then he could....

"No," Heather shouted.

The sheriff glanced over in time to see her reach out and knock Greer's barrel up. The muzzle spouted flame. Holes appeared in the floor all around English, raising tufts of carpet like a swarm of moths. And then the weakened floor gave and the sheriff was falling and Chucky was *not* immediately below.

He was really going to do it, Heather thought. Greer was really going to shoot Chucky, who deserved it, but he was going to shoot Chucky's hostage at the same time. She couldn't believe it. She knew Greer was one of those holier-than-thou sorts, sure his way was the only right way. He'd said all those terrible things about her and her sister and, especially, their dad. But she hadn't thought he was capable of outright murder. Not until now. Englishman would never do that. No lawman worth his salt would think of it, or permit it. No lawwoman, either.

"No," she shouted, and threw her arm out and knocked his muzzle skyward.

And then life turned into a slow-motion explosion. It was like sitting at home in front of the TV and watching film from Iraq. Another bomb going off in the middle of a crowded intersection. They slowed the images down, paused for effect, turned the horror of an instant into something that seemed eternal. That's how this felt.

Greer's gun went off, tearing into the ruined ceiling over Chucky's head. A section of ceiling gave, collapsing into the room. But it brought someone with it. Her father. She saw him fall, twist, drift down with the wreckage. For a moment, it felt as if she had time to take Greer's gun away and run over and catch Englishman before he hit the floor.

She didn't. In fact, Greer's gun was still chewing up ceiling when Englishman hit. His legs went out from under him and he pitched sideways, falling toward Uncle Mad Dog and Hailey. He had a pistol in his hand all the way to the floor, but it went flying when he landed—much harder than she would have expected, considering how sluggish time had otherwise become.

Chucky shoved his hostage toward Englishman and swiveled his gun toward the doctor and his patient. Greer's gun went quiet on an empty magazine just as Chucky's spoke. Twice. It wasn't on automatic anymore. One bullet exploded Aldus P. Goodfellow's head like an overripe melon. The second produced a crimson blossom in the middle of the doctor's abdomen.

"You get to go slow," Chucky told the doctor.

Greer tossed his rifle at Chucky and fumbled a pistol off his belt, diving for cover behind the end of Uncle Mad Dog's gurney. The pistol fired, once, but Chucky wasn't there anymore.

Chucky wasn't there because someone had tackled him from behind. A girl. Heather wondered what the hell Pam Epperson was doing here, and why Pam was able to move and accomplish things while Englishman's only deputy seemed to have lost the ability to act. Heather had become a camera. She was recording all this, taking it in and digesting it, but somehow no longer part of what was going on.

Chucky went down, but he still had his gun. It looked like it was aimed at Englishman, now, but Heather could no longer be sure because Pam was all over the boy, clawing, kicking, butting, biting.

Greer sighted down his pistol, up for another try. There was no open shot there. He'd have to shoot Pam to get Chucky. Heather thought she should do something.

She didn't have to. Mad Dog's hand shot out and took the pistol out of Greer's grip. Greer tried to grab it back but slipped on the liquid that was spilling out of the IV that had been patched into Uncle Mad Dog's arm.

How had Mad Dog managed that? He'd been unconscious, waiting to become the source for some horrible process of harvesting vital organs. But none of the wires and tubes that had been attached to him had survived Hailey's fury. And Uncle Mad Dog was back with them. Not enough to do more than grab the gun and hurl it across the room, but back.

Despite the surprise and savagery of Pam's attack, Chucky got a hand in Pam's hair and dislodged her. She tried to kick him in the face and he dodged it, caught her foot, and pulled it out from under her. He covered her with his gun long enough for her to back off a little while he regained his feet.

"I think I'm done," Chucky said. He looked around the room. Ruins would be a more accurate description. "And now nobody's left with a gun to end it except for you, Heather, the girl who can't shoot me."

He was right. Mad Dog, Greer, Englishman—none of them had a gun anymore.

Mad Dog could hardly move. Greer was on his butt near Heather's side. The doctor was folded over his wound, moaning softly. The televangelist and the last of the hired guns were dead. The guy with the bad hair wasn't moving or complaining anymore, though he still looked to be alive. The pale guy in scrubs had scrambled off of her father and assumed a fetal position, as if that might render him invisible. And her dad....

Englishman was trying to sit up, and not doing a good job of it. He'd hurt himself in the fall. One leg of his jeans was soaked with blood. He didn't look capable of making a dash for one of the discarded guns scattered about the basement floor.

"Too bad...," Chucky continued. Heather was still in that slow motion world where she had time to stop and evaluate things while he simply took a normal pause for breath. "...'cause I've got to die but I can't kill myself. You probably won't understand, but I think God may forgive me for everything I've done today. But not for suicide. That's what I've been taught. So I guess I just have to go on killing." He began to swing his muzzle. It was coming toward her.

"You're killing the people who're responsible, right?" Englishman said. "Or saving those they might have used the same way they intended to use you."

Heather hadn't thought Englishman was with it enough to talk.

"Then you know what this was about." Chucky made it a statement, not a question.

Englishman nodded. "That makes me next," her dad said. "This is *my* county. When people break the law here, I'm responsible."

Chucky's eyes went from Heather to her father and back again. The boy nodded. "I think I understand what you're saying."

Chucky's muzzle moved back to center on Englishman.

"Maybe...," Chucky began.

He didn't finish. He didn't pull *his* trigger. Time began moving again for Heather. She pulled *hers*, and turned Chucky's frail body into chunks of tissue and bone and a spray of blood that painted the remains of the wall behind him.

Heather sat in a waiting room in a Wichita hospital and held hands with Greer, of all people.

"I'm all right," she reassured him. But she knew, if she was holding hands with the man whose finger she had considered breaking earlier that morning, she was not all right.

"You did what you had to do," Greer said. "Just keep remembering that. It'll pull you through."

She wasn't sure if he was right. She thought so, but she just couldn't convince herself that Chucky would really have shot her dad. Not now, in hindsight anyway. At the moment, she'd had no doubt. Otherwise, she never could have broken free of the paralysis that gripped her while other people were shooting or trying to shoot or saving people from getting shot. Actually, she supposed, she might have saved the nurse when she knocked Greer's gun aside. But, like everything else, that hadn't worked out the way it was supposed to.

"I'm a marksman, Heather," Greer had told her later. "I've been through sniper training. I wouldn't have shot anyone but Chucky. That nurse and Pam, no way I would have harmed either one."

But that was later, after Englishman was stabilized and while they were waiting for the medevac helicopter to take her dad, and the other seriously wounded survivors, to the gun-shot trauma specialists in Wichita.

At first, she'd felt euphoric. She'd killed a man and saved her dad and it was a rush like she'd never felt before. Greer told her that was normal, too, as well as the horror she later felt about that reaction.

"Yes!" She remembered shouting it, because it was over. Her dad was alive and Chucky couldn't kill anyone ever again.

And then Greer was clawing his way up off the floor and saying something that reminded her of the reason she'd turned her radio off as she drove home from Lawrence that morning. It was a country rock station and they'd started playing a golden oldie that, after the terrible premonition she'd awakened to, just wasn't something she wanted to hear. How bizarre, she'd thought, that Greer should choose the moment after she'd killed a human being to tell her the name of the song.

"I shot the sheriff," Greer said.

She was so high on adrenaline and the moment that she almost sang the next line back to him. *But you did not shoot the deputy.*

And then she remembered the blood on her dad's leg and where Greer's gun had been pointing when it went off, and who was responsible for knocking the barrel up there in the first place.

A bullet had struck Englishman, in the thigh. The wound was pumping blood. "Artery," Greer said, and began cutting her dad's Levis away with the knife he'd had sheathed at the back of his neck.

"I'm all right," she told Greer again in the waiting room. A television was tuned to one of the all-news networks so people like her could reassure themselves that theirs was hardly a major tragedy. Since the news included coverage from Buffalo Springs, it didn't reassure her at all.

"I'm all right," was what Englishman had told her, and Greer, too, before he passed out.

Blood loss, that was what Greer and Neuhauser said, later, after the two of them treated the wounded and got everyone up out of that ruined basement. Englishman had come first—a pressure bandage and a tourniquet, and even a person-to-person transfusion after they checked his blood type and discovered Greer matched.

It was true, though. Englishman really was going to be all right. She could see it in the surgeon's face as he came into the waiting room.

"Sheriff English did very well," the doctor said. "He's coming around now and we'll have him ready for visitors soon."

"Thank God," Heather said. God was not someone she'd thought of or spoken with much since her mother died. Not until today.

"We saved the bullet fragment. Thought he might like a souvenir of what chipped a piece of bone off his spine."

"His spine?" Heather felt the dread seeping back.

"Spine?" Greer said. "That wound wasn't anywhere near his spine."

"First bullet went through his thigh without stopping. The second one, the one in his lower back, you never found. I'm not surprised. It didn't bleed much and you were so busy with the other."

"Will he be paralyzed?" Heather asked.

"Oh no," the doctor said. "That will only be temporary. Your father will have a full life. He'll have to put some real effort in with the physical therapists, but I fully expect he'll eventually walk again."

"Eventually?"

The surgeon reached out and patted the hand Greer wasn't holding. "Like he told me before we put him under. Maybe it's a good thing he lost that election today. He'll regain a lot of motion, but he shouldn't be trying to perform a sheriff's duties again."

Doc was beat. It was almost midnight and his day had started before dawn with a catastrophe and ended this afternoon in total carnage. Actually, it hadn't ended yet, but he knew he couldn't stay on his feet much longer.

He'd brought a speaker phone into the room in the Buffalo Springs Clinic he had made Heather Lane promise to occupy, at least for tonight. They'd finally persuaded the receptionist at the hospital in Wichita to put a call through to Englishman's room. The other Heather had pushed from her end, after long ago sharing the good news/bad news results of their father's surgery.

"Hey, honey," Englishman said. His voice sounded a little woozy. "Thanks for calling. They tell me I'm going to be a little gimpy, but fine. How about you?"

Heather was staying on her left side. The local anesthetic Doc had used to stitch up her shrapnel wound was wearing off and her right hip would be seriously sore by now.

"Let's just say I'll be sitting very carefully, if at all, for a while."

Doc piped in. "She'll have an interesting scar, but she'll only want to share it with really special friends."

"Hey, bro," Mad Dog called from the corner. He was sitting there with Hailey under one arm and Pam Epperson under the other. Doc still hadn't figured out what that was about.

"You're gonna heal faster and better than those doctors think. They don't know a Cheyenne shaman and his wolf spirit helper will cure you quick."

Englishman laughed. "How about you and Hailey, Mad Dog? No ill effects?"

"He's got mental problems," Doc said, "but he had those before."

"They tell me the transplant doctor died," Englishman said. "Galen, too. But that leaves the nurse and the guy with the comb over, Dunbar. And three of their four hired guns. Did the highway patrol get them to talk?"

"The nurse was talking long before the highway patrol got there," Mad Dog said. "Dunbar, bad hair and all, was manager for Aldus P. Goodfellow's televangelist empire. He's been channeling money into this county in order to control it politically for a couple of years. It was always about setting us up as the location for their Frankenstein-lab, a place to treat old man Goodfellow and his political cronies. God's care wasn't good enough for them. But the reverend had a stroke this fall and they started rushing things. Including the shipment of Goodfellow's fake clone this morning. Wynn-Some interrupted that."

"Was *our* Pastor Goodfellow involved?" Englishman asked.

"He knew about a little of it," Mad Dog said, "but he didn't approve. His boy though…."

"I know," Englishman agreed, "but the kid paid with his life."

"Dunbar hooked them up with this guy who'd been selling miracle cures for decades—stem cells and human growth hormones, even claimed he could clone people years before Dolly the sheep."

"Scam artist," Doc interrupted. "Mostly, anyway. Kept old man Goodfellow's heart beating. With enough transplants and gimmickry, he might have done that almost indefinitely. But his nurse admits the reverend's been brain dead from the moment they started treating him. Says that clone was actually one of a herd of unwanted children they raise for medical purposes at a clinic in Mexico."

"Any word on Wynn-Some?" Englishman asked.

"We thought you might know," Doc said. "He's in the same hospital as you. Still in an induced coma last I heard. But at least the people on that bus confessed Galen was driving without lights, too. Troopers said they wouldn't be charging Wynn-Some."

"There'll be time to go over all this later." Deputy Heather's voice sounded as tired as Doc felt. "Dad needs his rest now."

"Yeah," Heather Lane said, just as the door to the room opened and Mrs. Kraus stuck her head in. "Daddy doesn't need to worry about any of this. The state will handle things now."

Englishman's voice came back on the phone. "That's okay. The trials might be over before I heal up enough to help. And, by then, my term will have run out."

"Bullpucky!" Mrs. Kraus rasped.

"Hey, Mrs. Kraus," Englishman said. "Nice of you to come cheer me up, too."

"Nice, my ass," she said. "I just come from where they finished the vote count. I wanted to congratulate our new sheriff."

"Greer," Englishman said. "He's right here with Heather."

"Let me speak to the lieutenant," Mrs. Kraus said.

The phone changed hands and Greer said, "I'm here, Mrs. Kraus."

"Lieutenant Greer. You lost. They haven't even accounted for the fraudulent votes yet and it's two to one, Englishman."

Everyone in Heather's room was stunned into silence. Englishman had never won any of his previous elections by more than a few percentage points. This seemed impossible. And, of course, how would he perform his duties?

"But he can't…," Two began.

"Not now, maybe," Greer said. "But he's got a deputy, standing right next to me, who can handle anything. Anything at all."

◇◇◇

She could, Mad Dog thought, though he'd rather see Heather English go back and complete her law degree.

He was relieved to discover that the last of the reporters—they'd descended on the community like a plague of locusts this afternoon—was gone when Doc escorted Heather's visitors out of the clinic.

"I want this girl to get some sleep," Doc said. "And I'll be snoring away in the next room. I'm an old man, not up to all this excitement."

Mrs. Kraus scurried out to her car, which she'd retrieved from the Siegrist farm before the highway patrol got around to impounding it. "Might be it's time for a new generation to take over," she said as she opened her door. "Even I'm getting a tad past my prime."

Mad Dog felt that way, too. He'd been a long time without sleep. He opened the door to his Mini Cooper and let Hailey and Pam climb in.

"Can I take you home, Pam?" he asked, getting behind the wheel.

"Sure," she said. "If you're talking about your place. You and I have unfinished business."

He started to ask her, What about Mark?—who'd run for home at the first shot. He was going to remind her of their age difference. Before he could say a word she leaned over and nuzzled his ear and it became obvious he wasn't *that* old.

A good Cheyenne shouldn't do this, Mad Dog told himself. He glanced into his rearview mirror. From the way Hailey's eyes glowed in the moonlight, she clearly disagreed. And her toothy grin told him she thought it was about time.

Afterword & Acknowledgments

The last episode in the adventures of Mad Dog & Englishman, *Plains Crazy*, was released by Poisoned Pen Press in October 2004. That was just in time for the first Great Manhattan Mystery Conclave. It's held in the Little Apple, Manhattan, Kansas, and that provided the perfect excuse to go "home" again.

Barbara and I traveled about the state immediately before one of the most polarized presidential elections ever. I was keen on taking the pulse of my homeland because Thomas Frank's book, *What's the Matter with Kansas: How Conservatives Won the Heart of America*, had come out only a few months before. I thought Frank made many good points, but I also thought he hadn't quite got it.

My Kansas upbringing taught that religion and politics were *the* subjects to be avoided in polite conversations. Bringing them up, even in a novel, can be like trying to put out a fire by spraying it with gasoline. And yet, the Kansas I recall allowed for such conversations as long as you listened politely and, if you disagreed, did so without disparaging others' views. The Kansas I was educated in never doubted I should be exposed to good science any more than it limited what sections of religious texts could be discussed in houses of worship. But that was before the Kansas Board of Education inserted itself into the evolution debate.

Kansas has a history of conservatism, both politically and in the religious beliefs of its citizens. It's hard not to feel the need for a direct connection to God when your existence and the well-being of your family so tied to weather's whims. And whims is too gentle a word for the extremes Kansans face. Fewer families farm than when I grew up, but the state's economy still relies on how weather affects agriculture.

We attended another Great Manhattan Mystery Conclave just before the mid-term election of 2006, the day on which *Broken Heartland* is set. Those results prove, I think, that politics in Kansas are not as simple as Frank proclaimed. And that there's nothing the matter with Kansas that isn't duplicated in our nation at large. This story includes my small effort to demonstrate that, though the results of the 2006 election in Benteen County are as fictional as the locality itself.

Some readers of this series may wonder why Judy English had to die. She didn't, of course. The decision was easier to make than it is to justify. Part of my reason is because these books have so often been described as cozies. To me, that implies an effort to avoid controversy. This series has considered child abuse, incest, abortion, religious fanaticism, and the practicality of everyday democracy, to say nothing of brutal murder. And, though it may push real-world possibilities to the extreme (or beyond), I hope it has remained sufficiently grounded for readers to relate to my characters. People die. We may not like to be reminded of that, and yet there is comfort in shared grief. I grieve for family and friends who have died since this series started. Now, my characters join me.

No one should take the medical practices described here too seriously. You can't transplant eyes. Not so far as I'm aware, anyway. And there's no paralysis drug as selective as the one in this book, nor any legitimate purpose for it.

The Buffalo Springs Church of Christ Risen is an invention, as well. There may be real churches that share some of its name, but I have no reason to think they might be similarly involved in politics or illegal activities. Like picking names for characters, unintentional matches are unavoidable, and bear no resemblance....

Yes, I know Mad Dog is too old for Pam. So does he, but the heart seldom respects logic. Besides, Pam may be the more mature individual in the relationship, and anything that's all right with Hailey is okay by me.

The usual suspects must be rounded up for thanks. Barbara, my own "child bride," first and foremost. I've dedicated several books to her, but always along with others. Being an author's wife is no easy task. And I'm not counting all the reading, editing, and emotional support. She deserves at least one book, all her own.

Next, my critique group, without whom I literally couldn't do this. Elizabeth Gunn and Susan Cummins Miller were around for the whole ride. Sheila Cottrell, Liza Porter, and William K. Hartmann got off more lightly. Bill's wife and my dear friend, Gayle Hartmann, volunteered some careful editing as well as several wise suggestions. Karl Schlesier continues to provide guidance about all things Cheyenne. The Poisoned Pen posse inspires, especially Larry Karp with his thoughtful insights. Thanks to all!

Friends and family still in Kansas help keep me rooted there. Included among them are the folks behind the Great Manhattan Mystery Conclave. Their encouragement has been invaluable. So has that of the internet discussion group, Kansas-L. I owe Cheryl Brooks of that list for the idea about the black walnuts.

Finally, its impossible to adequately thank the fine folks at Poisoned Pen Press. Barbara Peters and Rob Rosenwald, of course, but also Jessica Tribble, Marilyn Pizzo, Jennifer Muller, Geetha Perrera, Nan Beams, and Monty Montee. The next generation, as well, including newcomer Eleanor Ann Muller. And, of course, Annette, whoever you are.

For any errors, flaws, or advice not taken, I alone am responsible.

JMH
Tucson, by way of Hutchinson, Darlow, Partridge,
Manhattan, Wichita, Sedna Creek, et Tabun,
Albuquerque, and a yellow brick road